SHRINK SOLVES MURDER

ALSO BY PHILIPPA PERRY

Couch Fiction: a Graphic Tale of Psychotherapy

How to Stay Sane

*The Book You Wish Your Parents Had Read
(and Your Children Will be Glad That You Did)*

The Book You Want Everyone You Love To Read
and maybe a few you don't

PHILIPPA PERRY
SHRINK SOLVES MURDER

HUTCHINSON
HEINEMANN

HUTCHINSON HEINEMANN

UK | USA | Canada | Ireland | Australia
India | New Zealand | South Africa

Hutchinson Heinemann is part of the Penguin Random House group of companies whose addresses can be found at global.penguinrandomhouse.com

Penguin Random House UK,
One Embassy Gardens, 8 Viaduct Gardens, London SW11 7BW

penguin.co.uk

First published 2026
004

Copyright © Philippa Perry, 2026

The moral right of the author has been asserted

Penguin Random House values and supports copyright. Copyright fuels creativity, encourages diverse voices, promotes freedom of expression and supports a vibrant culture. Thank you for purchasing an authorised edition of this book and for respecting intellectual property laws by not reproducing, scanning or distributing any part of it by any means without permission. You are supporting authors and enabling Penguin Random House to continue to publish books for everyone. No part of this book may be used or reproduced in any manner for the purpose of training artificial intelligence technologies or systems. In accordance with Article 4(3) of the DSM Directive 2019/790, Penguin Random House expressly reserves this work from the text and data mining exception.

Map copyright © Grayson Perry, 2026

Set in 14/17 pt Garamond Premier Pro
Typeset by Six Red Marbles UK, Thetford, Norfolk

Printed and bound in Great Britain by Clays Ltd, Elcograf S.p.A.

The authorised representative in the EEA is Penguin Random House Ireland,
Morrison Chambers, 32 Nassau Street, Dublin D02 YH68

A CIP catalogue record for this book is available from the British Library

ISBN: 978–1–529–15532–7 (hardback)
ISBN: 978–1–529–15533–4 (trade paperback)

Penguin Random House is committed to a sustainable future
for our business, our readers and our planet. This book is
made from Forest Stewardship Council® certified paper.

For the real Dorna Braddon and Prichard Knowles;
they know who they are.

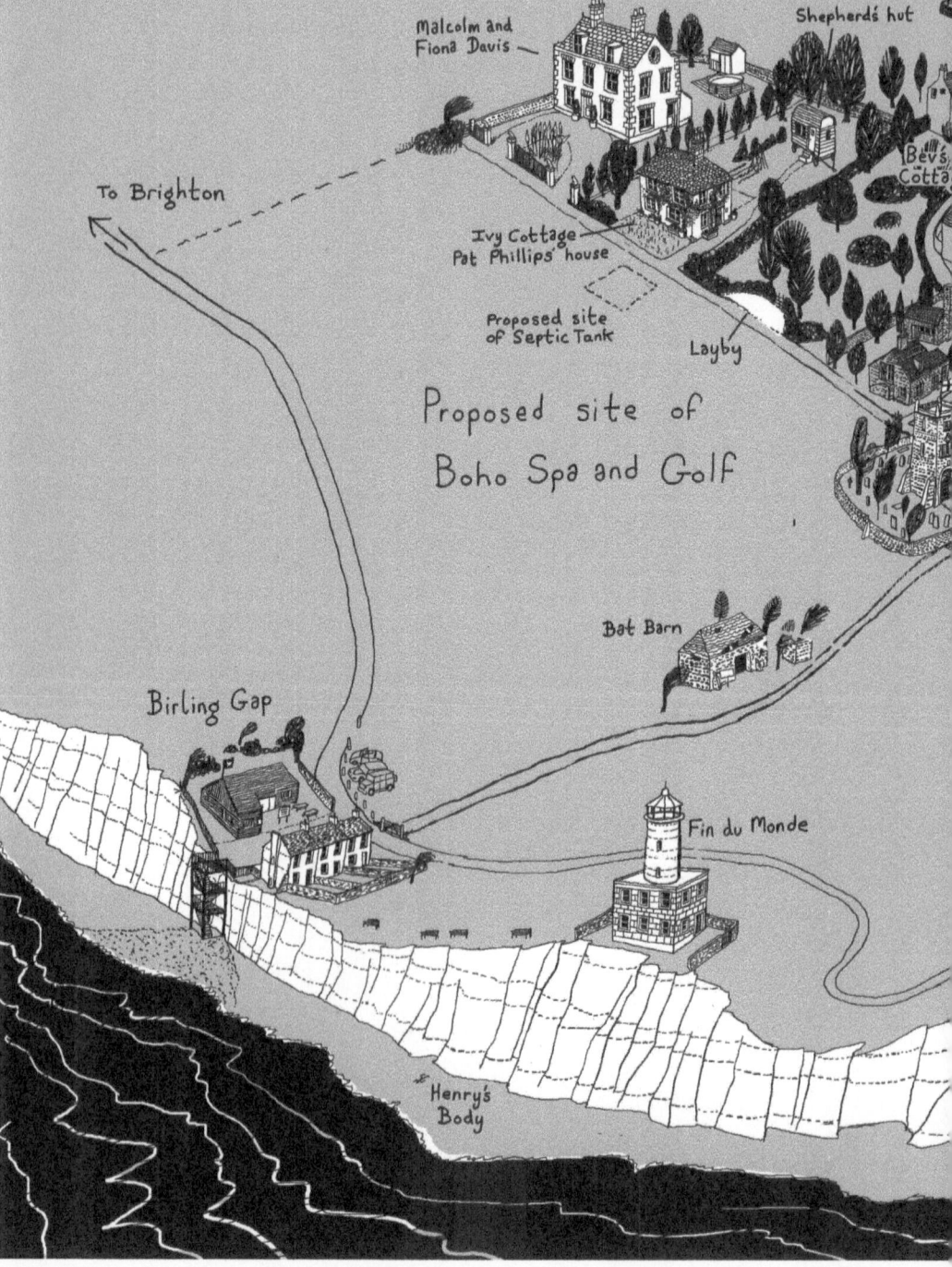

PROLOGUE

'Don't go so near to the edge!' yelled Patricia Phillips at a group of Korean tourists taking what appeared to be wedding photographs on the edge of the Seven Sisters cliffs. 'These cliffs crumble,' she shouted. 'It's not worth dying for. Get back!'

She planted her hands on her hips and waited. The tourists looked back at her blankly, then carried on posing not discernibly any further away from the white chalky edge. With a loud exhale, Patricia turned on the heel of her ancient walking boot and marched along the path across the Downs towards her cottage.

'Every bloody day,' she mumbled to herself, pulling her dryrobe tighter around her. 'Every bloody day, and no one listens.' She looked up. 'Put that dog on a lead,' she barked at a woman who had let her black Labrador loose in the sheep field. She got another blank stare in response. The dog lolloped in the direction of the flock and the sheep began to canter towards the cliff. 'Oh, for fuck's sake,' Pat said under her breath, then commanded, 'Sit!' with all the authority she could find. Luckily, the dog took more notice of her than anyone else had that morning.

'He's never chased sheep before,' began the Labrador's

owner, a short woman with cropped ginger hair. 'Normally he's very well beha—'

'Lead!' It was all Patricia could manage to yell back, with a dismissive wave of her hand. She couldn't even blame how furious she felt on the menopause any more, she thought, just as a sharp twang pierced her hip joint. She winced. The pain alone could have been justification enough for her mood, even if it hadn't been exacerbated by idiots.

The wind picked up as she crossed the brow of the hill and strode on towards her cottage. It was always blustery up here; the grasses were flattened, the elderly hawthorns and gorse permanently bent, buffeted and bruised by the prevailing wind. She tugged harder on her dryrobe, regretting having stayed in the water that bit longer than usual. The English Channel had chilled her to the marrow. She was of the opinion that no one could possibly get into the sea and come out in a bad mood, unless, of course, they needed a hip replacement and were too bloody-minded to admit it.

She eschewed the small wooden gate for walkers to the side of the cattle grid and picked her way across the metal bars. As she turned the corner towards her eighteenth-century brick and flint cottage, she stopped in her tracks. Not again! Every bloody day. There was yet another car parked on the grass verge. Right in front of her doorstep. She was just about to shout 'Get off my land!' like a crimson-faced farmer when a woman and a hefty-looking policeman got out of the Ford Focus. She inhaled deeply and downgraded her retort to an icily polite 'Can I help you?'

'Dr Phillips?' said the woman, flashing a badge. 'May we come in?'

CHAPTER 1

'I'm Detective Sergeant Amanda Stevens, and this is my colleague Police Constable Barry Footer,' said the woman, lightly patting the neat brown bun at the back of her head. 'We don't want to take up too much of your time.'

The officers followed Pat as she strode through the wooden gate and down the garden path. They watched as she bent down, picked up the flowerpot to the right of her bright yellow front door and took out the cunningly hidden key to unlock it. She led the way into the kitchen.

The sun was pouring through the window, the radio was on, the remains of breakfast were still in the sink and the small, round pine dining table in the centre of the room was covered in files and papers. There was a half-completed *Times* crossword lying next to a cup of cold coffee, an open *Financial Times* with some of the stocks and share prices underlined and a well-thumbed Sudoku booklet on top of it. A black and white cat raised its head from the dining chair cushion and took in the new arrivals. It yawned, stretched and settled down again, clearly unimpressed.

'Tea? Coffee?' Pat asked, switching off the radio. 'Biscuits?'

'Biscuits would be good,' replied PC Footer, rubbing his hands together in anticipation.

DS Stevens shot him a look, raising her heavily pencilled eyebrows. 'I wonder if we might ask you a few questions, Doctor,' she began, pulling out the cat's chair. The cat stayed put and emitted a warning hiss. 'It is a matter of sensitivity. So maybe a cup of tea might be helpful?'

What could possibly be helped by tea? Pat turned around to flick on the kettle. She looked back to find DS Stevens trying to edge the cat off its chair, but it stood its ground firmly.

'I wouldn't try to move him,' she warned. 'His bite is worse than his bark.'

'So, you're a psychotherapist,' DS Stevens said, pretending not to hear Pat's advice. She dragged a stool from under the table, sat down and nodded at PC Footer, who immediately took a seat next to her.

'I am,' replied Pat.

'Good,' said DS Stevens, looking around the kitchen. Her eyes darted from the row of mismatched chipped mugs that hung on hooks under the white wooden units to the collection of prehistoric orange Le Creuset pots on top of the fridge, the dying African violet on the windowsill behind the sink and the cork noticeboard overloaded with curled photographs, bent postcards, fliers, tickets and wristbands from numerous plays and concerts. 'Have you been here long?'

She was overdoing it with the small talk. Pat followed her gaze around the room. What was the woman looking for? What did she want from her? Was she about to be arrested?

'Eight, ten years, something like that.'

'And you moved from London to the South Downs, to Westlinke?'

'That's correct.'

'You live on your own?'

'I live with Dave.'

'Your husband? Son?'

'Cat.'

DS Stevens nodded curtly at PC Footer. Was he jotting all this down?

'Dave,' he repeated. 'The cat. So is that eight years or ten years, would you say, living here?' His round cheeks flushed as he looked up at Pat, his stubby pencil poised over his black notebook.

'Nine years and two months,' said Pat, watching him scribble away. 'And three days,' she added just for good measure.

'Three?' He looked up.

'Three,' she confirmed.

'And this is where you practise?' asked DS Stevens, gesturing to the papers on the kitchen table.

'Oh no,' said Pat. 'My office is a shepherd's hut in the garden.' She nodded towards the window. 'That's where I see clients. You wouldn't want to have them in here.'

'No.' DS Stevens laughed sharply. 'I can see that!'

'But it's mostly on Zoom these days.' Pat tried her best to be amiable and poised, the opposite of Stevens' brusque, uninterested delivery. 'People often prefer it. Zoom, that is. They don't have to leave home.'

'Yes, yes. Of course.' DS Stevens offered a dry smile.

'And I can see more people this way,' Pat added.

'Which brings me to this question.' DS Stevens paused, her face suddenly very sombre indeed. 'Do you know a Mr Henry Clayton?'

Silence hung in the air for a moment. The kettle came to a rumbling boil and clicked.

Pat poured hot water onto the tea bags, eyes fixed on the liquid as it turned dark.

'Henry Clayton? I'm afraid I'm bound by my code of ethics. I'm not really able to tell you.' She looked across at the round brass clock on the wall. He was due at three o'clock.

'Ah, well. Of course we know that you know him, at least in a professional capacity.' DS Stevens sighed before clearing her throat, her gaze now fixed on Pat. 'I have some bad news. You might want to take a seat.'

'I'm fine,' replied Pat.

'Well . . . I'm sorry to tell you that Mr Clayton's body was discovered washed up on the beach this morning. On the pebbles just below Birling Gap, to be precise. It's suspected that he died by suicide.'

'No!' Pat raised her voice. She pushed a mug of tea towards each of them. 'Milk? Sugar?'

'Yes, please,' nodded PC Footer. 'Both.'

'No, that can't be.' Her code of ethics was very much forgotten now. 'I've got a sense for this sort of thing. I did not see Henry as a danger to himself or others.'

'And why do you say that?' asked DS Stevens, her tone verging on the patronising. 'Is he not the type?'

'Type is not the right word,' replied Pat, grabbing a tin of biscuits that sat next to the Le Creuset collection on top of the fridge. The lid was sticky, clad with grease and dust, and the sell-by date was from the last decade, but she opened it anyway. 'We all have the potential to commit suicide.'

'Die by suicide,' corrected DS Stevens.

'Take our own lives, yes, but it is dependent on our state of mind. There is no type per se. Just as we are all capable of immense acts of bravery, love and self-sacrifice. But Henry – Mr Clayton – was not suicidal. He had expressed no suicidal thoughts whatsoever.'

'But he was in therapy, wasn't he?' DS Stevens tilted her head to express sympathy. 'So he did have some mental health issues?' Pat watched as the detective put little quotation marks around the words 'mental health' with her long, ballet-slipper-pink nails.

'That doesn't mean he wanted to commit suicide.'

'Die by suicide,' DS Stevens corrected again.

Pat bit her tongue and stared at PC Footer's dimpled hand as it dipped in and out of the sticky-lidded tin, clearly not noticing, or caring, that the biscuits he was polishing off were soft and damp and smelt very obviously stale. In the background, DS Stevens' voice was explaining that they'd found Henry at the bottom of the cliff, lying on his back, feet in the water, waves lapping over him. He'd been discovered at around eight o'clock that morning by some joggers from Westlinke Running Club, who passed by that stretch of shore every day at around that time. There was little suspicion of foul play, it being Birling Gap and all that, so close to the popular suicide spot that was Beachy Head. Henry Clayton was not from round here, so he had obviously made the journey to the Seven Sisters area to die by suicide somewhere between low and high tide on the night of Sunday 19 April.

Pat listened with increasing annoyance and frustration. Not that Henry was a friend, of course not. He was a client, whom she hadn't been working with for very long. Six, seven weeks, maybe; she'd have to look that up in her appointment diary. But he was a young man in his early thirties who'd had his whole life ahead of him. He was charming, good-looking, a nice boy. She began to feel irritated by the presence of DS Stevens in her kitchen.

She took a deep breath and tried hard to remain impassive. Stevens was likely in her mid-thirties, bustling with efficiency and freshly washed hair. She smelt of a cloying, heavy floral teenage perfume. She was made up, curled eyelashes, a bit of Kardashian contouring down the nose and across the cheeks, the sort of woman who always wanted to look her best. A small solitaire diamond glimmered on her engagement finger as she picked up her mug of tea. It was looking a little sad on its own without a wedding band. It'd been there a while, Pat was sure of it.

'How did you know he was a client of mine?' She interrupted the detective mid-flow.

'We found your business card in his wallet, with today's date and three p.m. written on the back,' said PC Footer. His tongue peeked out of his soft mouth as he leafed hastily through his pad. 'There were some other numbers jotted down there too, but we tried them and they all turned out to be taxi drivers.'

'What I don't understand,' Pat said, 'is why he was already here. He was supposed to be travelling down from London around lunchtime today and then taking a taxi directly here. He's always been a Zoom client, but this time he wanted to meet in person.'

'Did he now?' DS Stevens nodded meaningfully at PC Footer. 'Interesting. Why do you think that might be?'

'Well, without going into too much detail, he was struggling in his relationship. And he was worried about his privacy. He thought a face-to-face session would be more secure.'

'So he was paranoid?' suggested Stevens, a hint of triumph in her voice.

'No,' Pat replied sharply. 'He just wanted to come in person. It's not that unusual; in fact it was common practice to see people in the flesh before the pandemic.'

'Maybe he changed his mind; maybe he decided to just go straight to the cliffs instead. Maybe he was overwhelmed, don't you think? Overcome?'

'No, I don't think. As I said, he was not in that frame of mind.'

'Well.' DS Stevens shrugged, patting the back of her bun again. 'Perhaps he hadn't told you what his true intentions were. Maybe you just hadn't picked up on it. Maybe, professionally . . .' Her voice trailed off.

Pat stared at her, face purposely devoid of emotion. Her sea-soaked, wind-blown bobbed grey hair was sticking out at all angles, but her gaze was unblinking. She made sure of that. The kitchen was silent save for the quiet ticking of the wall clock.

DS Stevens smiled weakly. 'Well, um, maybe you—'

'To be clear. There are certain pointers for people who are at risk of taking their own lives.' Pat's voice was calm, her words measured. 'Low energy, low self-esteem, a hard, critical inner voice that won't go away.'

'That's as maybe,' countered Stevens. 'But things change, don't they? He was seeing someone for his mental health issues – you. And he was in the right age group to die by suicide. Between thirty and forty-four years of age. Male. He fits all the statistics. We have twenty-five to forty cases of death by suicide a year round here, so we're well used to these things. How can you be sure he's not one of those statistics?'

'People are not statistics,' Pat replied with growing exasperation. She leant forward and pinched her hip. A bolt of pain shot down her right leg, and she inhaled sharply. 'They don't fall into neat categories. We are all individuals.'

'You may say that,' replied DS Stevens, adding a light laugh. 'But at the end of the day, we're also statistics.'

'The reason why I believe he was not suicidal was because I asked him.' Pat placed both hands on the table. 'It's one of the first questions you ask as soon as a client sits down. Or at least I do. I also take a full history. There are pointers to someone's potential to self-harm, and Henry had none of them.'

'What pointers?' asked PC Footer.

'No previous suicide attempts, no desire to escape. Are you writing these down?'

Footer nodded.

'Not wanting to take vengeance. He did not think other people would be better off if he was dead. No magical thinking, no self-sacrifice, no suicide ideation, no evidence of alteration of cognitive function.'

'What?' Footer and Stevens asked in unison.

Pat continued. 'No aggressive or impulsive behaviour, no mental confusion. No drug-taking, no alcohol misuse, and he had no psychiatric history nor other comorbidities.'

'It's a tough one, though, isn't it?' said Stevens, standing up. 'Come along now, PC Footer. We don't want to waste any more of the good doctor's time.' She looked at Pat. 'Thank you, though, Dr Phillips, for helping us with our enquiries.'

'Are you speaking to anyone else?'

'No.' The detective shook her head. 'The next of kin have been informed. There will be a post-mortem, but that will be fairly basic. Just a confirmation, really, of the circumstances.'

'Which are?'

'That Henry Clayton died by suicide.' She nodded. 'We'll let ourselves out.'

The kitchen door clicked shut, followed by the garden gate, and then there was the sound of a car starting up. Pat sat at the table, her hands clasped in front of her, seething. Was she angry? Upset at the carelessness, presumptuousness? It just didn't feel right that Henry Clayton had killed himself. It didn't seem possible to her that he would go through with it. He had a seven-step skincare routine, for goodness' sake.

The two of them had laughed at the complexity of it. No, he wouldn't have wanted to damage himself like that. He wasn't planning to die. She stiffened, jaw tight with frustration. Why wouldn't the police listen to her? Why ask for her opinion if they had no intention of acting on it? Why contact her at all?'

She picked up a bourbon biscuit from the tin and sank her teeth into it.

'Jesus!' she said out loud. 'That's bloody disgusting!'

She leapt off her chair, ran to the window and spat the stale biscuit into the bin. How the hell could that young police officer have eaten his way through half the tin? What inner sadness was he compensating for? What void was he filling with sugar, trans fats and E numbers?

She stood at the sink, staring at her shepherd's hut. She'd been looking forward to talking to Henry. She'd put the heater on especially for him before she went out for her swim. She was used to the elements down here. She found the cold wind comforting, even the horizontal rain, and she loved the stone-grey waves of the English Channel no matter the season. But Henry was a London lad, and she'd wanted him to be comfortable in the hut, not shivering with cold sitting in the armchair beside her desk.

Some people were a little disappointed when they first walked into Pat's hut that she didn't have a couch for them to lie down on when they talked to her. That was the way it happened in the films. People were always horizontal in therapy, talking to the ceiling, or some slowly turning fan. But Pat preferred to look at her clients' faces. The way they moved. The changing expressions: small self-congratulatory smiles, or narrowing eyes and lips that indicated underlying anger; steady, impenetrable gazes or sad, lonely looks; seeking or avoiding eye contact. All these signs that she would miss if they were staring at the ceiling; and she especially wouldn't want to miss the look of recognition when they made a discovery that helped them understand themselves and their world a little better. She called those 'aha!' moments.

Henry had been doing well; he'd had several ahas! He'd been frustrated and annoyed when he realised how his behaviour had been fuelling the situation he had found himself in. Pat had thought he was finally ready to make changes, get his life back on track.

She left the kitchen and made her way over to the hut. If Henry wasn't coming, then she should at least turn off the heater. She walked up the three wooden steps and opened the door, letting out a guff of hot air. The shed was positively tropical, and there was that familiar singed-plastic smell, sharp and metallic. She left the door open, both as invitation to Dave, who had inevitably followed her, and to let the heat out of the room. Then she sat down in front of her ancient computer, with its scruffy keyboard that bore the crumbs of a recent luncheon eaten at her desk.

The rest of the space was surprisingly tidy. Her work area was clear, save for an old-fashioned Rolodex to the right of the computer that still contained the phone number of a gardener who used to mow her lawn when she was married to Martin and lived in Chiswick. Martin still lived there. For some reason, he never minded the commute into his barristers' chambers. Pat had always loathed it. The law, the commute, the long hours. She'd been a solicitor in a family law firm in the City before changing direction completely. A lot of that change had been down to Sue. Well, Sue and a desire to uproot her life and live by the sea. Surely there was only so much family law one could engage with without wanting to get into the nitty-gritty of what was really going on? Although Sue clearly felt differently. She was still at the coal face of law.

'Shit!' Pat exclaimed. She should telephone Sue. Sue was the reason Pat was treating Henry. Sue was the reason Henry was making the trip to Westlinke in the first place.

She picked up her mobile, hands shaking. She was suddenly overwhelmed with sadness. Somehow calling Sue and saying the words out loud would make the abstract concrete.

Her three o'clock was dead.

CHAPTER 2

'Yup?'

Sue was busy. She always answered the phone as if it were interrupting something important. Which it invariably was. She worked in a frantic, overstretched partnership of twelve solicitors, just off Chancery Lane, which specialised in family law, divorce and all things personal. She was a solicitor advocate, so was often in court, a horsehair wig on top of her smooth, sleek blonde blow-dry, and difficult to track down. Time was actually money. Her time was charged by the minute; even her thinking time was paid for, detailed as 'considering' on the invoice. As a result, Pat very rarely called her ex-girlfriend at work.

'Oh, it's you, sorry, I didn't see the number.' Sue's voice mellowed. 'Everything OK? I don't have long...'

'I'm not sure how to put this, so I'll just say it.' Pat swallowed. Her mouth was suddenly dry.

'What?' Sue was rustling papers on her desk.

'Henry Clayton was found dead this morning. Washed up on the beach at Birling Gap.'

There was a long pause.

'Sue?'

Silence.

'Are you there? Did you hear me? Henry Clayton is dead.'

'That's very sad,' replied Sue, before emitting a long, sombre sigh. 'That's very, very sad. He was such a lovely boy. Birling Gap? Near you? How?'

'Suicide, apparently.'

'Suicide? I doubt that.' She paused again. 'Sorry, you'd know best, of course, but . . . really? What d'you think? That doesn't sound right, does it?'

'I think the same. He showed none of the usual signs. Not that people haven't been shocked and surprised by suicides before, but I feel in my gut that he wasn't in that frame of mind. The police think otherwise.'

'Do they now?' Sue inhaled deeply down the line and then sighed again. 'The police taking the path of least resistance. Why doesn't that surprise me? Although I suppose they do get a lot of that down there.'

'How was Henry when you last saw him?'

Turned out Sue had seen Henry just two days before. He'd come to her office – an oak-panelled room at the top of a narrow, twisting staircase – for a coffee and legal advice about issuing a non-molestation order, a 'cease and desist', against his boyfriend, Derek, who'd been causing him some problems.

Henry had originally been put in touch with Sue by one of his stockbroker colleagues. She'd come highly recommended. Cool under pressure, a stickler for fairness, she was well known for championing the underdog and getting wronged women generous divorce settlements. She had taken Henry under her wing and suggested that he might want to remove

Derek entirely from his life. Legally force him to leave his flat in London. She had subsequently suggested that a few sessions with Pat might be helpful with the fallout from the breakdown of his relationship, as Henry kept wavering and getting back together with Derek and Sue kept having to put the legal work on hold.

'It doesn't make sense, though, does it?' she said now, clicking the end of her biro down the line.

'No, not to me, but the police aren't looking for anyone else. They seem convinced that he committed suicide.'

'How can they be so sure? And what did they want from you exactly?'

'They probably thought that the fact he had an appointment to see me was enough to prove their theory.'

'But you wouldn't have been able to confirm or deny he was a client.'

'Technically. But I slipped up. Don't tell my governing body.' Pat paused, a myriad of thoughts circling in her mind. 'But, you know, if he didn't jump, he might have fallen. An accident. What d'you think?'

'Or murder,' declared Sue.

'Oh God!'

'Well, you never know.'

'That might happen regularly in your circles,' said Pat, 'but down here, we mostly settle things over a glass of sherry in the pub.'

'Sherry!? And I'm afraid to say that domestic violence, a common cause of murder, is rife everywhere, and isn't necessarily anything to do with class either.'

'Yes, you're right.' Pat gazed out of the window of the hut, taking a deep breath. 'Are you really suggesting that Henry could have been murdered?'

'I'm not suggesting anything. I wouldn't dream of it. It's just a possibility.'

'A possibility? Murder! What am I supposed to do about that?'

'Find out who did it?'

'That's easy for you to say. I'm not a detective, I'm a psychotherapist.'

'I'd say that's probably better. You understand people, you see things no one else does. You're canny!'

Pat laughed.

'Well, you can't do any worse than the police, that's for sure. Listen, I've got to go. See you soon, good luck.'

Pat sat in the shed with her chin in her hands. Dave was curled up on the soft, fat armchair where Henry should have been. What could possibly have happened to poor Henry for him to have ended up dead on the beach? And why was he in Westlinke in the first place, when he should have still been at work in London? He was going to catch the 1.15 p.m. train from Victoria, if Pat remembered correctly. Why hadn't he done that?

She got up and crossed the hut, with its sheepskin rug and sage-green-painted floorboards. Opposite the desk and the window, three of her watercolour landscapes hung on the wooden wall. Next to a bookcase of academic journals and psychotherapy textbooks was a tall grey metal cabinet that contained the files on her past and present clients. Her professional code of ethics dictated that her client records should be filed under code numbers rather than names, but that was too far-fetched for maverick Pat. Technically she could've locked the cabinet, but she had no idea where the key was. She pulled out the top drawer and began flicking through the files. They were supposed to be stored in alphabetical order, but somehow that system had slipped. What was the point of having Mark Allen's file right at the front when he was no longer on her books and had moved to San Francisco at least eight years ago?

Although, to be fair, Mr Allen was something of an exception. Pat's patients rarely seemed to leave the practice. One of the problems of being a successful psychotherapist was that no one ever wanted to move on. They'd understand their issues, even make changes and improve their lives, but they seemed to like to stay on for maintenance. 'A bit like Hotel California,' had been Sue's response to Pat's conundrum. Scaling back the practice was one of the reasons why she had left London. Some patients didn't seem to make any progress but repeated the same patterns and circles and stayed in the same lane, no matter how many times they'd come to see her in her Covent Garden office. Obviously, as Pat would say many times over, you couldn't go to the gym once and expect to leave with abs. Therapy took time, but it also took effort. And there were a few stuck clients who wouldn't, or maybe couldn't, do the work.

She continued searching through her files. There was the angry banker who used to shoplift to help express his suppressed feelings. The unhappy loner who would physically 'dump his shit' at her door by using the lavatory in her office every Monday morning, leaving it in a terrible skid-stained state. The yearner who never felt she had her mother's love and had been chasing various unobtainable amours ever since; and the people-pleaser who attuned so acutely to everyone else she had lost sight of who she was. And then there was Henry.

'At last,' mumbled Pat, tapping the folder lightly, 'here we go. Filed under H for Henry rather than C for Clayton.' She pulled out the file, sat down and opened it on the desk. There was a printed copy of an email from Sue explaining the reason behind Henry's desire to contact her. There was their agreement that Henry would undertake eight sessions. There was his personal information form, which he had filled out in his sophisticated handwriting before sending it to her. She also remembered his first Zoom session. He was nervous, but quite talkative, as if all his worries and grievances were ready to burst out of him, like a fizzy drink that had been shaken before being opened.

His life was seemingly great. He enjoyed his job, had plenty of friends and got on with his family. His father had loomed large in his psyche, although he'd been in denial about that at first. His mother was a healthy, loving presence and he had a good relationship with his stepfather and stepsisters too. The only problem was his love life. He kept falling for men who went hot and then unfortunately cold on him, meaning he was hurt time after time. One of his aha! moments had been when he realised that these emotionally unavailable men were just a replacement for his father.

He craved his approval, his recognition, his affirmation and yet had no way to get it. He'd thought his latest relationship was going to be different, but Derek, for whom he had fallen hard, might have been his most disastrous love affair yet. Pat had been helping him become aware of the ways Derek didn't respect him, let alone love him.

The most important factors for a successful outcome in therapy were the client's expectations, motivation and hope. As well as, of course, the relationship between client and therapist. And Henry had thrived in both areas. He was excited for change. And Pat had really liked him. Looking at the file, she realised it didn't really sum him up. There was so much more to him than any piece of paper could ever convey. But she remembered what it felt like to be in his presence, and it was not how she felt when she was with patients who were likely to harm themselves.

'Knock, knock!'

'Jesus Christ!' she exclaimed, and leapt in her seat, smacking her knee on the underside of the desk.

'Almost!' replied a familiar voice.

'Come in! The door is open.'

'Here I am!' announced her friend and near neighbour Prichard Knowles, as if she'd been waiting for him for hours, days, indeed her entire life. 'And I bring libations.'

'Oh great,' replied Pat, her shoulders sinking a little in anticipation of the thunderous hangover that would inevitably wake her like a hammer to the head at 3 a.m. 'What is it this time?'

'Well,' said Prichard as he stepped inside with a flamboyant flick of his lengthy hand-knitted orange scarf, 'it's a bit of an experiment. I know!' he added, one of his hands in the air like he was stopping traffic. 'A word one never wants to hear when it comes to a beverage, but bear with, bear with. This one,' he pulled a sturdy bottle containing neon-pink liquid from his duffle coat pocket, 'is strawberry vodka. And this coquettish piece of *quelque chose* is pineapple and cheese – wait for it – gin!' He plonked both bottles down on Pat's desk. She recoiled as if faced with an unexploded bomb. 'Boom!' added Prichard for good measure, his machine-gun laugh erupting. 'Hahaha.'

'Cheese?'

'Cheese!' His long nose curled in amusement; a paintbrush of short grey hair shot out of each nostril. 'Who knew!'

'No one. And there will be a sound and solid reason for that,' replied Pat, inspecting the bottle. There appeared to be yellow crumbs swilling around at the bottom – quite possibly small hunks of Cheddar sediment.

A bit like the son of the Good Lord, Prichard Knowles could apparently conjure up alcohol out of anything. Most ingredients were fair game as far as he was concerned. He had yet to turn his hand to water, but so far he had produced beetroot wine, rhubarb wine, turnip wine, dandelion wine and – the least successful of all – nettle wine, which had brought them both out in some sort of allergic reaction and made their lips swell up so that they looked like *Love Island* contestants. It was one of those lockdown experiments that was never to be repeated.

'I'm not interrupting anything, am I?' he asked, scouring

the hut for evidence of activity. 'You look busy.' He nodded at the open file on Pat's desk.

'One of my clients has just been found dead on the beach,' said Pat, swiftly shutting the folder.

'Goodness!' Prichard perched, half-buttocked, on the fat armchair, where Dave was now staring at him with murder in his yellow eyes. 'That sounds bad.'

'Well, it's certainly not good. Especially for his mother.'

'A young chap, then?'

'Early thirties.'

'What a waste.'

'It is a waste. A terrible waste. And what's making me angry is that the police don't want to investigate it. They're writing it off as a suicide.'

'Suicide? Well, he's in the right place.'

'Surely not every bloody person who dies off the sodding Seven Sisters is trying to kill themselves!' replied Pat irritably. 'There are accidents, and then of course there's . . .'

'Murder!' Prichard's brown eyes were spherical as he filled the empty space of her words. He blinked slowly behind his smeared specs. 'D'you think your client was murdered?'

'I believe it to be a possibility, as does Sue,' Pat replied solemnly.

Prichard sat back in the armchair, prompting Dave to leave with an outraged meow, and exhaled loudly. Then he leant forward and grasped the stubby bottle of vodka. 'Well, stone the starlings!' He popped the cork. 'Nothing like this ever happens in a sleepy *vicus* like Westlinke.'

'*Vicus*?'

'Latin, keep up, hahaha.'

He picked up Pat's half-empty glass of stale water from the desk and chucked its contents into the pot of a parched spider plant before filling it with the pink drink.

'What do you think happened?' He took a swig, and his dark eyes watered.

'Someone might have pushed him, I suppose. An argument, maybe? I don't know.' Pat eyed the pink liquid with increasing suspicion.

Prichard raised his eyebrows, then took another shot. Pat quickly followed suit. She coughed and rubbed her nose, her throat on fire. Shaking her head, she admonished herself for such foolishness. Surely she should know by now not to drink anything that came out of Prichard's kitchen.

'Granted, it needs finessing,' agreed Prichard, his voice suddenly raspy. 'But I find it tastes better the second time.'

'It's like drinking Calpol,' Pat said. Prichard looked at her blankly. 'It's what you give children when they're ill.'

'Obviously I wouldn't know, being delightfully devoid of progeny.'

Pat took the glass out of his hand and took another swig. 'You're right.' She inhaled through her back teeth. 'It does taste better after a while.'

'So who do you think did it?'

'The murder?'

'The deed.' Prichard took another virulent sip. 'Is there a lover? A girlfriend? Something like that? It's normally them, isn't it?'

'There's an on-and-off boyfriend.'

'Well, it's him then, obviously.' He drained the glass and wiped his lips on the back of his hand. 'You should tell the police.'

'They're not interested. They're convinced it was suicide.'

'Maybe it was.'

'I have a persistent feeling it wasn't.' Pat got up abruptly, pushing her chair back.

'Now what?' asked Prichard, confused.

'Follow me,' she commanded. 'And bring those bottles with you!'

Back in the kitchen, the cold half-drunk mugs of tea were still on the table, along with the open tin of stale biscuits. Dave was nowhere to be seen.

'Right,' said Pat, clapping her hands together with sudden determination, 'help me clear this noticeboard.'

'What are we doing?' asked Prichard, putting his two lethal bottles on the table with a clatter.

'I'm making a crime chart of suspects.'

'Like they do in *Silent Witness*?' he asked with an excited grin.

'Like they do in every television drama and true-crime documentary.'

'Like a Pinterest board of villains?'

Pat grabbed her noticeboard from the kitchen wall. 'Probably.' She shrugged. 'Don't throw anything away,' she added as she unpinned a postcard of a Santorini sunset that Sue had sent her back in 2010.

Pat loved her noticeboard. It was organised chaos; she knew exactly what the story was behind every photograph or card or theatre ticket that might otherwise have seemed like random memorabilia. They each conjured up a memory, a moment.

'Oh, she was a gorgeous girl back then, wasn't she? Fearless,' she said, taking down a faded baby photograph of her daughter, Sofia, with cherubic blonde curls, up to her knees in a rock pool. She placed it carefully on the table.

'I didn't know you were a pot-smoking, drug-taking hippie, Pat! You dark *cheval*, you!' exclaimed Prichard, waving a piece of paper close to Pat's face.

'I'm not,' said Pat. 'Dulls the brain. Anyway, what's that?'

'Glastonbury tickets.'

She laughed. 'Glastonbury! I went with a corporate client back in my solicitor days, in 2002. I think I drank three Coronas, listened to Rod Stewart and witnessed a group of middle-aged men in a state of arrested development. Their nostrils were frosted like margarita glasses. Probably trying to recapture their youth.'

'Sad.'

'Very.'

'Although to be fair,' admitted Prichard, 'I am a fan of our Rod.'

Tickets, photographs, drawings in wax crayon, an amusing birthday card or two, Pat and Prichard piled them all on the worktop, next to a pouch of Dave's special organic chicken liver pâté, and set about organising their crime board.

'Henry is in the middle, I presume,' suggested Prichard, smoothing down the yellow Post-it in the centre of the board.

Pat looked up and nodded. A heavy black marker pen was sticking out of her mouth like a cigar. 'And let's put Derek right next to him,' she mumbled.

'Who's that?'

'The boyfriend. Our prime suspect.'

'Great!' enthused Prichard. 'I had no idea this amateur sleuth thing was so easy. Who needs Poirot when we have you, Pat! Now all we need to do is prove it's him.'

'Or possibly not. It's important not to jump to conclusions.'

'Jump!' said Prichard, before letting out another of his machine-gun laughs.

'Not funny,' said Pat.

'No, it isn't, sorry.'

Prichard stood back from the board and ran a hand through his salt-and-pepper hair as he admired his handiwork. In his mid-sixties, he still had quite a thatch in comparison to the gleaming billiard balls that Pat mostly saw in the Green Lion. Prichard Knowles MBE had probably been quite dapper in his day. He was good company, enthusiastic and well read. He had quite a collection of shoes. But now that he'd retired from his trucking business, where he'd been known as 'the Eddie Stobart of the south', he had gone to seed a little. He spent most of his time cooking, eating, watching daytime quiz shows and sporting flamboyant knitwear, the majority of which he'd crafted himself. Pat was not a big fan of the home knits, which did have a tendency to unravel, nor of his dangerous alcoholic concoctions. But there were many things that she did like about Prichard.

'What we need is a map,' he pronounced, tapping an index fingertip repeatedly against the corkboard. His love of maps was another thing she couldn't really buy into.

'I'm sure we don't,' she bristled.

'I think we do. How else are we going to know if he took the M23, the A22 or the A27 to the crime scene?'

'I'm not sure that matters.'

'Ooh, Pat, everything matters,' opined Prichard.

Neither did she enjoy his love of pedantry. 'Moving on,' she said briskly, 'are you willing to help with all this?'

'Tracking down a murderer? I should think so.' He nodded vigorously. 'Just so long as it doesn't involve violence, blood or huge amounts of physical activity. Like running of any kind. Or jogging. I might cope with a lively walking pace.'

'Fine.'

'And we might need a safe word?'

'What for?'

'In case we see something or . . . well, I don't know. A word that means we have to get back to yours. Or a red alert!' Pat looked even more puzzled. 'If we spot a clue.'

'OK. Like what?'

Prichard puffed his lips. 'Um. Chilli con carne?'

'Why chilli con carne?'

'CCC – can't converse calmly.'

'If we have to.' Pat shook her head.

With his terms and conditions set and agreed to, Prichard sat down at the pine table while Pat paced around the kitchen and explained why she had not come to the same conclusions as the police. Dave reappeared and curled up on Prichard's lap, ready for his forgiveness to be bought with a few head scratches.

'They're not asking the right questions,' she said. 'In fact, they're not asking any questions at all. Like why was Henry on the cliff? How come he ended up on the beach? And what was he doing in Westlinke hours before he was due to see me?'

Prichard did his best to keep up. But his home brew was beginning to make his temples throb, and his mouth was increasingly claggy and dry. He glanced up at the wall clock.

'Are we going to this thing?'

'What thing?'

'At the posh house. Mal and Fi's. Drinks.' He nodded out of the window towards a row of newly planted leylandii. 'I came to collect you. Remember? Or have you blanked it out like everything else you find *trop difficile*?'

'*Trop* boring, Prichard. Not difficult.'

'So, are we going?'

'With everything that's happened, I'd forgotten about it, but I suppose I must.'

'Well, I hope you're going to change?' He looked her up and down. 'You can't go in a dryrobe.'

CHAPTER 3

Malcolm and Fiona Davis had moved into the big house in Westlinke just over eighteen months ago, and since they'd arrived, their takeover had been nothing short of a *coup d'état*.

Within six months, they'd managed to persuade the local council to tarmac the old chalk and flint track from the ancient Tapsell gate of St Mary the Virgin church, past Pat's cottage and on to their swanky in-and-out drive that they'd carved into the hedgerow. The flint chips and flying stones were apparently an absolute bugger for the low chassis on Mal's Aston Martin DB9, and did little to preserve its glittering golden paintwork. They'd gone on to plant an extraordinary amount of pampas grass in said in-and-out driveway, the flamboyant fronds of which, whipped by the prevailing winds, had kept Pat up on windy nights ever since, as had the hooting laughter, the hysterical squealing, the awful music, the splashing, the naked running-about on the lawn and the gurgling bubbles from the newly appointed hot tub in the back garden. They'd also, worst of all, planted a fast-growing leylandii hedge between the end of their lawn and Pat's vegetable patch. It was apparently for privacy, but Pat couldn't help but think that they could have done with one less giant spotlight in the garden. Although she had to admit, the spotlight was useful if one wanted to stand upstairs in her 1970s avocado-coloured bathroom and train a pair of binoculars on the Davises' garden at two o'clock in the morning.

Having swingers move in next door was an endless source of irritation and, indeed, fascination. At least Pat suspected them to be swingers. She'd overheard Fi wax lyrical about 'tantric sex therapy', which sounded an awful lot like swinging. Fi was one of those people who tapped repeatedly on someone's arm when she talked, flicking her blonde hair about, laughing and pushing her bosoms towards her interlocutor's unsuspecting chin.

'Hurry up!' Prichard called from the bottom of the stairs. 'We're not even fashionably late now. We're rudely late. Hahaha! There won't be any vol-au-vents left.'

'Well, you can't expect a generous buffet from an orthorexic,' Pat declared as she descended the stairs. 'Fi controls food and probably everything else.'

She had changed into an elderly pair of black leggings that bagged at the knee due to wear, or loss of elastane, or both, and had donned some slightly newer hiking boots with odd laces, thick socks and a large navy ribbed jumper. She had managed to run a comb through her grey bob but was obviously, belligerently underdressed. Prichard took in her outfit.

'Nothing says "I couldn't care less" more than some old leggings and a jumper.' He laughed. He was used to her contrary nature and, indeed, secretly admired it. He was a people-pleaser himself. He knew it and it annoyed him.

'Wait,' said Pat, picking up a lipstick off the side. Looking into the large round mirror on the wall, she administered a slash of red. 'There. Now no one can say I didn't make an effort.'

A few minutes later, having walked down the path and round the corner, Pat and Prichard found themselves in Fi's remodelled sitting room, up to their shoe leather in a thick clotted-cream shag-pile rug that seemed to float above the polished mahogany floor. All Pat could think as she glanced down at her slowly disappearing feet was how tiresome it must be to vacuum and how impractical the colour was for seaside living. But looking around Mal and Fi's house, it was immediately clear that there had been little consideration paid to nature or the environment. The Georgian manor had been stripped of all its distinguishing features in favour of a neutral modern makeover that pleased no one and offended even fewer. White leather sofas, white hydrangeas, white trinket trays containing little golden coffee beans, and enough scented candles to perfume a spa; Fi had employed an interior designer from Surrey who specialised in doing up mock-Tudor mansions in gated communities.

'Pat!' exclaimed Malcolm as he approached, waving a bottle of cold champagne. 'Can I offer you a glass of fizz?'

In his late forties, with a pink open-necked shirt, a suggestion of chest hair and the faded tan of someone who'd recently taken very early retirement (due to good fortune, or indeed making one) and wintered on a lounger in the Caribbean, Mal was on the social end of the spectrum. Jovial, ebullient. If Fiona ever let go of her short, tight leash, he might even have been the life and soul of a party or two. But every time his face flushed with enjoyment, or he laughed too enthusiastically or slapped one too many backs with his flat, fleshy palm, Fi would announce, not even suggest, that it was time to leave. As a result, Mal was wary of appearing to have too much fun. The swinging appeared to be on Fi's terms or not at all.

'Very kind of you,' smiled Pat, watching as he poured champagne into a heavy cut-glass flute, then glanced furtively over at his wife before adding in a little more.

'Don't tell Fi, whatever you do,' he whispered. 'I'm supposed to be rationing the stuff. Prichard? Fizz?'

'It would be rude not to,' Prichard snorted, proffering his empty glass.

Mal took a step backwards and flashed a confident smile. 'Have you met your new neighbour yet?'

Standing with her back to the double-glazed sliding doors with a view onto the garden, the crazy paving and the permanently bubbling hot tub was a diminutive figure with cropped hair. Her silhouette moved forward.

'I don't believe we've been introduced,' she said in a husky voice, thrusting out her right hand, which was strapped up with a bandage. 'Dorna Braddon. I'm new round here. I'm the one who's been building the new house at the end of the lane, with the hedge.'

Pat squinted into the low sun. Ah yes, that haircut, that short stature. 'The woman who doesn't own a dog lead.'

'Oh, it's you.' Dorna laughed, withdrawing her hand. 'The self-appointed park warden.'

'The irresponsible dog owner,' Pat reiterated.

'I was very much in charge of my dog, actually.'

'Watching it herd a flock of pregnant sheep off the cliff?'

'Trigger was nowhere near doing that.'

'Trigger would have euthanised about thirty ewes and their lambs had I not intervened.'

'He was totally under control.'

'Just put him on a lead. It's not that difficult.' Pat sighed and shook her head wearily.

This Dorna character seemed to be very pleased with herself, with her henna dye and her forearm of jingly-jangly bangles. She even wore on her index finger, over the bandage, a thick silver ring, something you'd see on a teenage girl who'd treated herself to a shopping-centre afternoon with her friends.

'What do you make of her?' Pat whispered to Prichard while pretending to admire a display of cymbidium orchids, which turned out to be very convincing fakes.

'A middle-aged woman with a ring on her index finger is either recently divorced or going through a midlife crisis where she's trying to find herself.'

'Haha, Prich, they missed that out of my psychotherapy training.'

'Question is,' continued Prichard, 'which one is Dorna Braddon?'

'Maybe both, or none. Or something else entirely,' hissed back Pat.

'Right! Evening! Evening, everyone.' There was the tinkling sound of a knife tapping crystal. 'Shush, shush, if you will. You're not here to enjoy yourselves,' joked Fi, with a flick of her blonde hair. Her slim shoulders shrugged cutely up and down with self-satisfaction. Pat raised an eyebrow. Half the village was here, flattening down Fi's shag-pile rug and helping themselves to as much champagne as manners would allow.

There was Jacqui (with a *qui*) in her big long skirt, plonked on a white sofa close to the vol-au-vents on the coffee table. Jacqui was a jewellery designer, with a gimlet eye for detail and a myopic inability to see the bigger picture, which Pat had always thought was a bit of a shame, especially since she ran the weekly art club in the village. Standing by the door was the local member of Parliament, whose presence was clearly something of a coup. He was wearing his portcullis lapel pin just in case people didn't know how important he was. Over by the window was Peggy, with her Brillo pad of grey hair, who ran the post office cum village shop, the church committee and the shoebox collection for children in need at Christmas. She was also a fiendish Sudoku aficionado; she and Pat occasionally exchanged notes about this. Opposite was nosy Bev, who'd lived on the village green her entire life and patrolled it with vigour and a twitch of her curtains on a daily basis. No one managed to enter the Green Lion or stagger home without her knowledge. Then there was the couple from Brighton who'd just bought the rose-covered cottage on the corner. The pretty brunette wife, Lucy, was already something of a Fi Davis groupie. Standing by the drinks table was a youngish-looking dark-haired man with a glint of a golden earring, who'd recently arrived in Westlinke and lived next door to the pub. Pat thought he should just move into it and save on his heating bills. Next to him was Diccon and his wife Marcia, who were living proof that opposites did attract. He was extremely lean and she was large and fat, like something out of a nursery rhyme. They lived in the other big house up the hill, which rumour had it had once appeared on *Grand Designs*, although no one had ever been invited in to verify that. And then, of course, there was Prichard, who suddenly seemed to be enjoying Ms Braddon's company rather too much. He kept throwing his head back and honking at everything she said.

'Thank you, thanking you,' continued Fi, with another tap of her knife. 'Ladies and gentlemen, friends and neighbours – and we are honoured today with our elected representative too.' She looked over towards the door, grinned and bobbed a curtsey. 'I just wanted to say how happy I am that you are all here to celebrate a bit of a launch – the proper one was in London, obviously – for my new brand, Vibrant-Sea!'

She gestured grandly towards a short black metal rack of clothing behind one of the white sofas. There was a faint ripple of applause, which she acknowledged graciously.

'Vibrant-Sea has long been a pet project of mine, super close to my heart, as it combines my love of a vibrant, active, go-getting, positive lifestyle with the magic of the sea.' She glanced out of the window in the direction of what she obviously hoped was the coast, and then looked down at a scrap of paper she'd taken out of her trouser pocket. 'Sustainable athleisure is such a passion of mine. A big passion. A big, big passion. It is something I truly believe in and have been wanting to do my entire life. I would very much first of all like to say a big thank you to my beloved Malcolm, my rock, my husband, my inspiration, for helping to finance this total passion of mine.' She looked up as Malcolm raised his glass and then, catching her eye, didn't drink from it. 'Sustainable athleisure is something we should all be using these days. Too many clothes are put into landfill, and I feel passionately, ever so passionately, that everyone . . .' she looked around the assembled guests, 'almost everyone should be able to wear leggings that don't pollute the planet. Working out should not cost the world. There is no Planet B. So, here's to Vibrant-Sea!'

'Vibrant-Sea!' everyone toasted.

As a call to arms, it was perhaps not the most dynamic of speeches, thought Pat, wandering over to the rack and having a riffle through. But she was fond of a legging and these didn't appear to be that bad.

'They're two hundred and fifty a pair,' said Fi as she rushed to join her. 'Bamboo's expensive.'

'I'm sure it is,' agreed Pat, quickly removing her hand from the leggings as if touching them would imply she'd have to buy them, God forbid. 'Where does it come from?'

'China.'

'Mmm, very green,' she smiled. Luckily Fi didn't realise she was being sarcastic.

Fi was whippet thin, with a carefully curated tan and the sunny blonde highlights of someone who had also lounged in the Caribbean all winter. Despite, or perhaps because of, her regular tweakment trips to London, she looked older than she was. In her early forties, her body was a temple to moderation. No carbs, no sugar, no dairy, no caffeine, and she only drank champagne, which was apparently 'practically carb-free'. Walking behind her as she powered her way along the Sussex lanes with red weights strapped around her ankles, you could be forgiven for thinking she was in her early thirties. On Instagram, where she preferred to be, she glowed with the triple-filtered youth of a twenty-something influencer. In the flesh, however, she appeared to be most definitely heading towards half a century.

Pat picked up one of the grey zip-up hoodies with a scarlet lining and held it to her chest. Fi smiled and laughed and grabbed it off her, rapidly shaking her head as if saying 'a thousand times no'.

'This is, um, not for sale,' she said. 'This is for our youth market.'

'Oh, do you have it in a larger size?' asked Pat, mainly for her own amusement. Fi was suddenly reduced to a symphony of irritated tics. Her nose curled, her mouth pursed, and she aggressively scratched the back of her neck.

'We don't make clothes that big, I'm afraid. We're like all the luxury brands: Prada, Gucci, Versace. We don't go above a ten.'

'Well, good luck with it all,' Pat replied. 'Especially around here.'

'Actually, there are going to be quite a few changes around here. Aren't there, Dorna? Pat, have you met Dorna yet? She's doing this huge development on the Downs. It's going to be amazing. They're building a golf course. Boho Golf & Spa House Club.'

'Boho golf?' Pat frowned. 'How is that possible?'

'Boho Golf & Spa House Club is the full name,' corrected Fi.

'That does sound much better,' nodded Pat. Once again, Fi was oblivious to her sarcasm.

'Isn't it?! Dorna? Have you met Pat? She's a—'

'A park warden?'

'A psychotherapist.'

'Oh, fancy,' retorted Dorna. 'A psychotherapist near Beachy Head. Are you short of business?'

'I'm not really sure what you mean.' Pat's voice was icy.

'There was some poor chap only this morning,' Dorna continued, ignoring the Siberian situation unfolding in front of her. 'There were police and an ambulance. Yet another statistic.' She rolled her eyes. 'This whole area needs a rebrand, that's for sure!' She laughed and jangled her bracelets.

'And that's why you're here!' enthused Fi, patting her on the back. 'To turn the area into a luxury destination. It's just what we need. Some luxury. And a destination. Who doesn't like luxury? Who doesn't like elevating the ordinary? Thriving, not surviving. A lovely golf course and spa is perfect. I can sell my bamboo Vibrant-Sea leggings and hoodies and sports bra tops.'

'Exactly,' confirmed Dorna, raising her glass. 'To sports bra tops and leggings.' She sipped her champagne as Fi rushed back to her rack to see if she could persuade the pretty brunette, Lucy, to purchase a couple of pairs of leggings and a zippy hoodie top.

'Except he was probably murdered,' said Pat flatly.

'Who was?' asked Dorna, looking over Pat's shoulder for someone more useful to talk to.

'The boy on the beach.'

'Oh no he wasn't.' Dorna laughed. 'Don't be absurd. We're in the provinces. Nothing happens here. And anyway, the policewoman I spoke to said it was suicide.'

'It seems the police closed the case before they even opened it.'

'Well, they think it was suicide and they should know,' said Dorna.

'And I suspect murder.'

'I'd keep that quiet if I were you! Keep your little thoughts to yourself.' She leant over and lowered her voice, her warm champagne breath whistling in Pat's ear. 'Murder's bad for business. Very bad for business, Pat. Murder! No one wants to hear about that.'

CHAPTER 4

It was one of those mornings when the sky and the sea melded into a featureless grey. But still, undeterred as usual, Pat donned her black swimming costume, black bobble hat and thick dryrobe. It was 8 a.m. and she felt surprisingly spry. The drill to the temples that she had anticipated after Prichard's virulent pink drink and Fi's low-calorie champagne had failed to materialise, and she was relieved. In terms of hangovers, it appeared that Prichard's vodkas were less toxic than his wines. She smiled at Dave, who was sleeping on his favourite cushion, locked the front door, hid her key under the plant pot and grabbed her litter-picker, which was leaning against the wall beside the front gate.

Pat loathed litter almost as much as she disliked dogs off leads and feared for Korean tourists who leapt up and down on the cliff edge in the hope of achieving the perfect selfie. What was it with selfies, Koreans and Birling Gap? She found the whole situation intriguing. Apparently, so someone had explained to her once, some K-pop group (purveyors of fine Korean popular music) had shot a music video featuring the chalky white Seven Sisters in the background, and as a result, busloads of young girls in white knee socks, bare legs and tiny kilts or floaty dresses were deposited daily by the number 12 from Southbourne, making their way through the village and along the lane to the cliffs. They moved like pilgrims, bent against the coastal wind, before arranging themselves at the edge to leap, twirl and pose for the camera.

Pat knew that Instagram likes mattered to some people. Perhaps now more than ever. After the pandemic, when isolation had shrunk people's lives to screens and silence, the need to be noticed had sharpened into something urgent. What struck her most wasn't the posing itself, but the uniformity of it. The same angles, the same colours, the same places, repeated endlessly. A kind of aesthetic convergence that suggested not vanity but anxiety. Not *Look at me*, but *Do I belong here too?* The impulse seemed less about originality and more about reassurance. Proof that they were part of something, even if it was just the backdrop. She understood that in uncertain times, predictability could feel like control. And sometimes following the crowd wasn't thoughtlessness at all. It was a way of coping. A gesture of hope. A way of saying, quietly, *I exist. I was here. Just like everyone else.*

She strode along the tarmacked track, over the cattle grid, straight to the lay-by at the bottom of the hill, where she stopped, sighed, and used her litter picker to grab a Mars bar wrapper and drop it into the black bin bag she always kept folded in her pocket. Every day. Every bloody day. Someone pulled in, unwrapped a Mars bar, ate it, and tossed the evidence out of the window before driving off. Not once considering the possibility of the nearby bin. Not wondering what became of the wrapper. Not even curious. What sort of person did that? A tosser. That was her professional opinion. This particular tosser, she was pretty sure, ate a Mars bar for breakfast on his way to work every morning and considered that the beginning and end of his responsibilities. The wrapper vanished, the world reset and he drove on. He must think that the earth had a self-cleaning surface. She had resolved more than once to find out who he was. Camp out overnight if necessary. She'd bring a flask and a head torch. This was a long game now. And yes, she was convinced it was a man. Of course it was. Tossing was, she guessed, male behaviour. Women were usually brought up to be more accountable.

She turned to begin her march up the hill, keeping one eye out for dogs devoid of leads. Fortunately, the inclement weather and the early hour meant that there were no other walkers on the Downs. The field was empty, save for sheep. Pat inhaled deeply, filling her lungs, feeling her shoulders retreat from her ears and ignoring the occasional twinge from her hip. She liked it when the place was deserted. Walking over the hill and coming down the other side, she noticed a large rectangular sign hammered into the fence post next to the old red-roofed barn. That was new, she thought, wandering over. And then her heart stopped. Her mouth opened slowly. Her body went as stiff as the board she was staring at. What on earth? *Braddon Designs & Development*, read the gaudy orange letters. Surely it wasn't here, on this actual part of the Downs, that the frightful Dorna Braddon planned to develop her Boho Golf & Spa House Club?

'Fuck!' Pat exclaimed loudly. She pivoted away from the sign. 'Fuck!' she exclaimed again, grabbing her hip joint.

That really hurt. This was ridiculous! How could they have got planning permission in a national park? Surely the application should have been thrown out by the parish council. How could it have got through with no publicity? This was where her reluctance to open official-looking brown envelopes had got her, she thought ruefully.

Holding her head high, fuelled by a gritty determination, she carried on towards Birling Gap, the car park and the National Trust café, where she had arranged to meet Prichard at 8.30 a.m. sharp. She checked her watch and was pleased to see she was going to be early. By ten minutes to be exact. Pat liked to be early. She disliked tardiness almost as much as she disliked litter, dogs off leads, Braddon Designs & Development and the reckless antics of people dancing too close to the cliff edge.

The car park was empty. The wooden hut café was still shut; it didn't open until 9 a.m., and they had yet to put out the board instructing tourists how to stay safe on their visit. The new metal barriers were there, covered in their red signs advising caution, the risk of cliff falls and that people should stay five metres away from the base of the cliff. As if the erosion weren't self-evident enough, thought Pat, glancing to the left at a row of Georgian cottages. Exhibit A: one duck-egg-blue-painted house, half of which had already tumbled down the cliff, the other half being propped up by a flying buttress. She couldn't remember exactly when they'd installed the metal barriers. They were introduced after a tourist had fallen off the cliff to her death. Her boyfriend, his face to his phone trying to photograph her, hadn't noticed how near the edge she was. She took a step, lost her footing and fell over backwards. So now there were barriers just around the top of the stairs.

'Yoo-hoo!'

Pat turned around to see Prichard waving heartily as he strode towards her. Dressed in a long dark coat and another lengthy home-knit scarf, this time in multiple stripes, he was also wearing a Russian fur hat with ear flaps that stuck out at right angles like the handles on a saucepan.

'Am I late?' he queried.

'I'm early.'

'Of course you are!' he exclaimed, going in for a kiss on the cheek. '*Bon jonno, bon jonno,*' he said, pecking each side of her face. 'Oh, one second.' He pulled out a small book from his coat pocket and, opening it, stuck his finger on a page and pronounced, '*Jal jasseo.*' Pat stared at him. 'Korean,' he announced. 'I'm learning it, teaching myself obviously. That means "good morning", or, more precisely, "Did you sleep well?" Isn't that sweet? That's how they greet each other.'

'Endearing,' agreed Pat, sounding a little distracted.

'Are you all right?' Prichard arched his eyebrows at her.

'No. I've just seen the wretched Dorna Braddon's development sign next to the red barn.'

'The bat barn?' Prichard threw his multicoloured scarf over his shoulder with astonishment. 'How is that possible? Isn't it illegal to build with bats *in situ*?'

'Precisely. That woman is something else.'

'Never trust anyone with a hennaed pixie cut,' declared Prichard. 'And a ring on her index finger.'

'I'm beginning to come round to your way of analysing

people.' Pat sighed and looked up and down the coastal path. 'Shall we?'

'I've come prepared.' Prichard smiled enthusiastically and pulled a large magnifying glass out of his other pocket, accompanying it with his loud staccato laugh.

'Excellent.' Pat smiled. 'If I go down to the beach for a swim, I can have a look around on the shoreline for any clues the police might have missed above the high-tide line. And you should see if you can find anything up here.'

'*Joh-ayo*, which means "okey-dokey" in Korean.' Prichard paused. 'What exactly am I looking for?'

'Anything odd, I suppose,' answered Pat. 'Anything out of place. Henry was found right below these cliffs, so whatever happened would probably have happened right here. This is the crime scene.'

'Got it.' Prichard nodded vigorously.

'Are you sure you won't come for a swim?' asked Pat with a knowing smile.

'The only water I ever get into is bathwater, as you're well aware, Patricia Phillips.'

'I'm sure I'll tempt you one day.'

'When hell freezes over, and looking at that sea, it seems to be happening already, hahaha.'

Pat left Prichard on the clifftop and walked down the wooden steps to the beach. The sea looked cold as it swirled below. A milky-grey shot with patches of the palest blue. The water was never the same colour, which was one of the reasons she loved it so much. Standing on one of the last few steps down to the shore, she could hear the waves as they hissed and sighed over the pebbles, as if the sea was breathing. She looked up and down the empty beach. There was no one about. She must have just missed the sweaty, puffing joggers from the Westlinke Running Club who'd found Henry's body. There was no yellow tape, no cordoned-off area where he'd lain. Nothing. It was as if it had never happened. She looked up to the top of the cliffs over three hundred feet above. That was a long drop. A heavy fall. How terrified he must have been. The thought made her shiver.

She took off her dryrobe and left it in a discarded heap on the beach, then swapped her woolly socks for neoprene ones and strode across the pebbles, hardly limping at all, into the sea. This was always the worst bit, where her mind played tricks with her, suggesting it would be better not to bother, to give it a miss, that the water looked far too cold, why didn't she back out now and save herself the misery? Some cold-water swimmers used wetsuits, but Pat couldn't be bothered with the faff, the snapping-on and snapping-off, the struggle, the zip, carrying the sodding sodden thing back over the hill. It was easier to brave the full force of the cold, or not bother at all.

Speed was of the essence. She was not a sprint/dive person but more hop-hop-in-you-pop, but today she couldn't face rushing in. Today was cold. It was still April. Her ankles were freezing as she stepped into the water. Within seconds she lost all feeling in her toes. And then the icy waves rose over her knees, her thighs, and punched her hard in the stomach.

'Jesus!' She inhaled, before launching herself into the water, still wearing her black bobble hat. That was always the worst bit, stomach followed by chest . . .

It only took three strokes before it became bearable and she stopped hyperventilating, and then, after eight or nine, the water was pleasant enough. It was all right once you were in, as the saying went. She launched off and swam out a little further, kicking her legs, working her arms, and then looked back towards the beach. High on the cliff, she could see Prichard, with his distinctive ear flaps, bent forward apparently scouring the ground for clues. She continued to tread water, bobbing up and down in the waves. There were a few other souls on the beach now, much further up, towards Beachy Head, walking along the shoreline, arms linked, braced against the wind. She could see the old lighthouse, Fin du Monde. It had long since been decommissioned and was now converted into an Airbnb, popular with lovers and honeymooners alike. The views were said to be grand, although Pat had never been inside. The chalk cliffs were beautiful from the water; they shone a luminous bright white when hit by a shaft of sunlight. All along the beach, jagged piles of chalk lay where chunks had sheared off from the cliff's edge and crashed onto the pebbles below, white and fractured like broken slabs of marble or crumbled bones in the sun. Was Henry dead before he hit the water? Or had he survived the fall only to drown or die of hypothermia? Pat's stomach dropped. No one could last long out here, especially at this time of year.

She started to swim along the shoreline. She preferred breaststroke to front crawl, although it did nothing for the pain in her hip. Fortunately the water was so cold, and her body so numb, she couldn't really feel a thing. It had to be

Derek, she thought as she swam. Henry was going to remove him from his life; he might have made the mistake of telling him. He'd been due to sign the cease and desist order only a couple of days before. Surely that would be motive enough. Had the police even spoken to Derek? Done any sort of investigation at all?

She staggered out of the sea, buffeted by a wave. Her legs felt like jelly and her thighs and arms were scarlet with cold. Clutching her upper arms to keep warm, she stumbled over the stones towards her dryrobe and her socks and boots. The thick coat lined with moisture-wicking fleece was immediately warm as she wrapped it tightly around herself. She swapped the neoprene socks for her boots, then stared out to sea and smiled. Her body was awash with endorphins. That was why she did this nearly every morning. There was nothing quite like it.

'Did you find anything?' she asked Prichard when she finally reached the top of the cliff, panting slightly. 'Anything out of the ordinary?'

'Not that I can see, to be honest.' He sniffed. 'But then I'm not really sure what I'm looking for.'

'Well, I'm not really sure either,' agreed Pat. 'But maybe if we spread out and have a look in the long grass?'

'To see if the police missed something?'

'I'm not sure that the police looked at all.' Pat picked up her litter picker, which she'd left at the top of the steps. 'At least I can do some picking. It's always a mess around here.'

She spotted a lollipop stick immediately, tucked into a tussock of grass, and an empty crisp packet that had probably blown off one of the wooden picnic tables on the edge of the car park. She knew these clifftops well; there was not a dip or a curve or a brave bent shrub or hardy perennial that she wasn't familiar with. She could see the smallest changes, the shift in seasons, the tiniest soft green shoots. For when most people were standing on the edge, looking out to sea, taking photographs of either themselves or each other, Pat was scouring the ground, picker poised, looking for litter. One spot. Two entirely different perspectives.

'Do you think there might be a serial killer on the loose?' asked Prichard.

'I doubt it,' said Pat. 'This feels more personal than compulsive somehow. And we've only got one murder.'

'But serial killers have to start somewhere. Why couldn't this be the first?'

'From what I gather from all the true crime I've watched, even first kills usually show planning, fantasy, staging or some ritual or signature. This struck me as more messy and emotional. More rage than rehearsal.'

'Still,' Prichard frowned, 'if you were a serial killer in Westlinke, who'd you go after first?'

Pat raised an eyebrow. 'Tempting question. I've got a shortlist!'

They kept walking towards Birling Gap. Fortunately, Pat had her black bin bag in which she could deposit her collection. Prichard trotted along at her side, reading out Korean words and phrases from his book. As they approached one of the many memorial benches along the path, engraved with names of the much-loved departed, Pat, picking up yet another crisp packet with her picker, saw something that had been hidden behind it. A flash of light in the grass, near the black metal foot of the bench.

'What's that?' asked Prichard. He'd seen it too. 'Another can, do you suppose?'

Pat bent down to investigate.

'It's a telephone,' she said, picking it up out of the long grass. 'Someone's mobile.'

'Whose do you think it is?' Prichard whispered, hunching over and inspecting the iPhone more carefully.

'Why are you whispering?' Pat asked.

'I just am,' he whispered again. 'How do we find out who it belongs to?'

'Well,' Pat said, 'if there's any battery left, like this.' She tapped the screen hard, prodding it in the middle with a rigid finger. The phone sprang into life and a photograph appeared. They both recoiled with surprise. 'That's Henry,' declared Pat, squinting a little. 'That's Henry, and someone else.'

It was a grinning, happy photograph of two young, good-looking men with shiny smiles, gleaming skin and well-cut hair. Henry was dark, with regular features, a straight nose, a healthy set of eyebrows, and immaculate teeth he probably paid a fortune for. The other man was fairer, with thick blonde hair and pale blue eyes that stared straight out at the viewer. He was posing, his lips pouted a little, and his look to the camera was knowing. Henry was caught in the moment. The other man was very aware of the lens.

'Stone the starlings,' declared Prichard. 'They look like

they've stepped out of a magazine. I'd never kill myself if I was that good-looking!'

'We both know it doesn't work that way,' replied Pat, 'but yes, Henry was a handsome young man.'

'Do you think the other one is Derek?'

'I've no idea.'

'Do you think we should take it to the police?'

'Why?' Pat frowned in irritation. 'What are they going to do?'

'It's evidence in the case.'

'But there *is* no case.'

'It might be illegal.'

'What might be?'

'Us keeping the phone, withholding evidence.'

Pat stared at Prichard, trying to look incredulous. 'I had no idea you were such a conformist, Prich.'

But of course, she did. His picture-postcard-perfect cottage on the green was half home, half filing cabinet. He had a whole room dedicated to die-cast models of lorries, buses, tractors and cars, dating from the late nineteenth century to the present day, posing on their original boxes in glass-fronted mahogany cabinets. In the next room was his collection of twentieth-century studio ceramics, including a Bernard Leach and a Lucie Rie, neatly arranged on shelves in height order. And his brewery and distillery took over the pantry, utility room and half his kitchen. There was a place for everything and everything was in its place. And the place for that phone in Prichard's mind was the police station and nowhere else.

'I don't think anyone would mind if we took a look at it.' Pat shrugged.

'I don't want to go to prison.' Prichard threw one end of his scarf over his shoulder.

'Prison? You won't.' She tapped the screen. It went to face ID. She flashed the screen at Prichard.

'What are you doing? My face is never going to open that! Those two are young and handsome and half my age!'

'Password?' Pat looked up from the phone. 'What are the most common passwords, do you think?'

Prichard puffed out his cheeks. 'I'm not sure.'

'I can tell you the most obvious three, off the top of my head,' said Pat. '123456,' she tapped. 'Nope. The next one is 111111. No, that's not it. 000000. Damn, we're locked out for five minutes. What's yours?'

'Mine's quite hard, actually . . .' Prichard paused. '121212.'

'That's about the fourth most popular password.'

'Is it?' He sounded disappointed. 'I thought it had whimsy. I also thought people preferred dates like 1966. You know, when we last won the World Cup, that sort of thing.'

'Or their date of birth,' said Pat slowly. 'Let's go! Back to the house.'

'Can't we take it straight to the police?'

'What? Now?'

He nodded.

'Don't be ridiculous, Prichard,' snapped Pat, whipping out her damp swimming costume from her pocket and waving it at him. 'I'm not wearing any pants, and I refuse to go to the police station stark bollock naked.'

CHAPTER 5

Back in Ivy Cottage over a cup of hot coffee, a now fully clothed Pat opened Henry's phone in a matter of the few minutes it took her to grab his file from the shepherd's hut and type in his date of birth, 26 May 1992. He was thirty-three years old. He had so much to live for, she thought, tapping away at the screen, a dull ache in her chest. So many plans. So many dreams.

'Have you found anything?' asked Prichard, feeding cat treats to Dave, who was once again on his lap.

'Only this on his WhatsApp from Derek. By the way, it is Derek on the front of the phone,' she added. 'Look, it's the same photo as his WhatsApp profile thing.'

'Right.' Prichard nodded. 'I can't help but think . . .' His voice trailed off. He sniffed uncomfortably, scratched the side of his head and then leant forward.

'So earlier, Derek apologises for the argument they've had and asks Henry to forgive him.' Pat tried her best to ignore the guilty feeling of invading her patient's privacy, even in death. 'He says, "I was wrong about us. Shall we try again?" And Henry appears to be keen.' She sat back in her chair, staring at the messages, and slowly shook her head. 'That will annoy Sue, all that hard work she did to extricate Derek from the flat, only for Henry to agree to go back to him. It's classic coercive-control victim behaviour. The push-pull where someone feels mistreated but can't quite detach. They may feel hurt, but the hope for change keeps them tethered. Derek goes on to say, "Let me make it up to you. How about a night in this gorgeous little place by the sea, near where we were the other week." Look. It's Fin du Monde. Those are the double rooms with the view; I've seen the photos. So that's why Henry was here the night before! He was going to meet Derek.'

'So we have our man!' declared Prichard, standing up and vigorously tapping Derek's name on the Post-it note in the middle of the noticeboard.

'But Henry doesn't reply.'

'That doesn't mean anything. We were right! We *are* right! Derek is the prime suspect, and now we know why Henry was here and who he was meeting. Derek was the last person to see him alive. We should take all this to the police.'

It took Pat a little while to agree. The theory made a kind of sense, but she wasn't in the habit of leaping from plausibility to certainty. People were complicated, motives layered. Just because Derek had invited Henry to a night at Fin du Monde didn't necessarily mean he was responsible for his disappearance. Correlation was not causation, as she reminded her clients often enough. Her instinct was always to listen, watch, hold things lightly until the picture became clearer. Eventually, though, she agreed it might be best if she took Henry's phone to the police herself. It would, as

Prichard put it, arouse a little less suspicion. Of what exactly, she wasn't entirely sure.

Pat parked her never-washed, moss-growing twenty-year-old Lexus outside the old red-brick Victorian police station in Southbourne, the nearest town, just as another number 12 pulled up to take a party of tourists to Westlinke. As usual, none of them had prepared for the elements, opting instead for fashionable, photo-ready clothes: short skirts, knee-high boots, and the occasional floaty frock that offered no protection from the wind. She watched them through her filthy windscreen. Catching her reflection in the mirror, she forced a smile. There it was: her best approximation of pleasant cooperation. Her happy face. Or what passed for it under pressure.

As she walked into the station, she was immediately hit by the smell of old alcohol and a recent slosh of Domestos. Still damp after their daily mop, the light blue plastic floor tiles were tacky underfoot as she crossed the hall. She had always heard Sue talk about the 'modern-day Met' being institutionally this or institutionally that. But here in Southbourne, the police weren't institutionally anything; you could barely call the place a building, more like a neglected afterthought. Scruffy, shabby, with curling faded posters urging members of the public to *See it, say it, sorted* or to keep their distance due to Covid restrictions – that notice must be at least three years old, thought Pat – the reception area was in desperate need of updating. There were a couple of chairs pushed up against the cracked and peeling pistachio-coloured walls, and some glaring strip lights whose shades seemed to be housing a colony of dead flies. Opposite the main door, which slammed loudly as it shut, was the front desk. The pale cheap pine veneer was finished off with a thick glass half-barrier and a small cubbyhole window that the officer on duty was forced to peer through.

'Hello again!' breezed Pat.

'Oh, hello,' said the young man behind the glass. 'What can I do for you, Dr Phillips?'

'It's more what I can do for you, PC Footer,' replied Pat, bending forward to speak through the window.

'Oh yes?' Footer said, plucking a Rolo out of its golden foil on the desk in front of him and popping it in his mouth.

'I have found Henry Clayton's mobile phone.'

'You have?' He sat up. 'Where did you find it?'

'On the cliff near Birling Gap.'

'Well, of course. It must have fallen out of his pocket before he jumped.' He nodded.

How could they justify the lack of a proper search? Pat wondered. They would have found the phone had they made any sort of effort.

PC Footer pushed his dimpled hand through the gap in the glass and placed it on the counter. There was a smudge of chocolate along the side of his finger. Pat touched the outside of her anorak to make sure the phone was still in her pocket.

'It explains why he was in Westlinke in the first place,' she said. 'He was going to meet his friend Derek.'

'Right,' nodded Footer.

'They were going to stay the night at Fin du Monde – you know, the old lighthouse that's now an Airbnb.'

'I do. I think perhaps you should come and speak to the boss.'

'I think I should too,' agreed Pat, feeling strangely elated. 'I think that would be a good idea.'

PC Footer pressed a buzzer under the desk, which opened a side door to let Pat into the station. 'If you follow me,' he said, 'I'll take you to her office.'

Pat followed his back into an open-plan office containing ten or twelve desks each with a large square-screened computer. None flickered with any life. In fact, the whole room buzzed only with the sound of a broken air-conditioning unit, and exuded inactivity.

Two desks were manned by police officers, both of whom were eating sandwiches with their feet up, one reading the sports section of a red-top newspaper and the other scrolling his phone. PC Footer turned around to catch Pat's puzzled expression.

'It's nearly lunchtime,' he said, by way of explanation.

'Oh,' Pat replied. Note to self: don't become a victim of crime between 11.30 a.m. and 1.30 p.m. on a Tuesday in or around the region of Southbourne.

'She's just in here.'

Footer paused at the glass door. DS Stevens was on the telephone, her chair turned, her brown bun facing the glass. Pat watched as she pulled a strand of hair out of the bun and began to curl it around the length of her finger while her chair swung gently from side to side.

'She looks busy,' Footer said. Busy flirting, thought Pat. 'Shall we come—' But before he could finish his sentence, DS Stevens had turned around, noticed her audience and quickly put down the phone without so much as a goodbye. PC Footer knocked on the glass; DS Stevens nodded. They were allowed to enter.

'Footer,' she said as he opened the door. 'Dr Phillips? To what do we owe the pleasure?' she asked in a tone drizzled with annoyance.

Pat was immediately irritated. 'I have found Henry Clayton's phone. His mobile. On the cliff between the Fin du Monde lighthouse and Birling Gap.'

'Well, that's very helpful,' Stevens replied, in a manner that implied it was anything but. 'It must have fallen out of his pocket before he jumped.' She put out her hand, the one with the engagement ring, and wiggled her fingers.

'That's exactly what I said,' enthused Footer, his fleshy cheeks pinking. 'It must have slipped out before he jumped.'

'Or maybe it fell out of his pocket during an altercation.' Pat stared at the moving fingers. Was Stevens asking for the phone to be placed in her hand? 'It wasn't close to the edge. It was next to a bench.'

'Maybe he sat there before deciding to die by suicide,' replied the detective.

'Or maybe there was a struggle, and the phone fell out of his pocket.' Pat knew she sounded belligerent, because she felt it. 'And the reason he was in Westlinke in the first place was that he was meeting his friend Derek.' She toyed with the idea of saying 'boyfriend', but she sensed that might make

Stevens even less enthusiastic about investigating Henry's murder. If that were at all possible. 'They were staying at Fin du Monde,' she added. 'The lighthouse Airbnb.'

'I know the place very well,' said DS Stevens.

'Well, you'll be able to check easily then. Henry was going to patch things up with his friend. Without giving away too many confidences, the friendship had fallen apart, and Derek had asked that they meet to discuss it.'

Pat slowly took Henry's phone out of her pocket. Prichard had suggested she 'bag it' as evidence, so they'd found a ziplock freezer bag below the sink that had only been used once before, for cold chicken on a picnic. He'd rinsed it out and dried it with a paper towel, then popped the phone inside. Now Pat placed it carefully into DS Stevens' still open hand.

'And you found all this information out how?' Stevens' lips twitched with something too thin to be called a smile as her fingers clamped around the device.

'By looking at his phone,' replied Pat. 'It's got lots of evidence on it. The messages from Derek, the suggestion of the night at Fin du Monde, it's all in there.'

'You accessed his phone?'

'I found it on the grass and needed to find out who it belonged to.'

'And you knew the code?'

'I worked it out. I've written it on a sticky label on my evidence bag.'

'You were tampering with evidence?'

'Not exactly. And anyway, evidence of what? This isn't a murder investigation, apparently,' Pat shot back. 'But I think

Derek has something to do with it – a lot to do with it. You should at least speak to him.'

'The thing is, Dr Phillips, we have. Spoken to him. Derek.'

'When?'

'Before we came to see you.'

All the oxygen left Pat's lungs. They had already spoken to the prime suspect? She tried to compose herself but could feel her cheeks flushing.

'He was the one who told us that Henry was depressed. Very depressed. He was the one who said he was seeing a shrink for his issues. Mental health and all that.'

Pat's heart started to pound loudly, so loudly she felt Footer and Stevens might hear it. She dug her nails into her palms as she felt her face burn with the irritation that was coursing at great speed through her veins. If blood could ever boil, this was what it would feel like.

'Henry Clayton was not depressed,' she said very slowly, enunciating each word as if she were talking to the hard of hearing, or indeed, in DS Stevens' case, the hard of listening. 'He was just dissatisfied with a certain part of his life. That is all. There is a difference.'

'Well, his boyfriend, Derek Jones, said otherwise. And he knew him very well.' Stevens paused, then leant forward and patted the back of Pat's hand. 'I'm sure you tried your best.' Her nose wrinkled with contrived compassion. 'But we all have bad days at the office. I should know.' A little laugh escaped.

Pat reminded herself that she had to breathe.

'I'd like to see the photographs of Henry.'

'What photographs? The post-mortem photographs? I'm afraid that's not possible,' replied DS Stevens, crossing her arms.

'He was my client.'

'I'm sorry, Dr Phillips.' She smiled tightly. 'It's still a negative. Listen.' She stood up suddenly and glanced at her wristwatch. 'Thank you for the mobile. I'll be sure to return it to his next of kin. Forensics have yet to report, but just to repeat, we are not looking for anyone else in connection with the death of Henry Clayton. We have spoken to his partner, who confirmed he was depressed at the time, that he was on his way to see his psychotherapist. There's nothing more for us to do.' She shrugged. 'Now if you'll excuse me, I have some detecting to do. PC Footer will see you out.'

CHAPTER 6

Pat stood on the steps of the police station and sighed. That hadn't gone as she'd hoped or expected. She was accustomed to having a certain authority in the room, to reading situations clearly and knowing when to act. But this time she'd misjudged it. She'd handed over the phone, potentially their most valuable piece of evidence, too soon, and more importantly, she'd let herself be swayed. Prichard had meant well, but she should have known better than to act without clarity. What bothered her most wasn't the procedural outcome, it was the quiet sense that she'd betrayed her own judgement. And now, to find that the police had already spoken to Derek and ruled him out, that stung. She sighed again, this time more quietly. It wasn't disappointment in the police she felt so much as disappointment in herself.

The heavy door swung open behind her and slammed. She didn't bother to turn around.

'All right?' mumbled PC Footer as he walked past her.

'PC Footer, Barry?' she said, venturing with the familiar. He stopped. 'Where are you going?'

'I'm on my lunch break,' he replied.

'Lunch? Oh, let me buy you something.' Pat smiled. 'Are you going out?'

'Well, I've already eaten what I brought for my first lunch.'
'Right.'
'My mum made me some cheese and pickle sandwiches this morning, and I had those with a packet of prawn cocktail crisps and an orange KitKat, but I had that at about ten o'clock. I couldn't wait. I can never wait, to be honest.'
'An orange KitKat? Are they good?'
'The best. They're quite hard to get hold of.'
'I bet,' agreed Pat. She was matching him stride for stride as he walked across the car park.
'I could buy you a cup of coffee.' She nodded over at Costa across the road. He paused. 'Or a hot chocolate? I hear they make the best ones in there. With that spray cream.'
'Oh, go on then,' he agreed, his eyes lighting up. 'If you insist.'
Pat followed him across to the Costa. The doors swung inward with the soft hiss of hydraulics, and a warm blast came from a heater above them. It smelt of roasted beans and steamed milk, with a sweet undercurrent of caramel and chocolate. There were a few student types tapping on keyboards, but most of the customers were tourists, hunched over their hot chocolates and oat milk lattes; they'd be waiting for the next number 12 to Westlinke, or passing time before the train back to London. To the left of the till, in a glass-fronted cabinet that caught the light just so, were the sweet temptations: salted caramel brownies glistening under the glow like dark treasure; golden croissants flaking at the edges; pastel-toned muffins swelling with blueberries or

chocolate chips; slabs of lemon drizzle cake looking tender enough to fall apart at the touch of a fork.'

Despite living near Southbourne for a decade, Pat had never set foot in the Costa. Hers was not a coffee-house generation. Pubs, yes. Pints, absolutely. But coffee? That was something you made in a mug at home, without whipped cream or a loyalty card.

'Hello, Barry,' smiled the young woman behind the counter. 'The usual? There's a table free in the corner.' She nodded. 'I'll bring it over. Yes?' She looked at Pat.

'I'll have the same,' said Pat.

'With a hot chocolate?'

'Just a black coffee.'

'Sit yourself down over there.' She indicated the table with another nod.

'Thanks, Paulina,' replied Barry.

Pat followed Barry as he eased his way through the narrow gaps between square oak veneer tables and leatherette chairs. In the far corner, he sat down to face the room, leaving Pat to sit opposite, with her back to the door and Barry's face as her only view.

'Thank you for this,' she said. 'For agreeing to have a chat.' He hadn't specifically. He'd agreed to a hot chocolate, but now he was trapped here with no escape, and she was going to make the most of it. 'How long have you been on the force?'

Out came Barry's tongue. It appeared that his brain and his tongue were connected. 'Umm . . .' He paused for thought. 'Twenty-two months.'

'And you enjoy it?'

'It's all I've ever wanted to do, really. My dad's a copper in Brighton, due to retire next year.'

'Here you go,' said Paulina, plonking down two plates. 'Triple chocolate double muffins.'

Pat looked down at her plate. The idea of eating such a cake before she'd had any lunch didn't appeal. She glanced up to see that PC Barry Footer was already halfway through his. He'd inhaled one mouthful and was working vigorously on the next, melted chocolate bubbling in the corner of his mouth.

'And what is DS Stevens like to work for?' Pat was transfixed by his soft, shiny lips as they opened and shut, making short shrift of his 'usual'.

'DS Stevens? She's nice enough. She's very efficient, she likes to tick things off, solve things quickly. She's got one of the highest clear-up rates on the force. The big bosses like that. It's good for statistics. High clear-up rates make them look good. They make us all look good.'

'Yes, and I expect that's what it's all about these days, statistics, clearing up.' Pat nodded in hearty agreement, or what she hoped looked like it. 'So I suppose it's not a surprise that she thinks Henry's death is a suicide.'

'It's much less paperwork,' agreed Barry. 'That's for sure.' His voice trailed off. He appeared not to be concentrating on Pat's questions. She followed his gaze. It was obvious what had captured his full attention. The muffin on her plate.

'Much easier for everyone, for all concerned, if he jumped,' she ventured.

'Much.'

Such was the sugary siren call coming from the muffin, Pat sensed he was losing his hearing.

'Would you like it?' she asked, pushing her plate towards him.

'Oh no, no, no,' he nodded, his mouth saying the opposite of his body language.

'Really,' insisted Pat. 'I don't like them.'

'Don't like chocolate muffins!' Barry's face crumpled with incomprehension.

'They'll only throw it away otherwise.'

He didn't need asking twice. Out went the dimpled hand, and picking up the cake, he took a large bite before placing it down on his own plate. It sat there for no more than fifteen seconds before he took another chunk out of it.

Pat soaked up the atmosphere of Barry Footer, catching something of the sadness under his chocolate muffin enthusiasm. She'd seen a lot of people in their early to mid-twenties with that sadness. She recognised it.

'Was your parents' divorce devastating for you?' she asked. It was either that or one of his parents was no longer alive, which she could already rule out.

'I was six years old.' Barry paused as he took in her question. His eyes were round with astonishment, his open mouth frosted with granules of sugar. 'My life was never the same again.'

'Was it just you?' she asked, already feeling she knew his answer.

'Yes.' He sighed and put down the remainder of the muffin, then played with his plate, spinning it back and forth as he stared at the half-eaten 'usual'. 'My mum left my dad.' His lips pouted.

'She remarried and had other children?'

'How did you know that?' He sat back a little and looked at her. Was she a witch? A mind-reader?

'It's quite common.' Pat smiled.

'They both started new families, but mine, me, Mum and Dad, that family just stopped existing. Like we'd never been one at all. Like it never counted.'

Poor Barry, trying to feed a hunger that would not be satiated with food no matter how many times he sat at his corner table in the Southbourne Costa. Some chose alcohol to fill that void, some drugs. Sometimes people distracted themselves from an inner emptiness with dangerous sex in car parks with unsuitable, violent men. Or stealing. Pat used to have a client who was obsessed with shoplifting smoked salmon from Waitrose and was once found pleasuring himself in the bus lane outside the shop covered in hand-sliced slivers of fish. Barry's chocolate was tame in comparison. But the feeling was the same. The same sensation always: a hollow inside that demanded to be filled.

'I can help you with that if you'd like,' she suggested.

'With what?'

'The comfort eating. Only if you want. You might find it useful.' She smiled. 'Well, you know where I am if you do want to follow up.'

'Thanks,' he said quietly, pushing his plate distractedly away. 'You're the first person to ever ask that. To offer that.'

'Therapy?'

'Help.'

He turned and stared out of the plate-glass window, his gaze blank. There was a silence between them. In fact, the café was remarkably quiet for somewhere so busy, and Pat realised that most of the customers were sipping their drinks while scrolling on their phones. The only real noise was the clatter of mugs as Paulina stacked them on the coffee machine. Pat was being quiet on purpose; silence, she knew, could encourage people to talk.

'There's a suicide note, if you'd like to see it,' suggested Barry suddenly, his cheeks flushing pink. The silent tactic had worked.

'There is?' That didn't prove anything, Pat had to remind herself. Nothing. Unless . . . 'Does it have Henry's fingerprints on it?'

'It was quite hard to take his fingerprints, to be honest,' declared Barry. He leant across the table, his voice low, his eye contact indirect. 'He'd been in the water. It's not good for the skin, if you know what I mean. But anyway, the note has no prints on it. We've dusted for them, and nothing.'

'That's odd. If you're writing a note, in haste, in emotional distress, I would think it would have prints on it where you've touched the paper.'

'I agree. But Amanda – DS Stevens – is ambitious about targets and didn't think it was worth wasting any more time and money on that.'

'Right. And where was the note found?'

'At the Airbnb. Fin du Monde. It looks like he checked in, wrote the note and then decided to die by suicide.'

'Or not,' chipped in Pat.

'Do you want to see it?'

'The note?' She tried to mute her excitement. 'If it's not too much of a bother.'

'DS Stevens is out to lunch. She won't be back for a while. She takes the full hour allocated, as is her right, and sometimes even longer. We should be fine. Pop back to the station with me. No one will be any the wiser.'

Back over the road, Pat followed PC Barry Footer through the peeling pistachio hallway into the empty office, where they both elicited the most cursory of disinterested nods from the PCs with their feet up, still reading the sport and looking at TikTok. PC Footer pointed at what looked like an interview room.

'If you wait in there,' he suggested, 'I'll bring you the file.'

The interview room was small and airless, with pale beige walls and matching carpet tiles. Up against one wall was a table and four chairs, two on either side. On the table was an elderly-looking tape recorder with large buttons. On another of the walls was a large mirror. Pat walked slowly up to it, wondering if someone else was standing on the other side, watching her.

The door swung open. She stepped back, and in walked PC Footer.

'Is that . . . ?' she asked, glancing over her shoulder.

'A two-way mirror? Yup,' he nodded, pulling out a chair. 'Don't worry,' he added. 'Everyone's still at lunch.'

Pat was acutely aware of the mirror behind her. The idea that someone could be watching, listening, made her uneasy.

'Sit,' said Barry, pointing to a seat opposite. He was oddly commanding all of a sudden; in his natural habitat he'd taken on an unexpected air of authority, almost as if he knew what he was doing. 'So, here's the file.' He opened a beige cardboard envelope. It looked disappointingly thin. 'And here's the note.' He carefully took out a square piece of paper covered in a transparent plastic sheath and laid it on the table. They both stared at the large capital letters written in red felt pen or marker.

I WANT TO END IT ALL
HENRY

'Is that it?' Pat asked, sitting back in the blue plastic chair, a heavy frown on her face. Henry was educated, loquacious, verbose even. It didn't feel like something he would write. And in red marker pen, in capital letters. It didn't feel like Henry Clayton at all. 'Did it come with anything else? An envelope? Addressed to someone? His mother, for example?'

'Just that,' said PC Footer, staring down at the page.

'It doesn't feel very much like a suicide note.'

'I suspect you've seen a lot of them.'

'Normally my job is to prevent such a thing,' replied Pat, with a long, thoughtful breath. 'I don't think he wrote this. I really don't. I've seen his handwriting, it's elegant and fluid. This scrawl is completely different. Do you mind if I take a photograph and then I can compare it to my sample when I get back to the office?'

'The shepherd's hut?' PC Footer glanced up at the two-way mirror behind her. Pat spun around. Had he heard something? They both sat stock still, staring at their reflections in the glass. Pat didn't dare breathe. She strained her ears, but all she could hear was her own heart pounding. 'If you want,' he said eventually, pushing the page and the file towards her.

As he did so, a photograph slid out from the confines of the envelope. Pat looked down and immediately felt a wave of nausea flood over her, followed rapidly by a bolt of adrenaline. What was *that*? The bloated white face, the mop of dark hair, the deep brownish cuts and blows to the face, the puffy pale blue lips like a carp. One eye was half open, the lid pulled back a little. It stared, unfocused, filmed, grey-sheened, off into the distance. What was it looking at? What had it seen? She covered her open mouth with both hands. To stifle a scream? A cry of horror? A sob? It was hard to know which. Her blood ran cold.

'Henry,' she whispered. 'Poor Henry.' She stared up at PC Footer over her cold hands, which she slowly lowered. 'Is this how you found him?'

'Yes,' he replied flatly. 'You weren't supposed to see that.' He swiftly opened the file and pushed the large photograph back in. However, in doing so he flashed another full-length shot of Henry lying on his back on the beach, surrounded by pebbles, his feet in the sea. It was just as DS Stevens had described when sitting at the table in Pat's kitchen, except the detective had omitted one vital piece of information.

'How extraordinary,' declared Pat, as she leant in for a closer look. 'He's wearing his best suit – I've seen it before – and a tie; he looks like he's dressed up to go out.' For drinks, or maybe dinner, she thought to herself. She stood up and put her hands on her hips. 'Who on earth goes to commit suicide in an Armani suit?'

'It's *die by* suicide,' echoed a cold female voice over the intercom system, and both PC Footer and Pat turned to stare at the mirror and the disembodied voice. With a click of a switch, the mirrored glass disappeared, and they could both see DS Stevens staring back at them. Her face looked stark and harsh in the downward spot lighting.

'I'm not sure what you're doing here, Dr Phillips, but I think you should leave. We have tolerated your interference long enough. I could charge you with numerous crimes just by finding you here going through sensitive files – contaminating evidence in the process. We could start off with wasting police time.'

'But I don't think I am wasting your time,' retorted Pat.

'What you think has nothing to do with it, Dr Phillips. We deal with facts here in the police force, cold, hard facts. And the fact is, Henry Clayton was being treated for mental health issues, he was depressed, and he died by suicide. How many more times do I need to tell you? The case is closed.'

'PC Footer?' Pat turned to look at Barry in the hope of some sort of support. Instead, he put his palms in the air. His sugary hands were tied.

'Well . . .' She paused. 'If you won't find out who killed Henry Clayton, I most certainly will.'

She marched out of the interview room, hoping the door might slam behind her to dramatic effect. Instead, it closed achingly slowly due to health and safety concerns, leaving her with little option but to stomp loudly down the corridor.

CHAPTER 7

Outside in the fresh air, Pat got into her moss-mobile and drove the four miles back to Westlinke. She needed air, and she needed to think. She parked at Ivy Cottage, then marched with a barely discernible limp towards the village green with its flagpole, its Union Jack flag hanging listless in the lack of wind, and the nearby war memorial: a stone obelisk surrounded by a low wrought-iron fence, painted a shiny black. She walked along the path that bisected the green towards the village hall, where a busy community noticeboard advertised pottery classes, computing for the elderly, and a mums and toddlers drop-in coffee morning every Tuesday and Thursday, as well as detail-freak Jacqui's weekly art classes, which Pat and Prichard attended. She paused by the wooden bench in the middle of the green, which had an expansive view over the South Downs in all their majestic glory, and, on a good day, of the silvery shimmer of the sea.

She contemplated sitting down, but the oak slats looked wet, and they would play havoc with her hip. Out of the corner of her eye she caught a glimpse of Bev twitching her curtains in her pretty flint and brick cottage, its front door painted the uniform Farrow & Ball green, like all the other estate cottages. She contemplated a wave, but Bev scuttled away as soon as she'd been spotted. Pat smiled at Mr Bishop – at least that was what she thought he was called – who was fiddling about with a surprisingly fecund rosemary bush in his front garden. Then her gaze landed on the pub. Ah, a bit of lunch, she thought.

The Green Lion was something of a village institution, with its white walls and lichen-spotted slate roof, several large umbrellas outside and a row of four picnic tables with attached wooden benches. It sported a large hand-painted sign above the entrance depicting a bright lime-green lion, seemingly rampant and ready for anything. The infinitely smaller black and white sign in the glass window of the door declared the place to be open, and Pat walked in gratefully, ducking her head. Not that she was in danger of hurting herself – she wasn't tall, only five foot six – but the ceilings were low and the maroon decor gave the appearance of a much smaller space than it actually was. The two lit fires in the large grates on either side of the main room didn't help with the sense of claustrophobia.

It was hot inside. Pat undid her anorak as she approached the bar and leant on the dark wood next to a black beam decorated with a row of shining horse brasses. Just as she was about to speak, there was an explosion of laughter, a clash of glasses and some whoops of celebration, which all seemed rather a lot for a weekday lunchtime. She looked over her shoulder to see a grinning Dorna Braddon raising a flute of fizz towards the ceiling with her bandaged hand, surrounded by a group of men in suits, their striped shirts straining at their buttons. Two silver ice buckets of booze shone at the centre of their table. In one, the bottle was already positioned bottom-up, and the other was well on its way to joining it.

'How long have they been there?' Pat asked Johnno, the young barman, who had a trimmed Hoxton beard and two forearms of Celtic tattoos.

'Since before lunch,' he replied, glancing across. 'They're celebrating some deal or other, to do with a golf course, I think, I haven't been paying them much attention. So, what can I get you?' His accent was Antipodean, and everything he said sounded like a question. Although, to be fair, his last sentence was one. 'Drink?' he added, just to make sure.

'Hmm...' Pat had no idea what to choose. 'Can I have a zero-alcohol gin and tonic, and make it a double, then I'll be kidding myself I'm having a proper drink. And a sausage roll, please.'

'Right you are,' Johnno said, and disappeared.

Although Pat was standing with her back to the rowdy table, she tuned into their conversation, bristling as they laughed and toasted their good fortune one more time.

'To Boho Golf!' pronounced one.

'To Boho Golf!' they all agreed.

'They're a noisy bunch,' someone said.

She looked along the bar and spotted the young man with the earring who lived next door to the pub.

'Oh hello,' she smiled. 'Weren't you at the leggings launch last night?'

'Guilty.' He grinned. Dark eyelashes, brown hair; he looked as though he wouldn't be out of place strumming a guitar in a side street. 'I can't resist workout gear, or more truthfully the lure of free champagne.' It wasn't hard to believe.

'Are you a gym sort of person then?' It wasn't really a question. His toned bicep emerged from his T-shirt as he leant forward, elbow resting on the bar.

'I have my moments.' He smiled again and knocked back the shot in his glass. For an alcoholic, he did look quite well, Pat thought.

There was another explosion of laughter from the other side of the bar. The man glanced across in annoyance.

Pat extended her hand. 'I'm Pat.'

He stood up and shook it, his handshake firm but clammy. Must be the booze, she thought.

'Marcus. Good to meet you.' The Greek chorus of businessmen began clapping and shouting again. Marcus rolled his eyes, then offered Pat an apologetic smile. 'Forgive me, I'm afraid I must go. The noise.'

'More than understandable,' she replied. As he walked away, she reached across the bar to pick up a poorly folded, well-thumbed local newspaper. Anything to distract herself from the cacophony behind her. Were they really celebrating that wretched golf club development? Prichard had been at the preliminary planning meeting and had reassured her that there was no way it would go ahead; the Downs had always been protected. But then, after Mal and Fi's drinks party and the sign that she'd seen by the barn, right on her doorstep, it was all looking a lot more likely. And now this. Dorna's smug, shiny face, flushed with booze in the bright, unforgiving light of the window, and the circle of fawning suits surrounding her. Pat shook her head, turned over the newspaper and stopped.

There he was. Henry. Or at least his photograph. On the front page. *Tragedy of young man washed up on beach*, read the headline. Below were more details. The reporter had spoken to DS Stevens, and even PC Footer had got a mention, but the last line of the story was what upset Pat most. *The police are not looking for anyone to help them with their enquiries.*

'Of course they're not, the lazy bastards!' she mumbled, and pushed the newspaper to one side.

'I saw him,' said Johnno as he handed over Pat's fake gin and sausage roll.

'Thank you,' she replied. 'Saw who?'

'That bloke.' He nodded at the newspaper. 'He came in here before . . . you know.'

'Before he died? What? The night before?'

Johnno shook his head. 'Oh no. It was two weeks ago. He'd come in with some other bloke. They looked like they were friends, if you know what I mean.'

Pat took a large gulp of her fake gin; strangely, it seemed to give her a warm glow. Must be a placebo effect, she thought. The taste was not dissimilar to something Prichard might brew in his utility room, although hopefully less lethal.

'They sat over there.' He looked across to Dorna's corner. 'It's the cosiest part of the bar.'

'What did his friend look like?'

It was odd that Henry hadn't mentioned coming to Westlinke before. Perhaps it wasn't in the forefront of his mind during their sessions, or maybe he just hadn't registered that she lived here.

'Blonde, with very blue eyes. I remember the eyes. They

were quite striking – not that I'm a bloke who notices other blokes' eyes,' Johnno added hastily. 'I only really remember the two of them because they had a fight, well, an argument that they took outside. They had words, as we say at home. Words that then developed into some pushing and shoving on the green. Not very dramatic. They were both wearing posh shoes. You know, with leather soles. You can't get much purchase with a leather sole. If you want to fight, like properly fight, you need trainers.' He paused and looked at Pat. 'Not that I'm that sort of bloke either.' He smiled.

'Of course not,' said Pat, taking another slug of her drink. 'D'you know what they were arguing about?'

'I try not to listen to these things.'

'Of course not,' she said again.

'To Boho Golf!' came a shout from the corner.

Again?! Pat bit the inside of her cheek and resolutely did not turn around. Instead, she drained her glass and set it down on the bar.

'I didn't catch much of it,' said the barman, leaning in; he smelt of roll-ups. 'But the blonde one was upset because the dark one was involved with some environmental group; he didn't like him mixing with hippies. And I think maybe the dark one said something about debts mounting up.'

'To progress!'

Pat turned around just as Dorna leant over and picked up an empty bottle from the slushy ice bucket.

'Barman!' she called, waggling the bottle from side to side. 'Another one of these!'

CHAPTER 8

From the open window of the shepherd's hut, Pat could smell meaty smells and garlic. Prichard had let himself into her kitchen again and was clearly cooking up something delicious for supper. He was a good cook, enthusiastic and adventurous. He was wont to snip out recipes from the Saturday and Sunday colour supplements and give almost anything a go, the more obscure, flavoursome and complex the better. And he nearly always used Pat's kitchen, since his brewing equipment and distillery took up a lot of the work surfaces in his own. He'd complained once, years ago, that cooking for one was miserable and a frightful bore, so now he regularly turned up at Ivy Cottage, using every pot and pan, grater and whisk in the place. He was one of those extreme-sports chefs who demanded gadgets and bowls and feedback, applause and appreciation at every turn. Much like Pat's ex-husband, who used to cook one meal a week, usually Sunday lunch, which she and Sofia had to talk about in complimentary tones for the rest of the week. But Pat had to admit it, unlike his home brew, Prichard's food was excellent.

'Ox cheeks!' he declared as she walked in after her final Zoom session of the day, through a fug of fumes and steam and simmering jus. 'À la Tom!'

'Tom?' enquired Pat.

'Kerridge.'

That was the other thing about Prichard. All his dishes were authored by chefs he was apparently on first-name terms with: Nigel (Slater), Nigella (Lawson), Jamie (Oliver) or Otto (Lenghi). Pat had never had the heart to correct him on the latter. He found Otto's dishes to be complicated, requiring more herbs and spices than they had at the local Co-op, so he had to drive to Brighton when he turned his hand to such exoticness.

'Ox cheeks?'

'They had them on offer at the butcher's and I thought, waste not want not, so here we are.' He lifted the lid off a simmering stainless-steel pan and fogged up his glasses. 'I marinated them for two days; they've been on the stove for a mere four hours.'

'They smell absolutely delicious,' replied Pat.

'Hungry?' he smiled.

'Very.'

Prichard had laid Pat's pine kitchen table. He'd even gone so far as to put out some green paper napkins. He served up his braised ox cheeks, cabbage with cumin, and buttery mash, while Pat sat down and poured a glass of red wine. It was actual wine from an actual shop. Much as she enjoyed Prichard's efforts, sometimes it was safer to go with a Blossom Hill.

'Tell me about the police,' he asked. He pulled out a chair, saw Dave was on it, pushed it back and took another. Pat put down her knife and fork and rubbed her creased forehead.

'Well, it wasn't great,' she replied, before going on to

talk Prichard through her encounters with DS Stevens and the more sympathetic PC Footer. She spared no details of the photos of Henry's body, even though Prichard was squeamish.

'And the note?' he said with his mouth full.

'In capital letters, in red pen. It didn't look like it was written by Henry.'

'So a fake, then.'

'I was about to photograph it when we were interrupted by DS Stevens.'

Prichard's eyes rounded. 'How *dramatique*! I'm amazed she didn't try and arrest you.'

'Me too,' Pat sighed. 'She just reiterated that the case was closed and that if I carried on poking about she would charge me with wasting police time or messing with evidence or something along those officious lines. But to be honest with you, she strikes me as lazy, more interested in her lunch break than arresting anyone. You don't have long fingernails like that if you're rounding up criminals. She also seems strangely familiar with that Airbnb, Fin du Monde, for someone who actually lives around here.'

'What are you suggesting?'

'She doesn't take long lunch breaks for her digestive system. There's a reason why her engagement ring is a little tight. She's got no intention of going down the aisle with whoever gave her that tiny chip of zircon. I'm pretty sure she has a bigger fish in mind.'

'Nothing gets past you,' said Prichard, cutting into his ox cheek.

'Except who killed Henry.' Pat took a sip of her wine. 'Oh, and I saw that Dorna woman in the pub celebrating her golf deal.'

'That's not going through, surely?' said Prichard, putting down his knife and fork. 'I went to the meeting, it was laughed out of the parish council. That land is a nature reserve. You can't build on it. There have been protests about it. I know that. Save the Seashore.'

'That sounds familiar.'

'They're the local group who were going to glue themselves to something,' Prichard chortled. 'The cliffs, I think, but it turns out nothing sticks to chalk. They didn't need to in the end, as bats were found in that barn. You can't build with bats.' He chomped on a bit more cheek. 'That's the rules.'

'Who owns the barn?'

'That Dorna woman.'

They carried on eating in silence, both of them glancing up occasionally at the cork noticeboard with Henry's name in the middle and Derek's right next to it. After a minute, Pat put down her fork, picked up the Post-its and, grabbing the black pen, wrote the words *Fin du Monde* and *Dorna Braddon* and slapped them both up on the board before sitting down again.

'Really?' Prichard waved his knife at the board. 'D'you think?'

'Well, she was very anxious to dismiss Henry's death as suicide last night. And she has a bandage on her hand. Maybe due to a violent struggle? That deal is clearly worth a lot of money. And she's new to the village. And she was pleased with herself in the pub.'

'Are murderers generally pleased with themselves?'

'Murderers are many things,' Pat said thoughtfully, 'but often there's a certain grandiosity with dangerous criminals, a belief that the rules don't apply to them. You see a lack of empathy, a disconnection from consequence, sometimes a streak of paranoia or the sense that they're one step ahead. Violence doesn't always trouble them the way it should. And yes, control is often part of it. Needing to dominate the story. Stay in charge of the narrative.'

'And ordering too much champagne in the pub,' added Prichard.

'Not really, no.'

'No,' he agreed. 'But it might mean you're obnoxious, and I've got an idea how you could check out quite how obnoxious.' He had a grin on his face.

'Like what?'

'Book club?'

'What do you mean?'

'She's hosting a book club next week at her house, and she's invited a gang of people. We're reading *Intermezzo*. You know, the book by Sally Rooney?'

Pat took a sip of her wine. 'The sad one about being sad?' She took another sip. 'We? I didn't realise we'd all agreed.'

'We . . . um . . .' Prichard had the decency to blush, and looked down at his ox cheeks. He ran his hand through his salt-and-pepper hair and scratched behind his ear. 'It's on the village WhatsApp group.'

'The village group? The whole one? Or the other one?' It was Pat's turn to sound defensive.

'The one you were banned from.'

'Oh, that one.' She rolled her eyes and popped a piece of cheek in her mouth. Communal WhatsApp groups were something that tried her patience. They never stopped pinging on her phone. Pat liked to keep her phone for people she was fond of, and her clients. Fiona had even WhatsApped a complaint about the van that delivered Pat's papers waking her up at 8 a.m. on a Sunday. Pat had ignored that one.

Then there was Wi-Fi Gate. How was she to know that her practical solution to the piss-poor Wi-Fi problem in the village would have elicited such a pearl-clutching response? Unfortunately, she had mentioned on the smart village WhatsApp group that a broadband using satellites rather than wires worked better. It was more expensive, but Pat relied on a good connection for work. She could not spend hours staring at a frozen screen while her clients waited on the other end of the line with their audio going in and out. Jacqui posted that personally she didn't want to give her money to Elon Musk, who owned the satellite. No one branded Pat a Trump sympathiser to her face. If they had, she would have hooted with laugher at the foolishness of the idea. No, it was more insidious than that. A quiet tap of the tom-toms. It went around the village in hushed tones, and then she was quietly removed from the group. She didn't notice to start off with. It was something of a relief not to be updated about how to contribute to the sponsored walk, or where the next car boot sale was going to be. In the end, it was Prichard who broke the news to her after a glass of some unspeakable turnip wine. She'd been kicked off the group as she was apparently a MAGA fan. Pat had laughed so hard she could barely breathe. Prichard was worried and said that perhaps she should apologise or make it clear that she was not a Trumpian Republican. But Pat couldn't be bothered.

'How many people are going?' she asked now.

'Eight from the group.'

'Only eight?'

'It's women only,' he said. 'And me.'

'No husbands or partners?'

'Isn't that the point of book club?'

'Eight whole opinions on *Intermezzo*. What an evening!'

'You should come,' he suggested.

'I think I might be busy with my sock drawer. Or putting red-hot pokers in my eyes.'

'Come on,' he said, glancing up the corkboard. 'A chance to see the killer in her lair?'

'Well . . .' Pat cocked her head to one side.

'I can't imagine you passing up the chance to poke around that new glass-box house she's built.'

'The one with the phallic clipped bushes outside?' Prichard squinted across the table. His long nose wrinkled. 'Oh, come on!' Pat continued. 'You can't possibly have not noticed the enormous yew penises she's sculpted out of the hedge!'

'I can't say I have.'

'In which case, I shall show you! What day, what time?'

CHAPTER 9

It was 7.45 p.m. the following Monday, and Dorna was sitting on a mustard velvet button-backed sofa, her bare feet tucked up sideways, next to her buttocks, an English sparkling wine in hand as she held forth. She was explaining to the rest of the highly attentive WhatsApp group members exactly how she'd torn down the 1950s pebble-dash house she'd purchased two years back and updated the whole place with the help of a revolutionary minimalist architect from London, who appeared to specialise in removing all discernible features from a home and replacing them with acres of glass, polished concrete and every shade of beige.

'My favourite feature,' she explained with a jangle of her bangles, 'is this lovely little glass balcony at the front.' She pointed. Everyone turned their head to admire the vast glass balcony that ran the length of the house and jutted out at least twelve feet beyond the giant sliding doors. 'I just love the view of the Downs.' She smiled with evident satisfaction. 'You can see Birling Gap from here, with all those irritating tourists.'

'I find them endearing,' countered Pat, taking a sip of her drink. 'I think it's admirable that they make such an effort to come here to our inclement little part of the world.'

'You do?' Dorna sounded as if she had a whiff of pity in her voice.

'Prichard is learning Korean,' added Pat.

'I am!' grinned Prichard, appearing from a perilously low corduroy beanbag that he'd somehow landed in and was clearly thinking he might never get out of.

'It's just such a great view,' agreed Fi, who was wearing a pair of leather jeans tight enough to reveal every contour of her Pilates-peached backside, teamed with a white silk shirt that showed her lacy bra. 'Malcolm and I would love to upgrade, but there are so many rules and planning things it would be impossible. I have no idea how you managed with this place. You can't even plant pampas grass around here without people complaining.'

'Well, you certainly managed *that*! Hahaha.' Prichard's machine-gun laugh let rip from the beanbag and Pat watched as Fi winced. She'd never been fond of Prichard, mainly because he failed to flirt with her or give her anywhere near enough attention.

'You just have to know the right people,' said Dorna, tapping the side of her nose. 'More Chapel Down?' She rose from the sofa. 'Top-up?' she asked Marcia, who was standing by a bowl of olives the size of gobstoppers. 'Lucy?' She smiled at the pretty brunette, who was sitting so close to Fi their thighs were touching. 'Anyone else?'

Prichard proffered up his glass from the beanbag. 'I wouldn't mind a touch.' He laughed again.

'Would anyone like the tour before we start on the book?' suggested Dorna.

'Oh yes please,' declared Fi, leaping off the sofa. 'I'd love that. Where do you get your furnishings from?' she asked immediately, caressing a round sheepskin cushion. 'If you don't mind me asking. And please don't say London,' she giggled. 'None of us wants to hear that.'

'Well,' began Dorna, turning towards the door with her bandaged hand in the air, like a guide from a hop-on-hop-off open-bus tour. 'Quite a lot of them I source from antiques markets like Kempton. But you have to go super, super early to get there before the dealers. The ones from Liberty in London are always there, snapping up the best mid-century modern.' Her voice grew fainter as the tour began, leaving Prichard and Pat behind in the living room. Prichard would have happily joined it, but he was unable to extricate himself from the beanbag without rolling over onto all fours, and that was impossible while still holding his glass of wine.

'Pat,' he whispered, 'for God's sake give me a hand! I'm stuck fast.'

Pat spent what felt like a good few minutes trying to heave Prichard to his feet. Finally she managed to pull him out of the giant marshmallow, only for him to hurl himself into her arms, emptying his glass all over the mustard sofa. They both stared.

'Now what?' he asked in a panicked whisper.

'Just pop a soft furnishing on it,' replied Pat, picking up a cushion and covering the stain. 'She'll never notice it.' And they both sat down on the sofa opposite, backs straight, hands in laps, as if butter wouldn't melt.

'Oh Dorna, that's amazing,' said Fi as she walked back

into the sitting room a few minutes later. 'What you've done is beautiful. Truly. If only I had your sense of style.'

'I have a freakish eye for detail,' declared Dorna with another jangle of her bracelets as she curled a strand of short hennaed hair behind her ear. 'It can be overwhelming sometimes.' She shook her head a little before sitting down on Pat's swiftly moved cushion.

'I can see,' agreed Fi. 'We all can.' She looked over at Lucy, who agreed immediately.

'Yes, you've done an amazing job.' Lucy nodded.

'I think we should all go down to the kitchen to get a bite to eat, don't you?'

Fortunately for Pat, the party of book club ladies were already up to speed on the Bulthaup this, and the Gaggenau that, and the sprung cupboard doors with no handles that responded to the lightest of touches. So light, in fact, that Prichard managed to open a whole row of cupboards in his enthusiasm to get to the giant bowl of couscous that Dorna was teaming with her lamb stew.

'Do tuck in,' she said.

Once they'd all served themselves with stew, yoghurt-dressed salads and flatbreads, they sat at the long oak and resin table and book club was finally pronounced open by Dorna. She sat at the head of the table, of course, with Fi to one side and the lovely Lucy to the other. Pat and Prichard were down the far end with Marcia, whose plate looked strangely empty. Either she thought little of Dorna's cooking, or she was one of those women who didn't eat in public, Pat couldn't work out which.

'Right.' Dorna tapped her glass. 'I think I'll go first.'

'Oh, you should,' replied Fi. 'Tell us what you think!'

'I'm sure there are plenty of us who have something to say,' declared Marcia from down the other end of the table. 'I, for one, loved the book.'

'You did?' chimed in Prichard. 'So did I. I loved the concept of the two brothers talking to each other, I liked the dialogue, the deep thoughts, the ideas behind the book, but you know I was a big fan of *Normal People*, and indeed the other one.' He clicked his fingers. '*Beautiful World, Where Are You*. That's the one. Well, anyway, I really enjoyed the whole experience. I thought she was fascinating about grief.'

'Not too sad, then? Endlessly talking about sadness? To the point of possibly being dull about the sadness?' Pat asked.

'Good Lord, no, not too sad. It has, how can I put it, tender humour. Hahaha!' Prichard's laugh ricocheted around the glass and polished-concrete surfaces of the kitchen. It sounded like they were being hosed down by a sniper. Fi frowned. Dorna winced.

'Back to me,' Dorna said, and Pat knew that wasn't the first time those words had left her mouth. 'Well, I have to say I regret choosing it. I thought it was all a bit miserable. In fact it's pages and pages of misery with no light at the end of the rather boringly long tunnel. And I for one thought the brothers should stop being so rude about the women they were in a relationship with. I'd had quite enough of . . .'

Pat listened to Dorna and found herself agreeing with her, which was disconcerting. She had a large swig of wine just to make herself feel better.

'I think you're right,' she heard herself say. Prichard turned and stared at her, and slowly opened his mouth. Pat shot him a look. He kept quiet. 'I do. I'm afraid I found it all rather protracted.'

Dorna: 'I found it moralistic, conservative . . .'

Pat: '. . . and so emotionally cautious. I was longing for a clearer narrative.'

Dorna: 'Those brothers are so introspective and cynical.'

Pat: 'I just found them unlikeable. Impossible to empathise with.'

Dorna: 'Yes, and . . .'

And on they continued for at least ten minutes, exchanging thoughts and ideas as if in a tennis match up and down the lengthy table while Prichard and the rest of the book club looked on, following each serve, volley and backhand slice as if they were on the Centre Court at Wimbledon.

Out came more wine, cheese and a pile of Ferrero Rocher, at which point Prichard accused Dorna of 'really spoiling us', but it was true. She had made an effort. The woman was up to something, thought Pat, slicing off a corner of strong Cheddar. The book clubs she had attended a long time ago in London were mostly made up of large glasses of lukewarm Barefoot rosé and bowls of Bombay mix.

'Prichard,' Dorna trilled down the table. 'Could you possibly be a dear and open some more Chapel Down? My hand!' She waved her bandage. 'I simply can't.'

'That looks painful,' declared Pat. 'What did you do? How did it happen?'

She watched Dorna closely. Would the woman hesitate?

Was it anything to do with Henry's disappearance? The result of a violent struggle on the cliff? Had they fought, got physical? She would deny it, of course, but lying took effort, and there would be a pause while her brain searched for and plucked out a likely story.

'Oh God,' Dorna moaned. No pause. 'It's a recurring injury. Repetitive strain. I get it when I work too hard, and it flares up when I play tennis too. Or golf. It's so painful. Apparently turmeric works, but I never remember to take the stuff.'

'Oh, right.' Pat smiled tightly. That proved nothing. Only maybe that Dorna was possibly the best liar in the business.

'Talking of golf,' Dorna said, 'if you'd like to come with me, I have something wonderful to show you all. Truly wonderful.'

Pat pushed back her Perspex chair, safe in the knowledge that she was right: there had been an agenda to the evening all along, and this was it. Prichard arrived back from the kitchen island and stood watching everyone get up, a look of bemusement on his alcohol-flushed face. *Pop!* went his cork.

'Ah, Prichard,' said Dorna. 'Impeccable timing. Follow me!'

The party moved next door, to what appeared to be Dorna's study. There was a large beige-leather-topped desk, with a wide wooden chair with a beige-leather-padded seat. It was on wheels so it could spin and roll in any direction. On the right side of the desk was a low lamp that looked like a modern sculpture; next to that a large leather-trimmed blotter and a stack of expensive-looking black and gold-trimmed fountain pens and ballpoints. Perhaps you couldn't get beige pens, thought Pat. It was a power desk by anyone's standards.

The rest of the room had two large beige leather sofas placed opposite each other, with a low glass table in between, upon which was a carefully arranged collection of RIBA journals and *Architectural Review* magazines. The room was organised, uncluttered, the antithesis of the jangly bangles and vegetable-dye hair. Pat supposed the architect must have stopped short of styling his client's actual person. Dorna Braddon was serious about business, she thought as she looked around the room. There were a few books on the shelves, but the rest of the space was filled with silver-framed photographs of Dorna in various guises – long mousy locks, short red hair, a choppy blonde bob – wearing a hard yellow hat and a hi-vis jacket. They were all souvenirs of development projects. She had torn down and built or rebuilt a lot of buildings.

'Over here is something I have been very keen to show you all,' she said, beckoning the book group towards the window. 'Hang on a second.' She paused. 'Just let me turn on the light.'

One click, and a whole model complex was illuminated before them.

'Wow! Amazing,' enthused Fi, just as she did every day on Instagram.

'What a huge thing,' said Marcia. 'It's enormous.'

'Welcome to Boho Golf & Spa House Club!' pronounced Dorna. 'Isn't it fabulous.' It wasn't a question.

'There was I thinking she had a groovy new train set,'

Prichard whispered into Pat's ear. 'Champagne!' he added. 'This calls for champagne!' He lifted the newly opened bottle in the air as a serving suggestion.

'I think you'll find that's English sparkling,' said Pat.

'So over here is Beachy Head.' Dorna pointed. 'And here is Westlinke, and here is Boho Golf!'

'Wow! Amazing,' repeated Fi, who'd run out of superlatives. 'I mean truly wow! Amazing. Don't you think, Lucy?'

'Yes, wow,' Lucy agreed. 'Amazing.'

'So what's this?' asked Marcia, bending down to inspect the model development, complete with tiny cars and people as well as roads and the occasional tree or bush. Unless they were gorse or hawthorn, Pat knew nothing would ever be able grow in the poor chalk soil with the fierce prevailing wind.

'Oh, that's the swimming pool,' smiled Dorna.

'Right on the cliff edge?' queried Marcia.

'We might move that in a bit,' agreed Dorna. 'But it's essentially there.'

'And what is essentially here?' asked Pat, pointing to a small building that looked remarkably close to Ivy Cottage. It was, in fact, just the other side of the grass verge of pain, where everyone parked their cars.

'Oh, that.' Dorna thought for a second. 'That's the septic tank and pump room for the spa.'

'But that's right by my house!' Pat jabbed the building with her finger. 'It couldn't be closer. The smell of sewage—'

'Oh, it won't smell,' Dorna smiled. 'I can promise you that.'

'Can you indeed. And the noise?'

'We're planting some sycamores in front of it. It's all in tasteful flint, I'm sure it won't be a problem.'

'Certainly not for you. I see your house is nicely protected. And you have permission for all of this?'

'Sure.' Dorna shrugged.

'But aren't there bats in your barn?' asked Prichard. 'I know because I used to go and visit them and photograph them.'

'There were,' replied Dorna. 'But they have long since disappeared.'

'Long since?' he queried. 'I could have sworn I've seen them recently.'

'Not any more. They've migrated. Moved house, or barn, or whatever they do.'

'But isn't that why Save the Seashore were protesting against the development?' Prichard's innocent face looked puzzled. 'They said they found bats there.'

'They were mistaken.'

'But they can't have been.'

'Well they've gone now. *Pouf.*' Dorna was looking tense and shifty. It was clear to Pat that the bats had not gone of their own accord.

'Weren't Save the Seashore supposed to file an objection to the development?' asked Prichard. 'At least that's what I was told.'

'They never did. The deadline was last week.' Dorna's face was overcome with faux sadness. 'They must have decided not to.'

'Hence you celebrating in the pub?' asked Pat.

'So what if I did?' Dorna snapped. 'It's not illegal. Those Save the Seashore protesters are a nightmare. They've been on our case for months. They're a bunch of dozy busybodies, nimbies poking their noses into other people's business. Honestly, I felt like killing the lot of them myself!'

CHAPTER 10

Pat was sitting on the early-morning train to London, replaying the events of the evening before at book club. Dorna Braddon, in full campaign mode, had clearly thought she could butter up the village with lamb shank stew, a bucket of dry couscous, a wheel of Brie, a slab of Cheddar and a platter of Ferrero Rocher. Pat was incensed. Did Dorna really believe that people's loyalties, their attachment to the land, their sense of place could be softened with sparkling wine and impressive interior design? It felt calculated. Patronising, even. The psychology of it grated on her: the attempt to bypass thought with comfort, to grease resistance with indulgence. Flattery disguised as hospitality. What unsettled her most was how easily it seemed to work. And what had she done with her dog? There wasn't a trace of Trigger all evening.

Dorna had also admitted to wanting to murder all of the Save the Seashore group. There was a wide gap between wanting to murder someone and actually committing the crime, Pat was aware of that. But had Dorna slipped up? Had she blurted out something she really didn't want to; had she felt under pressure, under the influence of alcohol and the gaze of the assembled group, who were all hanging on her every word? Somehow Save the Seashore had something to do with this, thought Pat as she rested her temple against the train window.

She'd always found the movement of a train relaxing, the gentle sideways rocking motion, the rattle over the tracks; it was a place where she did her best thinking.

Save the Seashore had not filed their objections to the plan at the town hall. Why was that? Dorna had clearly forced the bats to vacate the luxury barn residence that had been their home for decades. Pat had gone there with Prichard one sunny evening when she first arrived down in Westlinke. He'd insisted on showing her the bats, if she remembered correctly. Bat-watching was a hobby of his. It was a decrepit, tumbledown building with a red tin roof that also had a resident owl. The place was full of straw and the remains of dead mice. It hadn't smelt enticing. But they'd spent almost an hour watching the bats and the owl. And now apparently they were gone. She and Prichard should definitely check to see if that were really the case.

Her telephone rang in her large handbag at her feet. She scrabbled blindly around in the capacious void, feeling old pens and pencils, crumpled receipts, tissues, hair ties, loose change, ChapSticks and keys, until she finally found it.

'Prichard Knowles!' declared the voice at the other end. Announcing himself on the telephone was another of Prichard's more eccentric habits. Pat suspected it was left over from the days when he was the Eddie Stobart of the south, and every time he rang his own company it ensured that the receptionist sat up and paid attention.

'Prichard! How are you?' she began.

'What a night!' he exhaled with excitement before cutting straight to the chase. 'So, do you think she murdered Henry? She admitted as much just before we left. Oh, and by the way, I forgot my coat, so I went back into the house and I could hear her complaining to Fi about your dislike of the Boho Golf plans. She said, and I quote, "She likes her view from the moral high ground, that's for sure!" To which Fiona replied, "Why do you think I planted all that leylandii!" Can you believe it? The two of them having a good old-fashioned bitch. But anyway, what do you think? I've been dying to ask. I've hardly slept. I had dreams about bats and spas and golf clubs. It was actually a nightmare!'

'Well, I think it's interesting that she said what she did.'

'Admitted to murder?'

'To wanting to murder, that's different.'

'Is it, though?'

The phone went dead as the train entered a tunnel. The window became a dark mirror, and Pat stared at her own reflection, the outside world lost to shadow. She straightened her glasses and smoothed down her hair with her fingers. She was in good nick for sixty-two, she thought. She could still touch her toes. Climb a cliff, swim well; she could probably still do a cartwheel given enough wine and a sunny day if her bloody hip wasn't irritating her. She smiled at her reflection and looked herself in the eye. Come on, Pat, she nodded, it can't be that hard. What did happen to Henry Clayton? No one puts on a glamorous suit to jump off a cliff.

A burst of light. The end of the tunnel. Her phone sprang to life and she called Prichard back immediately.

'Prichard Knowles! As I was saying,' he continued, 'I think we need to put Dorna's name more firmly in the frame, and also Save the Seashore. So Derek, Dorna, the Seashore tribe and the Fin du Monde.' He was listing them off.

'I shall do it,' agreed Pat, 'as soon as I get home tomorrow morning.'

'Roger that. Meanwhile I'll keep digging for proof of the missing bats.'

'Good idea. Also, there was another shock last night.'

'Really, what did I miss?'

'I have to say, Prichard, you surprised me with your take on Sally Rooney's book. I was amazed by what I was hearing. You seemed very enamoured by the whole thing.'

'Well, I didn't actually read a word of it, hahaha!' He laughed loudly.

'What?' Pat pulled the phone away from her ear. 'But you...'

'Amazon reviews,' he replied. 'That and the back of the book.'

'You dark horse, Prichard Knowles.'

'Aren't we all, Pat? Aren't we all! *Buenos noches!*'

Pat checked her watch. It was 9.16 in the morning.

She was on her way up to London for an evening with Sue. She looked forward to these trips into town. Not that she was ever bored with living in Westlinke. She loved the place and the beauty and freedom it gave her, but occasionally what she really wanted was the thrill of familiar streets, the bustle of the city, the greater variety of people to watch, or failing that, a brilliant piece of theatre and a late-night walk back to Islington. But mostly it was her friend she missed. Sue was intelligent, she was funny, witty and super smart, and Pat just loved how she felt when she was with her. Sue made her laugh and think, which was a rare and beguiling combination. Beguiling enough to give her another reason to leave her husband. Pat did not want to be married to a man any more. She could have settled for it, but just to settle when you only got one life didn't seem right to her. She wanted fresh air, literally and metaphorically. After she and Martin divorced amicably, she moved in with Sue. It worked for a while. But after a year, she realised that as much as she loved Sue, what she wanted more than anything was to live on her own in the countryside, near the sea. She enjoyed London from time to time, but it was the quiet of the country she longed for.

It had been the same years previously when she had been unhappy practising law and felt the pull to study psychology. She sat with that feeling for a while. Unpleasant sensations like restlessness, boredom, unhappiness were inconvenient, but people needed to listen to them because they showed what they might need to change about their lives. She did her courses at evenings and weekends while still working full-time as a solicitor: a counselling diploma, a master's degree in psychotherapy, then a doctorate in clinical psychology. Her daughter, Sofia, probably missed out on consistent time with her mother.

Pat knew she hadn't made a mistake when she married

Martin. He was a gentle soul who was still apparently loving his life in Chiswick without her, playing cricket, going to the pub with his many friends. He was also a regular for Sunday lunch at Sofia's house in Battersea. She and her husband, Adam, did a very good roast chicken, apparently. Not that Pat had been there for a while. Last time, she'd criticised Sofia's frilly pinny, worn while making the gravy, calling it a bit too 'trad wife' and derivative for her liking. The comment sparked an almighty row about feminism, autonomy and Nietzsche's idea of individuation in marriage. Sofia leant towards the romantic vision: two people becoming one, a shared identity forged in domestic harmony. Pat, by contrast, saw that as a slow erasure; she believed in a union of distinct selves, two individuals walking side by side, not merged. The fight ended with Sofia shouting, 'I don't want to end up divorced like you!' It was the kind of argument that stayed lodged between them, revisited silently in the early hours when neither could sleep.

Pat was looking forward to seeing Sue. Their affair had begun with heat, snatched kisses, breathless nights, a glorious, grown-up kind of passion, before settling into something gentler: a deep friendship with a side order of 'lesbian bed death', where laughter and loyalty gradually edged out lust. Whenever Pat came to town to see her psychotherapy supervisor, she stayed with Sue, and they even shared a bed, but the only joint activity that occurred there these days was grappling with the crossword.

She placed her handbag on the seat next to her, took out her laptop and put her earphones in, claiming as much space as she could in her corner of the train. She found the recorded sessions she was looking for on her crowded desktop, and up came a still of Henry's face. He was smiling, or at least about to, with a blue and white striped shirt peeking through his suit. His dark hair was neat, parted slightly to the side. He had his elbow on the desk in front of him, and he was resting his cheek in the palm of his right hand. He looked relaxed. There was a light in his brown eyes.

This was the recording of his last session before he died. Before he was murdered. Pat took a deep breath and turned up the volume.

His familiar voice floated into her ears as she pressed play, the tone still so alive, so Henry. It was strange how clearly she could remember the cadence of his speech, even before the recording began.

'It's like I'm two people,' he was saying. 'I can see that my boyfriend can be cruel, unsupportive, and maybe I should break up with him. But I love him.'

Pat's own voice came in response, calm, measured: 'What do you mean by love?'

There was a pause, then Henry continued. 'Well, when we do come together, it's wonderful. Better than any relationship I've been in before. He can be kind, you know? He remembered my birthday, only one day late, but still, it made me feel like we could turn this around. That we can be good together. Now I'm thinking, no, I don't want to leave him. Why throw away something that can be this good?' He gave a rueful little laugh. 'Tell me what to do, Pat.'

Pat heard herself deflect, gently. 'What does your heart say?'

'Stay,' Henry replied immediately.

'And your head?'

'Run.'

She had paused in the recording then too, before repeating his word. 'Run?' A pause. 'That's not even leaving amicably.'

'There's not really an in-between,' Henry had said. 'It's either everything or nothing.'

Pat watched herself nod slightly on the video. 'You said earlier that he was kind to you on rare occasions.'

'Yes,' Henry replied. 'Sometimes he'll leave a sweet note, usually after he's been less than kind. It's like he can't help the cruel side, but he also wants to change.'

She heard her voice lean in, slightly softer. 'Right. So, Henry... who else in your life was mostly not there for you, or overly critical of you, but sometimes did remember your birthday a day late?'

There was a beat of silence, then Henry sighed. 'I think... having talked about Dad with you, saying things out loud, he's sort of receding. I think I'm over him. I really am. He doesn't have the power over me he used to. I know what you said, that even adult children feel more worthy when their parents acknowledge them. And I do feel worthier now. I don't depend on his validation any more. I'm OK whether or not he's proud of me.'

Pat had simply replied, 'OK.'

Henry hesitated. 'You don't think I... I've replaced Dad with Derek, do you?'

'What do *you* think?' she asked gently.

'I want to say no,' Henry replied, 'because I don't want it to be true. But, you know . . . sometimes I think about it.'

Pat had given a soft 'Uh huh.'

'Maybe I haven't, though,' Henry added quickly. 'You want to make sense of things, tie them up in ribbon and give them back to me, hoping I'll use them. But life doesn't always work that way, does it? Not everything follows a pattern. I don't want to be a walking cliché.'

Pat heard herself say, 'I really hear you, Henry. You want this relationship with your boyfriend to work. You've experienced highs with him you hadn't felt since your dad turned up the day after your birthday with a Buzz Lightyear. And when I suggest you might be repeating something familiar rather than discovering something new, you don't like it.'

'No, I don't,' Henry had agreed.

There was a silence. Pat broke it. 'I'm still noticing something, cognitive dissonance.'

'What do you mean?'

'You know something in your head; intellectually, rationally, you know that your boyfriend isn't consistently kind, that he's borrowed money and not repaid it, that he can hurt you and doesn't seem to hesitate to do so. But in your body, you don't want to believe it. In your body, you want to believe this is love. That it can work. So your mind and your body are in conflict.'

Henry had gone quiet. 'Isn't the body always right?'

'It depends on how that body was trained,' Pat had answered carefully.

'You've lost me.'

'It depends,' she explained, 'on what you got used to growing up.'

Henry had taken that in for a moment, then said, 'I can feel you wanting me to leave my boyfriend. And it makes me want to stay with him.'

Pat's voice had shifted, firm but warm. 'You don't think it might be dangerous to stay with someone who's been violent with you?'

'It was only once,' Henry said quickly. 'We'd both had too much to drink. Our argument accelerated, and it got to him. He gave me a slap. To calm me down.'

Pat swallowed, even now, watching the screen. She heard herself say calmly, 'Even if it was just a slap, that's one red flag too many. You had a black eye, Henry.'

She paused the video.

There he was, staring straight at the camera. If she looked closely, she could still see the bruise, the faded green and yellow mottling his eye socket, the soft purple shadows clouding his cheek. Like a sunset turned stormy. It had been a hell of a thump.

She exhaled slowly, then clicked play again.

'I bruise easily,' Henry said. Then added, 'But you're supposed to be neutral, Pat. It feels like you've already made up your mind.'

Her own voice was quiet but clear. 'I care for you, Henry. And that, I'm afraid, makes it very hard for me to stay neutral. You are worthy of care. Worthy.'

There was a beat.

Henry grinned. 'How about a paradoxical intervention?'

'Are you on a counselling course or something?' Pat had asked, amused.

'Possibly.'

'How else would you know about the technique where the counsellor encourages the client to indulge in the very behaviour they want to change?'

'A boy can read, can't he?' he said with a laugh. 'I like the idea of the paradox. That by deliberately engaging in the problem behaviour, I might gain awareness or motivation to change. It sounds like it could work.'

Pat's tone changed. 'So you agree that staying with Derek is problematic behaviour?'

He paused, then shrugged. 'I don't have to decide right away, do I? I can just go back to him for a bit and see what happens.'

There was a silence before Pat answered. 'Sounds like a decision to me.'

She paused the video again, the screen frozen on Henry's face. She took off her headphones and stared at the image. At his bruised eye, at the traces of humour and hope still flickering behind the pain.

Then she sat back and took off her headphones, becoming conscious of the noises of the train again.

He looked alive on the screen. His head was down, he was rubbing his chin. Pat shook her head. What sort of decision had that turned out to be? The correct one? The one that got him killed? Had she aided and abetted that decision? He was a grown man and she was not responsible for his decisions, but could she have done something else? Guided him in another direction? Maybe he'd been right, and she ought to have given him a paradoxical intervention. But the black eye, that was a line crossed. Actual violence, not just threat or bluster, but harm done to another body. That took a particular kind of disconnection. Not just a lack of concern for someone else's pain, but a failure to regulate the self in the face of anger or fear. Pat had seen it before, that dangerous shift when frustration tipped into justification. When someone convinced themselves they had no choice. That it was provoked, deserved even! And she'd missed that Henry had justified it. Damn! The black eye had been the session before. Two weeks ago, if Pat worked backwards. Two weeks. Could the fight have been the same fight that Johnno the barman had witnessed? It seemed more than an argument about how they treated each other. Henry was proving to be the most unreliable witness to his own murder.

'We will shortly be arriving at London Victoria, where this train terminates!' The guard's nasal voice crackled over the loudspeaker. 'Please make sure you take all your belongings with you.' Pat sighed, remembering when all he used to say was 'Victoria station, all change.'

Therapists usually saw a supervisor or got together with other therapists regularly to supervise each other. Pat did both. She felt the need to discuss her clients, to see if she'd missed anything at any point. She might, she thought, be missing something with Henry. Her supervisor, Maria, had an office in Pimlico, above a pub on the main road going towards

Vauxhall Bridge. Pat usually walked there from Victoria, but today, she gave in to the hip and got the number 36 bus. A therapy centre above a pub; if one way of self-soothing didn't work, she could always try the other, she had thought when she first went there.

It all came pouring out of her when she sat opposite Maria, an eighty-year-old South African woman who appeared to have seen it all, twice. Pat told her everything that had happened in the past few days. Henry's death, the police writing it off as suicide, Pat being certain it wasn't suicide. 'I thought I had a good relationship with Henry,' she said, 'just because I liked him. I thought he told me everything. But actually, I've been going over Zooms I recorded with him and I don't think our relationship was as great as I thought it was. And I think I know why.' She looked up at her supervisor.

'OK, and . . .'

'I was telling him what to do and he was resisting me.'

'Ah,' said Maria, 'because you know best?'

Pat gave a sharp sigh, 'Well, obviously I know best. He was in a relationship with someone who hit him. I was keen that he should dump him.'

Maria put her head to one side and smiled. 'Maybe you'd make a better agony aunt than therapist. They tell people what to do.'

Pat began to get slightly worked up. 'Well now look what's happened. Henry is dead. I was right.'

Maria spoke slowly and calmly, as if she was trying to contain Pat's exasperation. 'You can't be certain it wasn't suicide.'

'There was a note left behind.' Pat was still speaking urgently. 'The police say he wrote it. But it didn't feel like that to me. It wasn't his handwriting, among other things. It doesn't add up.'

Maria spoke even more slowly, more calmly. 'You are quite quick to jump to conclusions.'

Her calmness appeared to seep into Pat, who answered her more thoughtfully. 'Yup, that's true.'

Maria knew now that Pat was more open to listening to her. 'You've got some facts, yes, you have your impression of Henry and what he was likely or not likely to do and you've filled in all the blanks, and now you feel as certain about what you filled the blanks with as you are about the facts themselves.'

Pat sighed. 'The thing is, I was a bit bossy with him. I think he was picking up on my bossiness and being bossy back with me. I don't think he told me everything either; perhaps he was scared of my disapproval. I hadn't picked up on his possible shame, but he picked up on my bloody-mindedness.'

'So where's the learning here for you?' asked Maria, and then probably wished she hadn't, because Pat started to go off on one again.

'It wasn't suicide. I saw the note, I told you. Henry didn't write notes like that. And he was fairly verbose, he would have said a whole lot more. He also wrote like a grown-up, in proper cursive writing, not scrappy capitals. And he loved his mum. A lot.'

Maria could see that Pat was working herself up, so she

said, 'No, I meant what's the learning for your ongoing development?'

Pat huffed. 'That maybe I should talk about some other patients. I have a potential new client who—'

Maria interrupted; she wasn't going to allow that. 'The learning is that you need to stay with "don't know" rather than jumping to conclusions by filling in the blanks.'

Pat gave in. 'Yes. You're right. Can I talk about a potential new client?' To herself she said, *I'm not going to accept that Henry's death was suicide.*

Maria nodded.

'This next one definitely is suicidal, and I care a lot about him already. I thought he would be a candidate for EMDR – a lot of unprocessed trauma in his childhood.' Pat told Maria about Stefano, who had signed up for six sessions since his initial Zoom. Then she went on to talk about Rob. 'Rob has a friend who is into conspiracy theories but who he cannot bear to dump. It would make him feel like he's a bad person.'

'What did you tell him about conspiracy theorists?' Maria asked.

'How d'you know I told him anything?'

'I know you quite well now.' She smiled at Pat.

'I told him they cannot bear the uncertainty of not knowing.'

'Ironic really. Pat, stay with the uncertainty around Henry's death.'

Pat slowly shook her head and went on to talk about another one of her clients.

CHAPTER 11

The sun broke through the thinning cloud as Pat pulled up outside Sue's Georgian townhouse in Islington. She paid the driver in cash and slammed the door, then breathed in the London air. Pollution, car exhaust, with a base note of fetid rubbish and the stale alcohol that seeped out of the pavement slabs. It smelt like home, another home. She'd never minded the chaos and the dirt when she lived in London full-time, but it was a different story now, coming back from the Downs. It was jarring, and yet familiar and comforting too. She'd spent years in the capital. She hadn't been born or raised there, but somehow London had got under her skin, and she would always love it.

And Sue's square, to Pat's mind, was one of the prettiest there was. Domestic in scale, the semi-detached villas boasted spacious interiors, generous fireplaces, sash windows and white plaster cornicing. All had been built in the 1820s and clustered around a well-maintained private garden that was, according to Sue, the perfect place for the local street gang to store their stolen mobile phones, in the bushes between the railings. It was the capital's equivalent of an oasis of urban calm, with the right amount of edge.

Pat entered the house with her key and punched in the number to turn off the beeping alarm. Sue was still at work and would not be home for a while. She put down her overnight bag and walked through to the kitchen at the back, with its French windows that looked out onto the two-tier garden. Sue liked to entertain. She had a large range gas cooker and a broad stainless-steel-fronted fridge that Pat opened to find it was full of half-drunk bottles of wine, jars of spices and sauces and gherkins and pickles. There were cookery books stacked on top of each other on a shelf with bits of paper and old envelopes sticking out, marking favourite recipes. Food and cooking were one of the few subjects that Sue and Prichard could talk about. But on the whole, she really didn't get him; she found that laugh too much.

Pat turned on the gas hob and picked up the Bialetti moka pot, filling it with ground coffee and water. Once she'd poured herself a cup, she opened the copy of the *Financial Times* that she'd picked up at the station, smoothed out the FTSE 100 pages and, after ferreting for a pen in her large bag, began looking up her shares. She was not a prodigious investor. But one of her aunts had bought Glaxo shares at the right time in the early eighties, when they were relatively low-priced, and had sold them high and shared the spoils with her nephews and nieces, passing the investing bug on to Pat along with the money.

Pat had invested in a budget airline at the beginning of lockdown, when all flights were grounded and their shares plummeted, and now they were finally showing a good profit. She had also followed the wellness industry closely and had bought shares in the pharmaceutical companies manufacturing the weight-loss injection pens that had now boomed in popularity. She was doing well. She smiled to herself. Perhaps she should think about replacing her car. But what was the point in that? It worked. It took her from A to B, she could park it and, most importantly, nobody would ever want to steal it. No, what she really ought to do with her money was donate it to the Samaritans or Crisis, and maybe jump the NHS queue and get her hip done.

She heard Sue's key in the lock. 'Hi,' she called. 'I'm in the kitchen.'

Sue walked through to the back.

'You're early,' said Pat as she hugged her ex-girlfriend-turned-good-friend.

'They let me out early – well, the court went into recess, some problem with non-disclosed evidence,' said Sue. She stepped back. 'Let me look at you. You look great, but how are you really? I've been so worried. Are you OK?'

Once they'd caught up on how the other had been feeling, the conversation turned, inevitably, to what came next.

'It's all so unsettling. Poor Henry.'

Pat nodded. 'It's terrible.'

'There were a lot of final straws and Henry seemed to want out of his relationship. And yet,' Sue let out a long sigh, 'and yet, I've seen it so many times. You try and save someone from an abusive partnership and they spend all this time and effort and money, and you do help them, only for them to go straight back into it at the earliest opportunity. It is so frustrating.'

'Yes, I see it a lot in my world too,' said Pat. 'You can do all the work with someone, and still they get pulled right back in. What they haven't learnt yet is that waiting for scraps of attention from someone isn't love. But the trouble is, when they do get a crumb, it gives them such a high it becomes addictive. The contrast between being dismissed and then suddenly wanted again, that can hook people. I think that's what was happening to Henry.'

'Yup, poor Henry. Anyway,' said Sue, 'I've come straight from court as I wanted to see you. Let me get changed, and we can go and have drinks and dinner. Do you want to help yourself to a glass of wine? There's some in the fridge.'

'I have never seen so many half-drunk bottles!'

'Oh, I know. I had some friends over last Thursday, all lawyers, and it ended up being quite heated, banging on about points of law.'

It hadn't occurred to Pat to bring smart clothes to change into for the evening, but she reckoned her North Face trousers and mismatched anorak and reasonably new trainers would do.

An hour later, they stepped through the heavy velvet curtain that hung around the entrance to Moro, the bustling Moorish restaurant on nearby Exmouth Market. The scent of cumin, grilled lamb and orange blossom hit them instantly, followed by the comforting sounds of clattering pans, chatter and clinking glasses. They made an odd pair walking into the restaurant, Pat looking not dissimilar to an Outward Bound instructor and Sue in a lilac tailored suit with a silk vest and black stilettos.

They were shown to a table near the open kitchen, where chefs moved with practised efficiency, flames flaring briefly over the grill and shouts of 'Service!' rising above the din. The table was close enough to catch the action, but tucked against a wall just beyond the whirlwind of the majority of the cooking.

Pat scanned the room as she shrugged off her anorak. It was full, boisterous, buzzy, packed with foodies, media types and dates in progress. She caught the eye of a young man at the next table, already flushed from wine, who gave her a slow once-over and then looked at Sue, clearly confused about what kind of duo they were.

A waiter arrived almost immediately, slipping a menu in front of each of them.

'Would you like something to drink while you look?' he asked.

Sue smiled. 'Pomegranate cosmopolitan, please.'

'Ooh,' said Pat, excited for an exotic drink, 'and I'll have a cocktail with sherry in it.'

'The rebujito?' asked the waiter.

'What's that?'

'Fino with mint and lemonade.'

'Oh no, something stronger, please.'

'What about the fabuloso? That's oloroso sherry, vermouth, brandy.'

'Absolutely, yes please,' said Pat.

'OK, I'll come back and take your food orders in a bit.'

Sue asked, 'Since when have you become so interested in booze, Pat?'

'Since Prichard started brewing wines and spirits during Covid. I need to know what a proper drink is supposed to taste like.'

'Cheers,' said Sue a few minutes later, raising her glass after the drinks had been delivered in elegant, sweating glasses. 'To absent friends, colleagues, clients, whatever we have to call them. To Henry.'

'To Henry,' said Pat, lifting her own glass and taking a sip.

As they were eating their chargrilled lamb (Pat) and wood-roasted chicken (Sue), Pat said, 'I saw the crime-scene photographs.'

'You did!' Sue sat bolt upright and her eyebrows rose in surprise. 'How? That's very odd.'

'The policeman on the case, or not on the case, showed me them.'

'I'm amazed. He's not allowed to do that.'

'Well, I took him out for a bun and asked about his childhood, and I suppose he wanted to reciprocate.'

'You make me laugh. Only you could do that. Get some poor copper to open up about his life and he gives you access to restricted material. You are amazing. You bought him a bun?'

'Well, cake. He's a comfort eater, unhappy childhood, felt out of place, filling the void with food.'

'Oh dear.'

'Henry was wearing his Armani suit and his best shoes when he died. He was dressed as if he were going out, not going to kill himself.'

'Who wears their smartest outfit to kill themselves?'

'Exactly what I said. I suppose it must happen, but it doesn't fit for me.'

'It doesn't make sense to me either. He was supposed to file a document the following day to object to some development plans for this group he worked for. Save the Seashore.'

'Save the Seashore?' Pat sat up straighter.

'He didn't really work for them; he helped them with their accounts when they first started fundraising, and since he already had a lawyer, me, he offered to help them with the legal stuff too. I gave it to my trainee solicitor, I didn't have a lot to do with it, but it was some planning objection to a golf course.'

'And was the golf course by any chance called Boho Golf & Spa House Club?'

'Yes! That's it!' Sue took a swig of her drink and waved a finger at Pat. 'How do you know about it?'

'It's right near me. I've met the developer, in fact. Terrible dog owner.'

'Right near you? In your part of the Downs? Oh gosh, I didn't realise. I haven't read the whole document, I didn't know whereabouts it was, and obviously the objection was never filed. It had something to do with bats and a barn. You can't build when they're present, or something like that. Do you remember the hundred-million-pound bat tunnel they built for HS2 that's apparently not even bat-proof?!'

'I do. Expensive.'

'So is that development. Thirty or forty million, something like that. It's a lot. I can show you the letter if you want, it's on my computer at home.'

'Thirty or forty, you say?' Pat swirled the ice around in her glass.

'Million. Thirty or forty million.'

She looked up. 'People have died for much less.'

'They most certainly have.'

CHAPTER 12

It was thirty-seven million pounds, to be precise, Pat learnt later as Sue printed off the letter that was supposed to have been filed the morning Henry died. Or at least when he was discovered washed up on the pebbles. His exact time of death was difficult to ascertain, as no one knew when he'd hit the water, and the sea had not given up its secret until he was discovered.

Pat managed to get a table seat on the train back down to Southbourne. She had pulled a large notebook out of her bag and was jotting down ideas, theories about who could have possibly wanted Henry dead. The principal suspects were Derek and Dorna. They both had motive and opportunity. It couldn't have been a coincidence that Pat had seen Dorna knocking back bottles of champagne in the Green Lion just a day after Henry's body was found and the planning objection hadn't been filed at the town hall. But Derek had form with violence; he had already been aggressive towards Henry, the black eye, the coercive control. Henry might have told him about the cease and desist order that he was planning, so Derek probably knew the game was up, and yet Henry had agreed to come and spend the night at Fin du Monde. Henry, what were you doing? Did you think one last attempt at romance would reform Derek's character? Maybe he'd thought it would make his trip to the town hall the following day easier. Only he'd never got there.

Her mobile rang in her bag, interrupting her thoughts.

'Prichard Knowles!'

'I know it is, I can see. Your name comes up on my screen along with your photograph.'

'So, I went to the barn,' Prichard ignored her completely, 'and I have to say that the bats are definitely no longer there. I'm not sure what our perp has done to get rid of them, but they are no more. Maybe she smoked them out. I don't know. It does smell a little of smoke, but that could just be the local teens, you know, indulging in the ganja.'

'The ganja? Where on earth did you get that from?' Pat laughed.

'The ganja? That's what it was called in my day. I don't know. I didn't partake, of course, but I knew plenty who did. Anyway, I did some further digging. I was looking through the pile of old guano at the entrance, just to check if there was anything fresh. But no.'

'What is your expert opinion?'

'I *am* quite an expert, actually,' declared Prichard, sounding a little defensive. 'I have been a member of the Bat Conservation Trust for the past twelve years and I have a bat detector that translates ultrasound into a frequency we can hear. Did you know a single bat can eat around three thousand tiny bugs a night? And there are fourteen different bat species in the UK . . .'

While Prichard continued to empty his knowledge bank

of everything he knew about bats, Pat stared out of the carriage window, her forehead pressed against the glass as the train slowed and stopped at Lewes station. She looked up and down the green and white Victorian platform. She had always liked Lewes. It was a pretty town by the River Ouse, historical, architecturally interesting, with a castle, and a little bit deviant at the same time. Most especially on Bonfire Night, when the townsfolk paraded through the streets holding the flaming crosses of the seventeen Lewes martyrs, Protestants who were burnt at the stake for their faith. They also set fire to an effigy of Paul V, who was Pope at the time of Guy Fawkes, just for good measure. It was quite the spectacle.

As was what was happening on Platform 2. The train began pulling away and Pat did a double-take. Surely not? DS Stevens, in some sort of passionate embrace with an older man! Pat could see his thick silver hair, a briefcase, a camel coat, a flash of a gold cufflink catching the sun. Were they leaving, or had she just arrived? Either way, they were not holding back. She was out of uniform, in stonewashed jeans and a baggy blue jumper. His hand was grabbing her backside, his fingertips digging into her denim-clad buttocks. She was standing on the tips of her trainers in order to reach his lips. It was definitely Amanda Stevens. Pat would recognise that tight little brown bun anywhere. The man looked familiar too, but she couldn't place him. Pity she couldn't see his face.

'. . . so the guano contains—'

'Prichard!' hissed Pat down the phone, free hand cupped

around her mouth. 'I've just seen DS Amanda Stevens kissing some man I am prepared to bet money on is not her fiancé on Platform 2 of Lewes station!'

'DS Stevens! Well I never. How do you know it's not her betrothed?'

'No one grabs someone's backside like that if they've been engaged for years. This was passionate, this was rampant. It was lust.'

'Does anything get past you?'

'I'm afraid it does, but this didn't, it was definitely lust.'

'Stone the starlings!' declared Prichard. 'So she's having an affair?'

'It does appear that she might not be entirely faithful to her partner.'

'Gripping. Will I see you at art club? I do hope so, we have a great deal to discuss.'

'I'm on my way.'

Pat collected her car from the station and pulled up outside the village hall in Westlinke a good twenty minutes early for art class. She sat in the moss-mobile in silence, digesting what she'd learnt over the past twenty-four hours. Henry had been involved with the Boho Golf & Spa protest, working for Save the Seashore pro bono. He'd mentioned an eco-charity and spoken about his love of nature, but she'd had no idea it was all happening right on her doorstep. Then again, he'd never been to her house, they'd only met on Zoom, so it was no surprise he wouldn't have made the connection. And why would he bring up his activism anyway? She wasn't a friend.

If Henry and Derek had argued on the green two weeks before his death, and that glistening black eye had been part of it, who else might have seen it? She looked at the row of brick and flint cottages in front of her, with their matching Farrow & Ball front doors. A tweak of a curtain caught her eye. Bev. Of course. She got out of her car and strode across the green, arms swinging, hip grinding, towards the beautifully kept cottage covered in blowsy fronds of pale purple wisteria in peak bloom. As she approached, she could see Bev at the window, with the guilty look of someone caught twitching the curtains. She rapped on the door and then hammered with the clawed knocker. The house was silent. The problem with being a peeking Bev was that you couldn't pretend to be out, particularly when your visitor had already spotted you.

'Bev! It's Pat, I know you're in,' she called through the letter box. 'I really don't want to bother you. I just want to ask you a question.' Silence. 'Bev, I saw you at the window, I know you're there.'

She waited. Eventually there was the sound of shuffling, and the door opened just a crack.

'Bev!' How are you?' Pat smiled widely in a manner that she hoped looked charming rather than demented. The door opened wider. 'Do you mind if I ask you a question?'

'I'm quite busy.' Bev smiled weakly on her doorstep. 'I've got a lot to do.'

'I'm sure,' agreed Pat. 'Thank you. I just wondered if, by any chance, you witnessed, or might have noticed, a fight on the green between two young men, well dressed, about two or three weeks ago. It would be very helpful if you could remember anything.'

'Hmm.' Bev looked upwards, pretending to think. 'I'm not sure.'

'Young men? Good-looking?'

'Now you come to mention it, I do remember something. It might have been two weeks ago, yes . . . two youngish-looking men. They came out of the Green Lion. They were already arguing when they left the pub. Their arms were waving all over the place. They were definitely yelling.'

'Can you remember what they were arguing about?'

'Well . . .' Bev pursed her pink lips, 'I don't like to eavesdrop.'

'No, of course not. But I imagine the noise they were making, the yelling, it would have carried. You couldn't help but overhear.'

'You're right, the argument was quite heated.'

'Go on.'

'One of them was apologising, said he'd made a mess of something. The other was shouting, "You owe me," and the first man was yelling back, "Just let me make it right!" Or something like that. I wasn't listening, obviously.'

'Obviously. Would you recognise them, do you think?'

'Well, it was dark, and you know my eyesight isn't what it used to be.' Bev put her hands on her hips, warming to her subject.

'Of course. But did they look familiar at all?'

'I'm not sure. But I kept on thinking of their nice shoes

in the mud on the green. D'you remember it was wet then? Early April, it always rains. And it was dark.'

'So what happened?'

'One of them hit the other and shouted, "You ruin everything!" Something like that.'

'Right. Go on.'

'Then he marched off, and the other one jumped up and ran after him saying, "I'm sorry! I can do better!" It was all very odd. I mean, I haven't seen a scuffle on the green for years. Not one like that, at least.'

'What do you mean?'

'It was proper emotional – like lovers in a film. Have you seen *The Notebook*? Wonderful film. One minute shouting, next minute one's chasing after the other begging him not to go. I said to myself at the time, "That's not a brawl, that's a drama."'

'Thank you, Bev, that's really helpful.'

'Oh good,' she smiled. 'I'm glad. Why are you asking?'

'I'm just looking into something for a friend.'

'That's nice. Are you off to art class?' Bev nodded over Pat's shoulder. 'I think that's Jacqui arriving now.'

Jacqui was indeed just pulling up in her immaculate pale blue Fiat 500 with white leather seats. Pat excused herself and strode back across the green towards the village hall.

'Do you want a hand with anything?' she asked Jacqui, who'd started unpacking the boot.

'Oh, that's very kind of you, Pat, but there's no need to worry,' smiled Jacqui, picking up a large bag containing various sizes of blank canvas. 'We've got a lot to do today. I've got an exciting announcement for the group.'

'I'll look forward to it,' replied Pat, almost meaning it.

'I do hope Fiona has remembered to bring the biscuits. See you inside.'

Pat walked through the double swing doors into the village hall. It was a well-used community facility, with a Sunday-school corner, beanbags and finger painting, a pile of mats for the new mums and tums yogalates class, and a line of desks with elderly-looking computers appropriately used for computing for the elderly. There was also a small kitchenette. As she hung up her anorak, she noticed there was a circle of red plastic chairs in the middle of the room, likely left over from last night's Alcoholics Anonymous meeting.

'There you are!' Prichard's head popped out of the kitchenette. 'I'm just making the tea to go with the biscuits.'

Biscuits played a large role in art club, much larger than Pat really thought they warranted. Each week, one of the students was required to bring enough for the whole group. Some took it very seriously and baked cookies when it was their turn; Prichard had made some rather delicious rosemary rock cakes last time and someone else brought home-made lemon curd tarts. When it was Pat's turn, she'd nipped by the Co-op and bought two packets of Rich Tea biscuits, which went down surprisingly well, especially with old Colonel Thomas, a retired army officer who'd moved to the village after his wife died. He seemed to have some sort of Proustian experience when she opened the packet, inhaling deeply, his rheumy blue eyes closing slowly with pleasure.

The colonel arrived at that very moment, walking stick in hand, dressed immaculately in a cream and brown checked

Viyella shirt, a knitted dark green tie and a tweed jacket, with brown cords and brown suede brogues. His thinning hair was combed flat, with a neat side parting. He had what had probably once been a jovial face, which was now etched a little in melancholy.

'Good morning, Patricia,' he greeted her. 'I gather we're in for a surprise today, according to our dear teacher.'

'Indeed we are,' said Pat. She was fetching the easels that were stored in the back room along with the optional smocks. They brought their own paints.

'Can I give you a hand?' he asked.

'I'm OK, Colonel,' she replied. 'I'm only bringing out a few bits.'

'In which case, I shall take a seat,' he replied, before joining the erstwhile Alcoholics Anonymous circle and watching Pat set up the easels in the middle.

'Tea!' Prichard came out of the kitchenette clutching a cluster of mugs, each containing pale-looking milky tea. 'Pat, Colonel.' He carried on around the circle. 'Lucy. Nice to see you. Margot.' He paused.

'Thank you,' Margot replied, nodding at the floor for Prichard to place the mug at her feet.

Pat had always found Margot a bit little imperious, with her aquiline nose, hooped earrings and purple turban that she tied on the top of her head like a Quality Street. It wasn't until the art club Christmas party, when she drank far too much white wine and found everything Pat and Prichard said to be beyond hilarious, that Pat realised the imperiousness was simply shyness, and she wasn't such a bad sort after all.

She had apparently worked in the theatre back in the day and fancied herself as a bit of an artist. Quite a few of the class did. Well, *all* of them did. Even Pat, who had wanted to go to art school but had ended up studying law and becoming a solicitor. Her father had told her there was no money in painting and she should get a proper profession. He was probably right.

'Oh good, we're almost all here now,' said Jacqui, entering the hall with her bags of canvases and dumping them in the middle of the circle, next to the easels. She sat down and then immediately leapt out of her seat.

'I feel I should be standing for this.' She smiled broadly and glanced at the door. 'I don't think we can wait for Fiona.' She looked back to the group. 'So, we, you – the art club – have been asked to paint the view from the village hall for a competition!' Her voice went up two octaves as she clapped her hands with excitement. She tended to speak to the club in the same sing-song tones employed by a kindergarten teacher.

'A competition?' asked Prichard, sipping his tea.

'I know!' Jacqui grinned and nodded at the same time. Her enthusiasm was palpable. 'It's being organised by the parish council and will be judged by our honourable member of Parliament.'

'Oh, I know him, he came to my launch,' declared Fi, trotting through the door in a pair of box-fresh trainers and head-to-toe athleisure, including a very fetching pair of leopard leggings. 'So sorry I'm late, I had meetings.' She shook her blonde hair, exuding importance.

'Thank you for joining,' trilled Jacqui. 'I was just telling the class that we've been asked to paint the view outside the village hall for a competition.'

'Great,' said Fi, only half listening, as she bent down and pulled out a large Tupperware container. Prichard sat up and peered across. Whatever she had there, it looked home-made. Pat could tell he was salivating. His cup of weak tea was certainly in dire need of something to soak it up. Fi clicked open the lid and offered up the Tupperware. 'Carrot, anyone?'

'Tea and carrots?' The colonel looked bemused.

'You don't have to eat them with tea,' she smiled, producing a giant sipping cup with a straw attached and the word *Yeti* emblazoned down the side. 'They work equally well with water.'

Before anyone could say anything, the doors opened again and in walked Dorna Braddon. Pat glanced over at Prichard, who had his mouth wide open – at the carrots or Dorna, she couldn't be sure.

'Dorna!' exclaimed Jacqui. 'I was hoping you'd join us after our conversation the other night at Fi's. Welcome, welcome. Everyone, this is Dorna Braddon and she'll be joining us from now on. Say hello, everyone.'

'Hello, Dorna,' the majority of the group chimed.

'Why don't you come and sit next to Pat,' suggested Jacqui, 'and I can tell you what's happening today.'

Dorna took her seat without so much as a sideways glance or a nod of acknowledgement. While Jacqui talked her through the exciting news of the competition, Pat observed her furtively. Dorna was dressed in blue trousers and a navy jumper, an expensive-looking watch peeking out from under the cuff. But most interestingly, as she put her hands in her lap, Pat noticed that the bandage was gone. Straining to see the state of the hand, she leant forward and picked up her tea from the floor, then glanced up. It was red and swollen across the knuckles, with faint scabbing and bruising, the kind of injury you might get from punching a wall. Or a person. Or falling on gravel. Pat wasn't sure. But RSI it wasn't. She coughed in the hope of attracting Prichard's attention, but he was too busy listening to the rules of the competition.

'So if you're ready,' said Jacqui, 'gather your things and let's meet outside the front of the hall. Choose your canvas, any size, and may the best man – or woman – win!'

There was a scraping of chairs as everyone stood up.

'Oh! I see your hand is better.' Pat approached Dorna.

'At last.' Dorna smiled. 'Let me tell you, RSI is a right bitch.'

Maybe a little too much emphasis on the word *bitch*, thought Pat.

CHAPTER 13

Outside, the art class set up their chairs and easels, chose their views and proceeded to settle down and begin their masterpieces. Pat deliberately put herself one side of Dorna, while insisting that Prichard sit the other side. Prichard wasn't quite sure what her intentions were, and after a lot of vacillating about which angle of the green he wanted to paint, he finally settled for a rather dull view of the car park. Fortunately, however, he could, if he craned his neck, just about see past Pat's moss-mobile and Jacqui's baby-blue Fiat 100 to the daffodils, tulips and wisteria beyond. He took out his box of watercolours and picked up his paintbrush, then, closing one eye, began to measure distances and angles. Eventually he started to paint with the tiniest, thinnest strokes, as if he'd taken a leaf out of Georges Seurat's school of pointillism.

'So how long have you been painting, Dorna?' he asked, looking over at Dorna's canvas. She appeared to be focusing on an increasingly phallic-looking war memorial, with long, dark, thick straight lines reaching towards a pointed apex.

'Oh, years,' she replied with a rattle of her bangles. 'I thought about it as a career, actually.'

'You did!' Prichard had always been terrible at hiding his

feelings. He squawked, then coughed and tried to control his voice. 'You did?' he said, a little lower.

'I considered art school, the Slade, St Martin's, I even looked at a foundation course at Brighton art college. Just think, I could have been here, on the coast, a few decades earlier.' She laughed.

'But instead you went into property,' said Pat. 'Quite a difference.'

'Well, no, not really, it's all creative and artistic in the end, isn't it? It's about making something out of nothing.' Dorna raised her shoulders with pleasure.

'The Downs aren't nothing,' replied Pat sharply. 'They are an area of outstanding natural beauty, and should be owned by the nation rather than sold off to the highest bidder.'

'Nothing's sacred, is it, though?' Dorna looked over at Pat and gave a tight little smile. 'If we were all nimbies, nothing would ever get built, not even the pyramids.'

'You're not seriously likening Boho Golf to one of the Seven Wonders of the World?' Pat was biting her tongue; this was by far the most polite response she could think of.

'What is it everyone's saying these days, Patricia? "Build, baby, build." I think that's the motto.'

'They also sang: "They paved paradise and put up a parking lot."'

'I think you'll find that was in the sixties. A bit before my time.'

They sat and painted in silence for a few minutes.

'So, I went to have a look at the bats in the barn yesterday, and you're right, Dorna, they appeared to have moved on,' Prichard said, his chin in the air as he peered over the cars and concentrated on Bev's cottage.

Dorna's brush stopped moving and she turned to look at him. Pat held her breath and involuntarily raised an eyebrow.

'But I own the barn, Prichard, so therefore you were trespassing.' Dorna's voice was cold, hard and clipped. The hairs on Pat's arms stood up. Dorna's hand looked as if it was shaking a little, her knuckles white on the back of her scratched, puffy hand as she gripped the paintbrush.

'Oh, I'm so sorry,' said Prichard effusively, with a wide smile. He could be very charming and beguiling when he wanted to be. 'But you see, I'm a bat enthusiast, just ask Pat.'

'He is,' confirmed Pat, looking straight ahead.

'And, well, I was just a little bereft that they had gone. I've been watching and monitoring that community for years. So I do apologise.' He nodded slowly. 'I should have asked you. The previous owners didn't mind, you see. They were also happy with the local teenagers using the place as a smoking den. Very dangerous, obviously, with all that straw.'

'Not to worry,' replied Dorna, still bristling.

'But I suppose it's only because you own the barn that you're allowed to build there anyway, now that the bats have gone,' Prichard continued.

'And now that the Save the Seashore Group have also gone, we're free to move ahead,' replied Dorna, starting to fill in her phallic war memorial column using fifty different shades of grey.

'Gone?' asked Pat.

Dorna turned swiftly to face her, a snap of irritation

flickering across her face. 'They seem to have run out of puff; they failed to file an objection in time. Well, that was it.' She smiled again. 'So all's well that ends well.'

'Except not for Henry Clayton,' retorted Pat. 'All is not well for him.'

'No, perhaps not,' replied Dorna, turning back, and as Pat watched, she gave her right hand the briefest glance.

Pat eyed Dorna's canvas. The obelisk rose starkly, thick and pointed, like something that wanted to assert itself. It didn't look much like remembrance. It looked like dominance.

'How's everyone getting on?' asked Jacqui, rubbing her hands together as she walked between the painters in her voluminous skirt. 'It's all about the details, remember. It's the tiny things that make a painting. Find something that excites you and concentrate on that. Oh, Prichard!' She paused placing a hand on his shoulder. 'That's coming along nicely. I love your elegant, delicate strokes and your beautiful use of colour. The wisteria is beautiful.' She moved along the group. 'Colonel, you never let me down.' She sighed loudly. 'Your eye is always impeccable. Dorna? Well! What can I say? What a great grey obelisk you've painted. Don't forget to put a little bit of green in there, and perhaps some flowers. And Pat . . .' Jacqui paused and simply stared. 'I see you've painted all the cars. And the wheelie bins. It's very, um, interesting.'

'Just painting what I can see,' replied Pat.

'Er, yes,' said Jacqui. 'Margot . . .' She moved on.

It was just before lunch when they started to pack up. Their paintings were still very much works in progress, but as they brought their canvases back inside the village hall, it was apparent that the entire class had gone the chocolate-box route with cottages and flowers and a pale blue spring sky. Except Dorna, whose war memorial looked increasingly like a Scud missile the more detail she added, and Pat, who had painted the car park, which was, technically, the actual view from the village hall. Pat didn't think of herself as contrary; she simply focused on things others seemed to prefer to overlook.

It was only when she was packing away the easels that she realised Fi had disappeared, her Tupperware box of carrots still sitting in the kitchenette next to her handbag.

'Where's Fiona?' she asked. 'She's left her things.'

'I think she's in the lavatory,' replied Margot.

'Oh, thanks, Pat.' Fi appeared as if summoned, sailing through the swing door. 'I still can't believe that no one ate my carrots.' She picked up the box and looked piteously into its depths. 'Will you have one?'

Fiona had done her face in the ladies': thick layers of mascara and a golden shimmer to her eyelids, some heavy blush complemented by bright pink lipstick. She had also ditched the leopard leggings and zipped top and was wearing a short white frilled skirt, with bare brown legs, a wedge heel and a low white blouse unbuttoned right to the middle of her cleavage.

'Are you going somewhere?' asked Pat, crunching on her carrot stick.

'More meetings,' replied Fi with another shake of her blonde hair. 'For Vibrant-Sea.'

'Sounds good.' Pat nodded and chewed.

'Oh, it is. I'm working with a guru. He's like a marketing king. I'm sure he'll be hugely expensive, but Mal says he doesn't mind just so long as I'm happy.'

'That's nice of Mal.'

'I know. A happy wife is a happy life, as they say.' Fiona grinned, before turning around and throwing the carrots into the nearby pedal bin, where they landed with a hollow clatter. 'I'm going to wait outside.'

Prichard and Pat both followed her slowly out of the hall, blinking in the sunshine, just as a red sports car pulled up, roof down, loud music playing. There was a young man with dirty-blonde hair at the wheel.

'A Toyota Supra,' mumbled Prichard out of the side of his mouth. 'Nice suit, terrible car.'

The engine stopped, the music died and the young man took off his sunglasses. Pat's heart most definitely stopped for a moment. She moved her hand to take hold of Prichard's forearm. The blonde hair, the nice suit, the bright blue eyes.

'Derek!' cried Fiona as she flew down the steps like a teenager and leapt straight into the passenger seat. The car quickly roared off round the green and up the hill.

'Prichard!' said Pat loudly. 'Chilli con carne!'

'What?' He looked at her blankly.

'Chilli con carne, Prichard! Jesus!' Pat rolled her eyes. 'What's the point of having a safe word if you can't bloody remember it!'

CHAPTER 14

Back at Ivy Cottage, Pat and Prichard sat down to a hastily heated bowl of tomato soup for an emergency meeting. The unexpected arrival of the chief perp, Derek, required the highest degree of urgency.

'Fi's reaction was exuberant, that's for sure,' said Pat, spooning up some hot soup. 'I haven't seen that much youthful enthusiasm in someone over the age of forty in a long time.'

'Well, I'm not surprised,' said Prichard. 'He's a very good-looking man. His car was a little, well, low-rent, but apart from that, you can see why she sprinted down the steps like a gazelle on heat.'

'Except when you suspect who he is, and what he might be capable of.'

'What is she doing with him? And how do they know each other?' Prichard looked up at the board and squinted at the new 'Fiona' Post-it that Pat had scrawled as soon they'd raced through the door. 'And is she now in the frame, d'you think?' He bent forward and slurped his soup. 'What's she got to gain from Henry's death?'

'Not a lot, so far as we know,' agreed Pat. 'Unless there's something more sinister about her connection with Derek.

What did she say he was doing? Helping her with her brand? That he was a marketing guru? Marketing? Henry never mentioned that.'

'What did he say Derek did?'

'He didn't, I don't think. I'll have another listen to some of the sessions. But I'm usually focused on other things – emotions, responses, patterns of thought – not the finer points of someone's partner's job. I'm not sure I even asked.'

'And what about Dorna?' asked Prichard, raising a thicket of an eyebrow.

'Did you see her hand? That's definitely not an RSI injury. It was scratched and swollen, like she'd been in a fight.'

'So you think it's her?'

'I don't know. But it does seem very useful for her that any objection to her thirty-seven-million-pound development died along with Henry.'

'Is that how much it is?' Prichard scratched his chin. 'That's a lot of cash. Certainly worth smoking some bats out of a barn, that's for sure, and if she's capable of that, well, who knows what else she's capable of. I've seen a documentary about that, it's called *Don't F**k With Cats*. A man tortured kittens on video. Posted it online. A group of internet amateur sleuths hunted him down by tracking plug sockets, vacuum cleaners, hotel carpets.'

'Ugh! But why is this relevant to us?'

'Because it escalated. He started with cats – in our case it's bats – and then progressed to murdering humans. Kittens were the gateway drug, like with the ganja.'

'What do you mean?' Pat's brow furrowed.

'The ganja is the gateway to the heroin, obviously. No one just jumps straight to the smack.'

'I'm not sure that's always true,' she said mildly. 'But anyway, statistically speaking, Dorna's far less likely to be a murderer. Men do most of the murdering.'

'But she's a feminist,' Prichard opined. Pat stared at him. 'She told me as much. She believes in equal opportunities, and that can't mean just the good stuff like jobs and money and promotions and trousers.'

'Trousers?' Pat laughed. 'So you think murder should be an equal-opportunities employer?'

'Yup,' he said, sploshing his spoon back into his soup.

'Well, statistically women are less likely to kill for personal gain. When they do kill, it's often in response to sustained threat. Self-defence or desperation. And they tend to use methods that don't involve direct physical violence. Poison is more common than blunt force. What happened to Henry looked brutal. Up close. Personal. The kind of violence that comes with rage. There were cuts and bruises, signs of a struggle. That suggests something sustained. Something physical. Derek's got history for that. Dorna? I'm not so sure.'

Rat-tat-tat-tat! There was a loud banging, a rapping at the kitchen window, and both Pat and Prichard leapt in their seats and swiftly turned their heads towards the sound. Three white faces were pressed flat against the glass, their noses snubbed, their black eyes peering blindly into the kitchen.

'Jesus!' exclaimed Pat.

'Oh goodness! *Jal jasseo!*' yelled Prichard, jumping out of his seat and waving. '*Jal jasseo. Jal jasseo!*' He whipped open the front door and hurried outside, repeating his phrase, grinning and nodding. He was met with what sounded like giggling. '*Jal jasseo. Jal jasseo!*' he said again, to more giggling. 'Pat,' he called. 'Come here!'

Outside, on the grass verge of pain, were three Korean girls, all clutching short denim jackets around them.

'Birling Gap, Seven Sisters?' one of them asked, and pointed down the track past Pat's cottage and on towards Malcolm and Fi's house. The other two looked blankly at Prichard and then more questioningly at Pat.

'*Jal jasseo*,' Prichard repeated again, and the girls laughed, covering their mouths with their slim hands.

'I think you might stop asking if they slept well,' said Pat. 'As it's half past two in the afternoon.'

'It really is most unfortunate that I have forgotten my phrase book. The one time it might be useful.'

'Never mind,' replied Pat. 'Birling Gap?' They all nodded in unison. 'Yes? Follow me.' She led them back up the path towards the cattle grid and pointed towards the Downs, making a walking gesture with her fingers. 'Twenty minutes.' She looked down at their wedged fashion shoes. 'Thirty-five minutes,' she corrected. 'Thirty-five.' She showed them on her watch, and then added another finger-walking sign.

'Thank you.' The talking girl gave a grateful smile and a nod.

'*Jal jayo!*' Prichard replied with a forty-five-degree-angle bow.

'*Jal jayo*,' the girls replied before almost tripping over themselves in their desire to escape.

'What does that mean?' asked Pat.

'Goodbye,' said Prichard. 'Or more specifically, "sleep well".'

'Great,' replied Pat, giving his shoulder a squeeze. 'That doesn't sound creepy at all! Maybe you can learn some more appropriate expressions next?'

Prichard set off over the Downs about fifteen minutes later, after confirming with Pat that he would be back for an actual, non-safe-word chilli con carne. Now that she had planted the seed in his head, and the semi-final of *The Apprentice* would be airing that evening, it had to be done. The two of them often watched television together. It was like wine, they had both concluded one day, better consumed with other people than alone.

Pat sat in her kitchen in silence and stared at the board with the yellow Post-its. What was Derek doing with Fiona? And how was she related to all of this? What was Derek doing in Westlinke at all? Surely he would prefer to distance himself from the scene of the crime. That was what a cold-blooded killer would do. And yet here he was, less than a mile from where he might have pushed his boyfriend off the cliff. Was it an accident? Had Henry fallen off because they were in a physical fight? Or had he really taken his own life, just as the police believed?

And was Pat's insistence on it being murder, or at least not suicide, rooted in something else? Guilt, maybe. Guilt that one of her clients had died on her watch. She'd handled plenty of complex cases over the years. Maybe it was more luck than skill, but she'd never lost a client before.

Some people were hard to reach. That was part of the job. The ones who'd learnt early that letting anyone in was dangerous, who lived instead with the inner-critical voice planted there in childhood. But even with them, Pat usually managed to find a way through. Somehow.

But Henry hadn't seemed like that. He'd been engaged. Responsive. Willing to work, even when they disagreed. But now she wondered, was he just performing? Trying to be the 'good client'?

Had she misread him?

She stood up from the table. She needed a swim to clear her head. She peeled her thick black swimming costume off the warm radiator by the front door. It was stiff like roadkill, but she folded it and put it in the pocket of the dryrobe she'd thrown on, along with her black knitted bobble hat, goggles and swimming socks, then headed out across the Downs, litter-picker in hand.

She walked slowly up the tarmacked track and over the cattle grid, pausing by the lay-by on the corner. Had the tosser been this morning while she'd been travelling back from London on the train? She paused and scoured the ground. There it was! A crumpled Mars bar wrapper. She grabbed it with her picker and popped it straight into the bin. Come Armageddon, the only thing to survive, along with the cockroaches, the rats and the fleas, would be the tosser, she thought as she turned and marched up the hill.

It was colder than she expected as she reached the top, and there was a sharp wind blowing off the sea that whistled into her ears and made her hunch her shoulders. She rummaged in her coat pocket, pulled out two plugs of cotton wool and popped them in her ears. That was better. She could do without earache on top of her hip ache. It was always unpredictable out here on the Downs. She could be sitting in the garden in her dressing gown, eyes half closed, soaking up the sun, only to be buffeted like a kite on a string as soon as she crested the brow of the hill. Pulling her hat low, she walked up to the neon-orange sign hammered into the fence by the old barn with the red roof. *Braddon Designs & Development*. She scoffed to herself. It was already looking a little tatty. She exhaled deeply to try and calm herself down. How was that Braddon woman allowed to get away with all this?

Despite the stiff breeze and the gunmetal sky, the platform at Birling Gap was, as usual, teeming with tourists lining up for their close-ups. Pat stood in the car park, hands on her hips, bracing herself for the litany of 'sorry' and 'excuse me' she was about to come out with on her way down the steps to the beach. But she suddenly found her attention drawn to the tall white column of Fin du Monde. Henry had checked in expecting a romantic make-up night with Derek. Perhaps he'd left something behind other than his supposed suicide note. Perhaps there was something the police had missed. If they'd even bothered to look around his room in the first place. Maybe it was worth having a conversation with the owner.

    As she turned to walk up the coastal path towards the lighthouse, she spotted someone familiar sitting alone at one of the wooden municipal picnic tables, tucking into what appeared to be a cream tea. Scone. Jam. Cream. And a small stainless-steel teapot sitting next to a thick white cup and saucer.

'PC Footer?' she said, approaching the table. 'How unexpected to see you out here.'

'I'm on a break,' he replied defensively, dabbing the corners of his moist mouth with his paper serviette.

'It's one of those things, isn't it?' declared Pat with a jovial laugh. 'You live in an area for years never seeing someone, and after you're introduced, you bump into them all the time! Mind if I sit down?' She straddled the wooden bench that was joined to the table. 'How are you? How are things?'

'Good,' he nodded, taking a sip of his pale, milky tea. 'No more news of your client's suicide, if that's what you're asking.'

'I was just on my way to Fin du Monde, to ask the owners if they can remember anything.'

'Right.' He nodded before sinking his teeth into his jammy, creamy scone. A small blob of jam gleamed on the tip of his nose. He paused and munched and ruminated. 'I could come with you if you like?'

'Really? Are you sure? I don't want to put you out. But that would be very kind,' replied Pat.

'Not in an official capacity, mind,' he added quickly. 'But, you know, if they see the uniform, they're more likely to answer questions.' He took another bite of his scone and made as if to stand up.

'Take your time,' said Pat, her hand reaching across the table and touching his. 'You should enjoy your tea. It looks delicious.'

She watched as Barry finished off his scone and ran his soft finger around the edge of the white plate to clear it of the last vestiges of cream and jam. Then they set off together along the coast towards the old lighthouse. While Pat picked litter off the path, she threw out a few general questions about how Barry was feeling, how DS Stevens had reacted to Pat being in the police station and how she hoped he hadn't got into any trouble. Apparently not. He had told DS Stevens he was just trying to prove it was suicide, and she had bought that. She was keen to keep the matter quiet. 'Don't rock the boat,' she'd told him. The case was closed. No one wanted any feathers ruffled.

'I mean, he fits the profile,' Barry went on, huffing and puffing along the path. 'Thirty-three years old. Single. A bloke. She seems happy with all of that.' He bent forward, his hands on his thighs, to catch his breath. For a man in his twenties, he was not nimble on his feet. Pat didn't fancy his chances in pursuing any fleeing criminals, even arthritic ones with Zimmer frames. A sheen of sweat shone on his smooth top lip. 'Shall we?' He nodded towards the lighthouse.

Arriving at the door to the Airbnb, it suddenly occurred to Pat that there might not be anyone there. Drilled into the side of the building was a row of miniature metal key safes, the bane of all historical sites everywhere, from Barcelona to Budapest. Every doorway was now peppered with these little metal boxes, accessible night and day by the traipsing tourist trundling a wheelie suitcase through cobbled streets, their nose in their mobile, trying to find the correct code.

She rang the main bell. It took seemingly an age for

someone to answer. There was a shuffling and a clicking of locks, and the door opened.

'Hello? Can I help you?'

A smiling woman with neat blonde swingy hair stood in the doorway. She glanced from Pat to Barry and Barry to Pat. A flicker of confusion briefly bothered her face, but she managed to cover it quickly with a nice, bland, inclusive service-industry smile. 'Have you booked? A double with a sea view?'

PC Footer convulsed with embarrassment. His ears turned puce as he choked, coughed, guffawed. 'No. No. No!' he blurted, waving both hands in front of him in abject terror, like he was about have all his teeth extracted at once. 'It's nothing like that!'

Definitely a virgin, thought Pat.

'Thank you,' she smiled. 'Not today. We're actually here to ask a few questions about a friend.'

'Oh, what sort of questions?' asked the landlady. 'This is a discreet place.'

'Of course,' nodded Pat. 'I understand. A friend of mine, Henry Clayton, booked in here ten days ago.'

'The young lad who committed suicide?'

'Died by suicide, yes, that's the one,' replied PC Footer, his cheeks still scarlet with embarrassment. 'This was the last place he was seen alive.'

'But you've been here already, asking questions.' The landlady looked at Footer. 'You came with Amanda. DS Stevens, your boss.'

'I did,' agreed Barry.

'But I was just wondering if I could have a look around and see where my friend stayed.' Pat pushed forward. 'I'm Pat.' She put her hand out.

'Grace,' replied the landlady.

'Do you mind, Grace, only it would make the world of difference to me.'

'Of course, of course. I'm sorry for your loss,' Grace added quickly. 'His suite is empty today anyway. It's been cleaned since he left with his friend, but you're welcome to take a look.'

'His friend?' Pat paused on the threshold. 'The handsome Derek, with blonde hair and bright blue eyes?'

'Oh? I didn't catch his name, and I'm not sure about the blue eyes or the blonde hair, to be honest.'

'The chap who made the booking?'

'Mr Clayton made the booking,' corrected Grace. 'His credit card paid for it all. I've told the police all this already.'

'But his friend, the chap he was staying here with, was blonde with blue eyes?'

'As I said, I'm not too sure about that. But then I can't really remember, I was in a hurry to get home. Once you've got your key, I don't really see you again, you see. Sometimes if you arrive late, I don't see you at all. That's the point with the key safes. I do try mostly to meet the guests, give them a feel for the area, some tips. But it was about five p.m., and that's normally when I go home.' She shrugged. 'The room is on the second floor, if you want to take a look. It's open.'

'Do you have any CCTV?' asked Pat, as she walked towards the spiral staircase.

'Amanda asked the same question.' Grace smiled.

'Do you know DS Stevens?' asked Pat.

'Not really.' Grace shook her head. 'We've met a few times. I told her that unfortunately the Ring camera's not working. I keep asking my husband to fix it and he keeps saying he will, and he keeps not doing it. But that's husbands for you, isn't it?' She gave a nervous laugh. 'Full of promises they can't keep.'

'Yes. Indeed.' Pat nodded. 'Husbands!' she said, echoing Grace's laugh. Easier always to agree when someone was doing you a favour. She smiled. 'PC Footer?' He looked at her. 'Are you coming?'

Pat and Barry wandered around the neat bedroom on the second floor, with its double bed with a leather padded headboard, two leather chairs and a bricked-up fireplace. There was an ensuite galley shower and bathroom, decorated along nautical lines, and views out onto the new lighthouse, lower down the cliff at Beachy Head.

'I thought the room would be round,' said PC Footer. 'Like a lighthouse.'

'Did you not come in here before?' asked Pat.

'No, the boss did the search. I waited outside.'

'And she was the one who found the suicide note?'

'On the desk over there.' He pointed.

'You can see where the paper came from.' Pat looked down at a white pad pushed up against the wall. 'But not the pen.' She picked up a blue and white plastic biro with a jaunty yellow flag on the side and clicked the end. 'This one has black ink.'

'Well, she found it here.' Barry nodded.

Back downstairs, Pat and Barry found Grace waiting for them in the corridor, sitting in a small bucket seat next to a slim occasional table.

'Everything OK?' she asked. 'Did you find anything useful?'

'Not really,' replied PC Footer.

'I didn't think so. Sorry,' shrugged Grace. 'He didn't bring any luggage or anything, but that's quite usual here.'

'Do you rent by the hour?' asked Pat.

'We're not that sort of place, Pat.' Grace smiled tightly. 'Our minimum stay is one night.'

'And what's that?' Pat glanced at the table, on which was a leather-bound book with gilt edges, and next to it what appeared to be a marker pen.

'It's our visitors' book, which we encourage our guests to sign,' replied Grace.

'With this?' Pat picked up the pen and took the lid off.

'Oh, I know.' Grace rolled her eyes. 'That's another thing my husband is supposed to fix! Who wants to sign a book with a big fat red marker pen! Look.' She opened the book. 'No one has signed it for months. The pen is putting them off.'

'That's the same pen as the one used in the suicide note!' declared PC Footer.

'Is it?' exclaimed Grace.

'It is,' confirmed Pat. 'Except if you were going to kill yourself, I'm pretty sure that you'd use the pen that's already in your bedroom, rather than coming downstairs to pick up a red pen, writing the note and then going back upstairs to leave it there.'

PC Footer stared at Pat as she talked, his moist lips gently ajar.

'However, if you were running back into the lighthouse after having pushed someone off the cliff and wanted to cover your tracks, you'd grab the first thing that comes to hand, this pen. Then you'd hurry up the stairs, tear a piece of paper off the pad on the desk and scribble the most cursory of suicide notes as quickly as you could, being careful not to leave fingerprints on the note. Then apparently you'd return the red pen on your way out.'

She paused for a brief moment to catch her breath.

'Henry would never have used the red marker pen. He would have used the biro in the bedroom if he'd written a note. He would have written in cursive, something profound, erudite, something for his mother, some sort of comfort. The person who used the marker pen didn't care; they were in a hurry, they weren't sitting at a desk in an unfamiliar room while their tortured soul was being torn in two. They were covering up a murder using the tools they had to hand. Which were a thick red pen, a weak intellect and a poor imagination.' She sighed and put down the pen, replacing the lid. 'I suppose it's impossible to get this fingerprinted. Especially now I've been holding it.'

'I would say so,' agreed PC Footer.

'And I suppose they let themselves into the building using the key from the key safe?' asked Pat.

'Well, yes,' nodded Grace, a shocked expression on her

face. 'It's orange, with the words "Cabin Room" written on it,' she added.

'And do you have the key now?'

'It was lost the night of the suicide.' She paused. 'I presumed it was in Mr Clayton's pocket when he jumped.'

'No keys were found in his pockets,' said PC Footer.

'Well then,' said Pat. 'It's still with the murderer. Or disposed of after they wrote the note.'

CHAPTER 15

Prichard's face was incredulous as the police car pulled up outside Ivy Cottage and Pat got out of the passenger seat, still dressed in her dryrobe with her black bobble hat and litter-picker. He watched through the window, craning his neck over the sink for a better view, as she appeared to walk round to the open driver's door and chat, nodding and turning before giving a little wave and making her way through the gate, down the path and in through the kitchen door.

'Have you been arrested?!' he exclaimed as she pulled off her hat. 'Don't tell me, you've been accosting tourists again, or shouting at people who don't have their dogs on leads, or bothering the police with your enquiries.'

'Well, actually, the police have been helping me with my enquiries.' Pat pulled out a chair and sat down at the kitchen table. 'I've been to Fin du Monde to check out the last place Henry was seen alive.'

'How exciting,' replied Prichard, turning round and picking up a bottle. 'Wine?'

Pat paused. This was always the risk of having Prichard over for a TV supper; he never minded hugely about tomorrow so lived very much for today. A bon viveur was probably a good way of describing him. But she didn't take much persuading to join him.

'Elderflower,' he added hopefully. 'I've changed the recipe. It's a lot less sweet than it was last time.'

'Sure,' said Pat. 'Just a little one.'

For the next half-hour, Pat and Prichard sipped their acid-reflux wine while the chilli con carne simmered and fogged up the kitchen windows. They discussed the merits of the red marker pen, and Prichard, after two glasses of elderflower, decided it would be good to dramatise the act of leaving the bedroom to head for the clifftop.

'If he were sad, Henry would have walked straight past the hall table and out onto the cliff. Surely? Once your mind is made up to do something like that, there's little that can distract you.'

'Well, yes,' said Pat, staring at the corkboard on the wall. 'There's often a kind of hyper-focus, a narrowing of perspective. People who are suicidal can become so internally withdrawn that all they can hear are the critical thoughts, looping endlessly. It can feel like there's no other voice left.'

'So you wouldn't notice the red pen on your way out, pick it up, go back upstairs, write the note and put the pen back on the table on your way to the cliff's edge.'

'Unlikely.'

'How do you know he didn't take it when he first arrived at the Airbnb?'

'I don't, but I think Grace, the landlady, would have noticed and said something. She was there when Henry checked in. In fact, she checked him in.'

'OK, so the note is bogus,' declared Prichard. 'We should write that on the board.'

'Do,' agreed Pat. 'There was something else too. Grace said Henry left the Airbnb with another man.'

'Well, Derek,' said Prichard, as he wrote *Suicide note = bogus* on a Post-it note.

'Except she said she couldn't remember him being blonde, nor having blue eyes.'

'Oh.'

'Do you think you could miss the hair colour in poor lighting?'

'His hair is fair and his eyes are blue. You don't forget those in a hurry. But I suppose in the dark it's all much of a muchness.'

Pat nodded and took a sip of her wine, then winced a little. 'How dark is it at five p.m.?'

'I mean, the clocks have just gone forward. I could probably tell someone's hair colour at that time of the afternoon. The light isn't even fading, is it?' He looked out of the window at the mottled purple sky. 'Though Derek's not a white blonde, a sort of Boris Johnson blonde, is he? Do you think Boris dyes his hair, by the way? It's very blonde for someone of his age. I know he always says he's got Scandi roots, but I'm prepared to wager he does something to it!' Prichard laughed.

'Let's not get distracted. Our two prime suspects have more than enough evidence stacked against them,' said Pat, still mulling. 'And yet Derek is still here, as is Dorna. If I'd killed someone, I would put a big distance between myself and the scene of the crime. Unless I didn't think I was guilty, of course. I suppose if someone believes they're above everyone else – above consequences, above the law – they'd have a sense of entitlement, even superiority. They'd expect special treatment, they wouldn't see a problem with using people to get what they want.' She exhaled. 'Henry was in the way. That's what it comes down to. Collateral damage.'

She paused. 'Derek was exploiting him long before that, emotionally and probably financially. He was controlling. Henry had been diminished for some time. I doubt Derek even saw him as a full person, just a means to an end. And when empathy's missing, when you stop recognising the other person's needs or value, it doesn't take much to cross the line. Especially if you've built your identity on being powerful, admired, exceptional. You don't see a life, you see an obstacle.'

'Well, yes, now you put it like that,' said Prichard. 'Poor Henry.'

'Poor Henry indeed.'

Prichard walked over to the bubbling pot on the stove. 'Are we eating Jamie's chilli in here? Or are we having supper on our knees?'

There was always something a little rebellious for Pat about watching television while eating off her knees. She had not been brought up that way. In that large, draughty house just outside Macclesfield, down the lengthy tree-lined drive, they hadn't quite dressed for dinner, but they'd certainly put on a cardigan (mainly for the warmth) and washed their hands. Meals were not meant to be enjoyed; they were to be tolerated and got through, with a straight back and no elbows on the table. So to sit watching *The Apprentice* with a glass of wine, even if it was elderflower, and a bowl of chilli on a tray felt like indulgence.

They had a sofa each, and they sat discussing the quality of the candidates, the extremely glamorous outfits the ladies were wearing, the impressive eyelash engineering, and how many times everyone could say 'Lord Sugar' or 'Suralan', which now seemed to have fused into one breathless word. Prichard, being a retired successful businessman, was mostly hypercritical of their business plans, their apparent lack of financial nous, their shaky grip on accounting, and their inability to pitch the idea they'd supposedly nurtured for years like a beloved house plant.

Pat, meanwhile, was quietly fascinated. She couldn't help admiring the sheer nerve, the willingness to be judged publicly in pursuit of a dream or maybe just a decent Instagram following. There was something almost endearing in the mix of blind ambition and telegenic meltdowns.

'Honestly,' declared Prichard, a spoon of chilli poised, 'is that the best they can do?' He shook his head sadly at one of the teams' non-existent profit. Then his expression changed, spoon of chilli still in mid-air.

He turned to look at Pat. 'Did you hear that?'

'What?'

'That squeal?'

'Yes, I thought it was on the television,' replied Pat.

'No, listen.' Prichard's head slowly moved to the side. 'There! I think it's outside.'

'I definitely heard that,' replied Pat. 'That's proper squealing and laughing, and I would say the sound of... what?'

'High jinks!' pronounced Prichard. 'And it's coming from Mal and Fi's garden. I wonder what they're doing?'

Pat looked at him and raised her eyebrows. 'Want to find out?'

Prichard followed Pat up the stairs and into the avocado-coloured bathroom, which she had meant to have renovated over ten years ago but had since become resigned to, and in fact rather fond of. It was a small room with a long, narrow window above the bath that looked out onto Mal and Fi's garden. However, to admire the view required a certain amount of gymnastic balance and skill, which Pat had mastered over time. One had to stand on the side of the bath while holding onto the windowsill with one hand and crunching the neck at the same time to get the correct angle. She assumed the position with the speed and agility of an arthritic mountain goat, then slipped her free hand behind the short white curtains and pulled out her binoculars.

'Well I never, Patricia Phillips,' said Prichard with a wide grin, nodding his head. 'I never had you down as a peeping Tom.'

'Piss off, Prich,' hissed Pat, squinting. 'They're all naked in the hot tub.'

'They're what?' he exclaimed.

'Naked. All of them.'

'Who's "them"? How many of them?'

'Eight? Ten? I can't really count as they keep moving around.'

'Budge up,' said Prichard. 'Surely there's room for two up here.'

'There is,' she replied. 'It'll be a tight squeeze, but not as tight as the hot tub.'

He clambered up next to her, clinging onto the windowsill, his chin on the edge of the open window. 'Crikey,' he whispered, 'is that what an orgy looks like?'

'I'm not sure why you're asking me,' Pat replied. 'I'm an authority on many things, but orgies are not one of them. But I can possibly, probably, assert that this might be the start of one.'

'Impressive.' Prichard stared. 'Is that Fiona?'

'It sure is.'

Pat and Prichard watched as a lithe, naked Fiona leapt out of the hot tub and ran across the garden and back into the house, cheered on by her fellow swingers. It was hard to tell who was who in the pale blue uplight of the bubbling jacuzzi, or which arm or leg belonged to which person as they bobbed up and down in the water like lobsters in a pot. Or indeed a human soup. A few seconds later, she reappeared by the large sliding doors, her figure silhouetted in the light from the kitchen. She shrieked loudly to garner the attention of the hot tub, then waved two bottles of champagne in the air and jogged towards it, bosom bouncing up and down, to the delight of the occupants. She leapt into the bowl of bubbles and bodies, and resurfaced in the middle still holding her two bottles of champagne.

Pat and Prichard looked on in stunned and fascinated silence.

'Here,' said Pat eventually, handing over the binoculars.

'Thanks,' replied Prichard, placing them up against his eyes and then quickly removing them. 'Crikey,' he added, 'it all looks a bit much in close-up.'

'It does,' agreed Pat.

'How often do they do this?' he asked, looking through the glasses again.

'Quite often. Every few weeks or so.'

'You've told me about it before, but I never really believed you. I've got all the sexuality of a spider plant, but even I can see this is a swingers' party! I thought you were exaggerating.'

'Me!' Pat looked surprised. 'Exaggerate?'

'You're the only one who doesn't. I thought they just liked a knees-up in their jacuzzi.'

'I think this is a little more than a knees-up,' replied Pat, just as one naked man scrambled out of the tub to chase an equally naked squealing woman around the garden. His stomach was fortunately low and large enough to cover his swinging nether regions. 'Christ,' she whispered. 'Is that Malcolm?'

'Yes, it is,' said Prichard, lowering the binoculars.

As Malcolm and his catch leapt back into the tub, to much applause, an athletic young man eased himself out of the water and walked across the garden towards the house.

'Who's that?' asked Pat.

'I'm not sure,' said Prichard, his elbow on the windowsill, the binoculars trained on the garden. 'I can only see his back.'

'Let me have a look,' said Pat, grabbing the glasses. But she was too late; the shiny wet body had disappeared into the house.

They were both silent for a few minutes, watching the sliding doors. At last the young man reappeared, carrying several wine glasses in his big hands.

'Wow!' said Pat, slowly lowering the binoculars and looking across at Prichard with a feverish glimmer in her eyes.

'What?'

'It's Derek.'

'It can't be.'

'It is. Take a look.' She handed over the binoculars.

'Gosh,' said Prichard. 'You're correct.' He glanced across at the hot tub. 'And Fi can't take her eyes off him. Look at her!'

'They certainly appear to be working well together.'

'They do,' agreed Prichard as the naked Derek slipped back into the bubbling water.

'And he doesn't look like a man who's grieving, that's for sure.'

CHAPTER 16

'How are you this morning?' asked Pat as she walked into her garden carrying a hot mug of strong, milky, sugary tea.

Caroline checked her watch. 'Is it still morning? Almost twelve, just about. I'm fine. You? Good swim?'

Caroline was Pat's Lady Gardener – at least that was what her company was called – and she came once a week to mow the lawn and try and keep on top of the weeds, as well as maintain the small vegetable garden. In her mid-forties, with long copper curls, freckles and the hearty complexion of someone who spent all day outside, she mowed quite a few of the lawns in the village. She was a font of knowledge and possessed a guileless indiscretion.

'Cold,' replied Pat.

'Well, yes, it would be,' agreed Caroline. 'I don't understand the appeal myself, freezing your nipples off in the grey English Channel every day. I know it's supposed to be good for you, but so is being vegan, and they always look *so* unwell. I went to one of those healthy food places in Southbourne the other day to get some Burt's Bees for my chapped lips, and this skinny bloke on the till was so white, so pale, like he'd just been dug up. Honestly.' She shook her mass of hair and shoved a thick chunk of it behind her ear. 'What's wrong with a bacon sandwich? Do you want me to plant out those lettuces?' She pointed to a black plastic tray of seedlings that she'd planted a few weeks ago. 'Or are you worried about a frost?'

'Not unless you are,' replied Pat, handing over the tea.

'Nah,' said Caroline, taking the mug in her large mud-stained hands with their short blackened fingernails. 'I put Mal and Fi's in early this morning, before I came to you. Not that they were up, or I don't think they were. The state of their garden, though.' She blew on the tea and took a large gulp. 'I mean, the hot tub.' She scrunched up her face. 'It was full of bottles, plastic wine glasses and the weirdest-looking things... you know,' she dropped her voice, 'sex toys. Everywhere!'

'Really?' said Pat. 'Go on.'

'I don't know what half of them do, Pat. That's not my bag. But even so, I had to tidy them up. They made me feel quite unwell, and you know me, I'm not the squeamish type. I'm happy with a spider, a rat, a dead fox, a rabid old badger, but one of those pink plastic rabbit things from Ann Summers. Please!' Caroline mimed putting her fingers down her throat to make her point. 'And there was this young man lying on a sunbed the whole time, covered in baby oil like he was on *Love Island* or something, and he did bugger all to help. Bugger all!'

'Oh, what did he look like?' Pat didn't really need to ask, but she thought she'd make sure, just in case.

'Blonde, good-looking, tanned, blue eyes. I mean, he was a handsome lad, that's for sure.'

'Too handsome to help.' Pat laughed. 'I've come across that combination before.'

'I'm sure you have.' Caroline smiled.

'What was he doing there, I wonder?'

'I asked him that.'

'Go on...'

'He said he was an old friend of Malcolm and Fiona's. That he knows them from Brighton.'

'How does he know them from Brighton?' wondered Pat.

'That's what I wanted to know. They met at some place called Hotel du Cocktail. I think that's right. He said it like I should know where it was. Like it was well known or something. Never heard of it myself. Have you?'

'It's not a place I have come across,' said Pat. 'It's the sort of terrible name I would remember.'

'Yeah,' Caroline agreed. 'Is it supposed to make you think of something else, d'you think?' She winked and laughed.

Pat smiled. 'I think yes to the lettuces.'

Back inside, she began to pace around her kitchen. What was she not getting? What had Mal and Fi and Hotel du Cocktail have to do with any of this? And why on earth was Derek now staying next door? It made her feel deeply uncomfortable. There was something hugely disconcerting about someone she had in the frame for Henry's murder sunbathing in plain sight through her avocado-green bathroom window. It was like a weird, warped modern take on *Rear Window*, with sex toys.

She climbed the stairs just to check on exactly what was happening in Fi and Malcolm's garden.

It was one of those rare warm spring days when the blossoms rocked gently in the breeze and the sky was a perfect cornflower blue. Standing on the bath with her binoculars, she could see Derek cooking himself in the sun, his oiled body catching the light like polished bronze. He seemed to be wearing earphones, feet tapping to a beat, one hand occasionally conducting an invisible orchestra. Pat was transfixed. There were as many circles of grief, she sometimes thought, as there were circles of hell in Dante's *Inferno*, and she'd seen most of them. The manic. The catatonic. The mute. The crumpled figure in the foetal position. The bottle as confessional. The textbook Kübler-Ross cycle: denial, anger, bargaining, depression, acceptance. But Derek seemed to have whipped through the lot at astonishing speed and landed somehow in what looked suspiciously like acceptance, glossy, tanned and musically inclined.

Grief took many forms, she reminded herself. But this was a new one on her.

Fi suddenly appeared, dressed in what could only be described as a black dental-floss bikini. Pat had to give her her due. All the athleisure-wearing had clearly paid off, because from the angle of the avocado bathroom, Fiona looked lean, toned and definitely younger. Derek patted the sunbed cushion. Fi sat down and ran her hand over his chest. It could have been a finger, but Pat couldn't quite see due to the top of the leylandii that kept frustratingly swinging in and out of her view. Whatever was going on, it looked intimate. So, Derek apparently played for every team, she concluded. Henry, Fiona, whoever he fancied. Perhaps he was a hobosexual, any gender so long as it came with a roof, or indeed fancied him, and he seemed to have very little problem mixing marketing and pleasure. And judging by the spring in her step, the constant flicking of her hair and the brevity of her bikini, Fiona had been working very hard on her brand all morning.

Pat's mobile suddenly rang at full volume, its cacophonous bell echoing around the bathroom, and likely outside too. Fi turned to look up at her neighbour's window just as Pat slipped, swore and landed flat on her back in her bath. Writhing in pain, she answered.

'Argghghg. Yes?'

'It's me,' said Sue. 'Are you all right?'

'Oh God, I've just slipped over and hit my coccyx.'

'Ouch. That sounds bad. Are you in the bath? It's all very echoey.'

'I am. God, that hurts.'

'Oh, OK. It's an odd time of day to be having a bath.'

'I'm not.'

'Oh? Well, anyway . . .' True to form, Sue didn't have time to ask more questions; she was at work, on the clock and busy. 'I've just had a phone call from Henry's mum. She called to say that his bank accounts have been emptied. Cheque account and savings account, both empty.'

'Really?' Pat sat up slowly in the bath.

'Thousands of pounds.'

'How many thousands?'

'Tens of thousands. About a hundred and twenty grand in all.'

'Wow,' said Pat. 'That's a lot for a young man.'

'He worked hard, he was successful; that's why Derek targeted him, I suppose.'

'True. But how did they get the money? Surely everything was frozen as soon as he died? Isn't that what happens?'

'Normally. As soon as the bank is informed, the account is shut. But these accounts were emptied just before he died, hours, maybe minutes . . .'

'And his mum has only just noticed?'

'Well, she's been grieving the loss of her beautiful son, hasn't she?'

'And the police? What do the police say? Or the bank, how about the bank?'

'Priya, my trainee solicitor, is working on that, but I suspect they will only care if we can prove fraud. Who's to say that he didn't just spend it?'

'Has it all gone to the same account?'

'Yes, but it's not easy to trace, it just seems like a holding company. It's really quite sophisticated. I'm bizarrely impressed.'

Pat sat in the empty bath and scratched her head. Her silver-grey bob was still damp from her swim. 'Murder and fraud. That is some charge sheet.'

'Well, yes,' agreed Sue. 'The problem is, you need proof. *We* need proof. Otherwise they will simply get away with it. Got to go. I've got a meeting. Speak later.'

She hung up, leaving Pat in the bath, the base of her spine still pulsing with pain. However, as she lay back down against the cold, hard plastic and stared up at the white swirl-patterned Artex ceiling, she found comfort in the knowledge that more evidence was piling up against Derek. Much as she disliked Dorna Braddon and her bustling energy and her bloody lead-less, sheep-worrying dog and her complete disregard for the beauty of the Downs, or bats, or nature of any kind, Derek remained the prime suspect.

She grabbed her phone and dialled.

'Prichard Knowles,' he answered in a sing-song voice.

'It's me.'

'Who?'

'Oh, for God's sake Prichard, it's Pat.'

'Sorry, Pat. I'm driving, you see, and I have all eyes on the road. I just pressed a button and your voice came through, rather loudly I might add.'

'Where are you?'

Pat immediately regretted asking the question, as Prichard launched into a protracted explanation of his exact whereabouts on the A259, right down to the bridge and which junction he'd just driven past.

'Where are you going?' asked Pat.

'To Brighton,' he replied. 'The doctor.'

'Right. OK.' Prichard was being remarkably coy. He had not mentioned an appointment at all, which was unusual; Pat was mostly across all his appointments, be they the hairdresser or the hygienist. 'Well, I hope everything's all right.' She paused. 'How long will you be?'

'I can't really talk, Pat. I'm driving.'

'Sure,' agreed Pat.

'But I've been having a few problems with my prostate.'

'Prostate? Good. I mean, not good.'

'Well, it's the age, my age, you see. I mean, it's not serious, but I need to keep it monitored. I'm having a scan and a blood test just to check PSA levels and all that. Every man should have one, you know, like breast cancer screening for ladies. "A scan for every man" would make a great slogan. Anyway, that's where I'm off to. My doctor is such a nice chap, he really is, and it's not that big a deal, as I said. I just have to keep monitoring it and all that jazz, as they say.' He laughed. 'I tell you, the traffic on the A259 is so much better than I thought. I was going to take the A27, but it looked like it was going to be eight minutes slower. So I'm on the A259, and I have to agree the traffic is moving surprisingly well . . .'

Pat lay and listened to Prichard describe his journey, the number of caravans and lorries; he always liked an update on the lorries he saw. None of them were ever driving up to the standard of his old fleet of three hundred vehicles. Mr Stobart had something like two thousand seven hundred lorries at his peak, so Prichard was never quite in his league. Anyway, for a man who could not apparently talk, thought Pat as she shifted in the bath, Prichard sounded as if he had enough chat in him to power him all the way to Brighton.

'Prichard,' she said eventually, interrupting his flow.

'Yes? Sorry.' He paused. 'I might have to hang up soon as I'm approaching the outskirts. I'm through Rottingdean and just coming up to the Brighton Marina.'

'Listen,' said Pat. 'Sue just called me. Apparently all Henry's money has disappeared.'

'Stone the starlings!' exclaimed Prichard.

'I know. It vanished a matter of hours before he died, and his mum has just discovered it.'

'Hours?'

'Yes. So that puts Derek more in the frame than Dorna.'

'Do you think?'

'Well, Dorna doesn't need a hundred and twenty thousand pounds, which is the amount of money taken, when she has a thirty-seven-million-pound deal on her doorstep.'

'And judging by his car, Derek certainly could do with some cash,' chipped in Prichard.

'He's still at Fi's,' Pat told him. 'It's like he's moved in or something. He's lying on a sunbed covered in baby oil and she's flirting with him and wearing the tiniest bikini I have ever seen!'

'Is it itsy bitsy teenie weenie?' chortled Prichard.

'Something like that, yes,' replied Pat. 'But could you do me a favour while you're in Brighton, if it's not too much trouble and you're all right after your tests and all that?'

'Sure.'

'Apparently Derek met Fiona and Malcolm in this place called Hotel du Cocktail. Have you heard of it?'

'Do they sell cocktails, hahaha?' Prichard's machine-gun laugh came hammering down the line, and Pat winced and moved her phone away from her ear.

'Probably,' she replied.

'Leave it with me,' he said. 'I have to go now.'

'Thank you, and good luck.'

CHAPTER 17

The sky had clouded over by the time Pat came out of her shepherd's hut. Prichard was clearly taking his time in Brighton, and she hoped he was all right. She had grown extremely fond of him over the years. His enthusiasm for all things and all people was charming and life-affirming and kept her tendency to misanthropy in check. She thought about how he still got on with Dorna, even if he didn't like her building plans or what she might have done to the bats. Sue used to joke that Pat had misjudged her career, a misanthrope in the service industry, and really should have trained for something that didn't involve speaking to people at all. But Pat disagreed. It wasn't people she disliked; it was some of their behaviour, their neuroses, their passivity, their refusal to think for themselves. The great thing about being a psychotherapist, she thought, was that helping other people grow often fed into her own personal development. When she managed to stay open, which was not every time, she could feel herself evolving alongside her clients; not in spite of them, but because of them.

She walked down the hut's steps and went to inspect the lettuces Caroline had planted that morning in smart, straight virulent-green rows. Pat seemed to remember they'd chosen romaine, but as she looked at them, she wasn't entirely sure. They were still alive, which was good. Four hours in and still standing. It was only a matter of time, she mused, before her involvement, and that of the thriving local rabbit community, would prove to be the death of them. Some people were born with green fingers, some people had green fingers thrust upon them, and some people's fingers, in the case of Pat, were resolutely the kiss of death.

She was just wondering whether she should give them more water when her mobile rang in her back pocket.

'Dr Phillips?'

'Yes? How can I help?' Pat was always wary of answering an unknown number; equally she was mindful that the person on the other end could be a client, an ex-client, someone in trouble.

'I'm sorry to bother you,' the female voice continued.

'You're not,' replied Pat, sitting slowly down on the steps. 'Go on.'

'My name is Rebecca Clayton. Henry's mother.' The woman paused. 'Henry Clayton was my son.'

'Hello, Rebecca,' replied Pat, breathing in deeply. 'How can I help you? Other than to say that you had a very lovely son, and I am so sorry for your loss. I know people say that often without meaning it, but I really do mean it.'

'Thank you. That's very nice of you.' Rebecca's voice was quiet, soft; it was obvious that she was silently weeping at the other end of the line. 'I'm sorry to call you out of the blue,' she started.

'It's fine,' said Pat. 'Go on.'

'And I know you can't tell me, and I know there's patient confidentiality and all that, but you have children?'

'Yes.'

'You'll have an inkling then of the pain I'm in.' She sighed so heavily that Pat could almost hear her heart breaking. 'So I want to ask you one question, which you're probably not allowed to answer, but from one parent to another, was my beautiful, amazing, perfect boy suicidal?'

'He was my patient, and I was helping him with lots of things.'

'Depression?'

Pat grimaced. What was she supposed to say? 'No,' she replied finally. 'I didn't see depression as being one of them.'

'Really?' Rebecca sounded desperate. She was clutching at any hopeful straw. 'And as one parent to another, do you think he committed suicide?'

Pat's heart was racing, her hands sweating as she strengthened her grip on the phone. She inhaled deeply. 'I find it hard to believe that he did.'

'No?'

'No. I don't think Henry committed suicide.'

'Thank you,' Rebecca sobbed. 'Thank you so very, very much.' She hung up.

Pat stared blankly at her vegetable patch, phone in hand, as if the rows of seedlings might offer an answer. There was grief, and then there was raw pain, the kind that even stripped away language. What she'd just heard was visceral; not just loss, but something ruptured. She sat silently on the steps of the hut, as if her body needed time to catch up with the weight of it.

The phone rang again.

'Hello?' she said weakly.

'Mum?' came a familiar voice.

'Sofia?' Pat looked up. 'Is everything OK?' Her daughter was not a frequent caller.

'I love the way you ask me that. There's no drama. I'm just calling, you know, to catch up. How are you, Mum? You sound odd.'

'No, no, I'm fine.' Pat sniffed and rubbed her nose. 'Just had a sad call to do with work. I've been, um, gardening.'

'You! But you notoriously kill everything.' Sofia laughed, and it made Pat smile.

'Now you're being rude,' she replied.

'You were the sort of parent who couldn't even keep cress alive!'

'That is true,' agreed Pat. 'But that's only because I couldn't see the point of it.'

'Well, that's where you're wrong. Egg and cress is very popular in a sandwich these days; it's having a retro comeback, as are all those seventies dishes. Prawn cocktail, vol-au-vents. Even cheese and pineapple.'

'Oh my God. Don't. Prichard made a gin out of that the other day. It had bits of cheese floating about in the bottom of it, like something you'd find on the floor of a teenager's bedroom!'

'Not *my* teenager bedroom.'

'No, not yours, the average teen bedroom.'

'Anyway, it sounds disgusting. Making me feel sick.'

'Be thankful you weren't forced to drink it! How is your food thing going?'

'My Instagram feed?'

'That's the one.'

'I have over six hundred and fifty thousand followers.'

'Is that a lot? It sounds a lot.'

'It's not bad.'

'Good, great, and they're all following your . . .'

Pat hesitated. She still didn't really get it. Watching someone film their dinner, narrate the making of jam or recommend the best brush for painting a chair – it was hard to see the point. She'd watched Sofia's account, or feed, or stream, whatever it was called, and found herself torn between mild admiration and disbelief. There was something strangely soothing about it, yes, but also deeply curated, weirdly detached from real life.

Still, people watched. A lot of them, apparently. And they commented too, endlessly warm and affirming, about how beautiful Sofia was, or how delicious her Thai salmon curry looked.

Pat didn't exactly disapprove. But she couldn't help feeling that something vital was being flattened, that a kind of performance had replaced presence, and that connection now ran through filters.

'. . . your great recipes and things,' she finished finally.

'They are, and I'm getting sponsorship offers all the time. I think once you reach a critical mass with your number of followers, you become a valued influencer.'

'I'm sure,' Pat agreed. Influencer of what? Salmon and feta dishes? She didn't rightly know.

'I was calling, actually, to ask if I might come down and stay next weekend.'

'In Westlinke?' Pat found it hard to suppress her surprise. Sofia had been to stay once, along with her husband, Adam, and they had lasted just one night. They'd found the house too uncomfortable, too chilly to walk around barefoot, and Adam had not enjoyed the company of Dave, who had bitten him when he tried to remove him from the kitchen worktop. He was not a cat kinda guy; in fact he didn't like animals or the country per se, and they had left early on Sunday morning, not staying for the leg of lamb Pat had prepared, leaving her and Prichard to eat it for the rest of the week.

'Well, I thought, why not? Adam is away working – he's got some corporate bonding weekend in Scotland – and I thought it would be lovely to come and see you.'

'It would!' Pat smiled. 'It really would. I would love that.'

'I have something I need to talk to you about, as well.'

'That doesn't sound good.'

'It's nothing to worry about.'

'People always say that when there is something to worry about!' Pat laughed loudly. It sounded gauche. She stopped. 'So, um, I'll see you next weekend, then?'

'I can't wait. I'll set off first thing Saturday morning. I'll text you my arrival time.'

Pat was astonished. She couldn't remember when she'd last had any quality time with her daughter. A year ago? Two years? Well, she'd been married to Adam for over four years, so it must have been before then, because since the wedding, Sofia's life had become entirely Adam-centric. She couldn't see Pat because she was cooking Adam's supper, ironing Adam's shirts, doing something for Adam. This was supposedly a new face of feminism, according to Sofia. The nineties domestic goddess idea had always been laced with post-modern irony, thought Pat – knowing, naughty and overtly flirtatious – but apparently not any more. Still, nothing was going to put a dampener on her excitement. A whole weekend with Sofia. What could she possibly want to talk about?

She picked up her litter-picker. She still had a few hours of daylight left, and Prichard clearly hadn't left Brighton yet, otherwise she'd have been listening to a blow-by-blow traffic report worthy of BBC Radio Sussex as he wended his way back to Westlinke. She needed to process her call with Henry's mother, and the fact that Sofia had asked to come and stay.

She walked across the cattle grid and up over the hill onto the Downs. Sofia wasn't getting divorced, was she? Surely not? Well, Pat was divorced, and children of divorced parents were statistically more likely to go the same way. No. Pat dismissed the idea. Her voice hadn't sounded upset or divorcey. She walked on along the coastal path, which was clearer than usual. Henry's mother. Poor, poor Rebecca. What a call that had been. There was something in her voice that clung to Pat like a fog, heavy and impossible to shake.

Suddenly it began to rain and hail. Pat looked up. She'd been so absorbed in her thoughts and theories, concentrating on the footpath and the odd bits of litter that she'd been picking, she hadn't noticed the weather, the clouds, the storm that had flown in from France. No wonder the coastal path was empty; the sky was black and the heavens had truly opened. It wasn't a light drizzle that could be shrugged off, or even just fat raindrops; these were stinging pellets, ricocheting off the ground and bouncing off her shoulders like shrapnel. She had been so distracted she'd come out in a T-shirt and the thin padded gilet that usually hung on the back of the door in the shepherd's hut.

Where was she? She looked up and down the path as the rain hammered down, pouring off the end of her nose and running like a river down her spine and into her underwear. It was biblical. It was the sort of storm people got lost in. Through the curtain of rain, she made out the silhouette of the Beachy Head pub. She'd walked that far? She hurried towards it as best she could through the heavy wet grass. Her hip began to play up, but she made it to the car park. She glanced at the chaplaincy next door to the pub, staffed every day of the year by people quietly keeping watch, looking out for those who'd run out of road. Then she hurried into the Beachy Head and heard the door thud shut behind her.

She was dripping wet. Her white T-shirt clung to her like an elderly swimming costume, devoid of elastane. The place was not quite packed, but there were plenty of walkers and tourists gathered around the tables, drinking Coca-Cola and trying to work out the time of the next bus back to Southbourne. Pat walked slowly towards the bar, conscious that her trainers were seeping, squelching water with every step. She found a high stool at the end, and waited, wiping the steam off her black-framed specs with a paper napkin she lifted from the pile in front of her.

The staff were busy – there was obviously something of a rush on – but she wasn't in a hurry. She was happy just to sit there, out of the rain, hoping to dry out a bit. A youngish-looking man came to stand next to her. Dressed in a black zip-up, with his hood pulled low over his head, he placed a hand on the bar. Pat couldn't really see his face, just his sharp nose, peeking out from underneath the hood. She looked down at his hand. His fingernails were bitten painfully short, and the cuticles around the edge had been chewed, ripped, stripped off by his teeth.

'Excuse me!' he said, his partially bearded chin jutting out. 'Excuse me!' He waved a big pink fifty-pound note. 'I'd like a double brandy.'

'Double brandy?' checked the old chap behind the bar, with a white beard and wisps of white hair attempting to cover his shiny domed head. 'Courvoisier? On ice? Or as it comes?'

'Yup,' agreed the young man, 'as it comes.'

Pat watched as he waited, shifting from one foot to the other, scratching his already sore-looking hands. His brandy arrived and he picked up the glass, left the banknote on the bar. 'Keep the change,' he said, and walked over to an empty table in the middle of the room, where he sat down and stared at his drink. The heavy cloud of sadness that accompanied him was overwhelming. Pat could feel it in her gut.

'Excuse me,' she said to the barman. 'Please may I have two Cokes and a packet of crisps?'

Two minutes later, she arrived at the central table.

'You might want a mixer with that,' she said, placing one of the Cokes next to the young man's untouched brandy. He didn't respond. His forearms formed a triangle in front of him on the table, and his head was bowed. 'A packet of crisps might go down well too, if you fancy. Do you mind if I sit down?'

She didn't wait for him to reply. She pulled out a chair and flopped down opposite him.

'So,' she began, 'it's pouring with rain outside, what's the plan? Wait for it to stop, finish your drink and then go to the cliff? Or drink the brandy and go straight to the cliff and to hell with the rain?'

He still didn't respond, but his head lifted, maybe just a centimetre. Pat glanced round to see one of the chaplains walk through the door. He met her eye for a split second, his benign face etched with concern. Pat smiled at him and gave an imperceptible nod that told him she'd got this. He backed off towards the bar, hovering. He was there if she needed him.

She opened the crisps. 'Oh dear,' she said, pushing them towards the young man. 'I think these are stale. Just my luck.'

'They're cheese and onion,' he replied quietly. 'They always taste stale.'

'Do they?' asked Pat, helping herself to another. 'The ones I really hate are prawn cocktail.'

'I quite like those,' he mumbled.

'You can't!' She looked at him. 'Prawn cocktail are the devil's work. Do you want one of these?'

'No.'

His head went down again. Pat paused and glanced over at the chaplain in his black shirt, white dog collar and yellow hi-vis jacket.

'I always think someone doesn't care very much about their future when they say "keep the change" after passing over a fifty-pound note. What's in your future?'

The young man looked up at her then. 'I have no future, no job. I live with my mum, no friends, no qualifications.'

Pat replied, 'And since you told the barman to keep the change, no money either.'

He shrugged and looked away.

'Tell me a bit more,' she said.

'About what? I have nothing else to say.'

'Nothing at all?'

'Well, there's my mum.'

'Tell me about her.'

'She'd be better off without me.'

'Your phone's ringing.'

The young man took his phone out of his hoodie. 'It's her. It's the twentieth time she's phoned today.'

'Answer it?'

'No.'

'D'you feel like this a lot?'

'I feel awful all the time.' His fingers played with the crisp packet as he spoke, his gaze fixed down.

'Yeah, hard to go on when you feel like that.' Pat paused, and then said, 'When did you feel less awful?'

'I think I was born like this. No good to anyone, no good to myself.'

'Tough carrying that kind of belief around.'
'It's really hard.'
'Yes, really, really hard.'

She left another long pause before saying, 'When did you last feel OK?'

'I used to play computer games, but what's the point?'

'They can distract you, I suppose, but they're not very sociable.'

'I haven't got any friends.'

'Except me and your mum.'

'You're not a friend.'

'You're right, but I'm trying.'

His phone went again. He looked at it, hesitating. Pat didn't move, just watched him, calm and unwavering. Perhaps he could feel her focus pressing in. It was as if her stillness alone compelled him.

'She doesn't give up, does she?' she said. 'Answer it.'

He looked up at her, then, fingers shaking, brought the phone to his ear.

'Hi, Mum . . . No, I didn't, I was driving . . . Oh, you can see that I'm at Beachy Head. No, don't worry . . . Yeah . . . I'm talking to a lady . . . A date?' He looked at Pat with a hint of a smile.

'She wants to know whether we're on a date?' Pat asked. 'It's too early to say as yet.'

'She says it's too early to know,' he repeated into the phone. 'Yes, that's right . . . Yes, sorry about this morning . . . Yes, one of my moods . . . OK, see you tonight. I'll be late.'

He ended the call, put his head in his hands and started crying in silence.

Pat said nothing, just gave his forearm a pat and waited.

'She does care, you know,' he said eventually.

Pat smiled at him.

'Sometimes I think nobody does, but I just don't let them in.'

'Yeah,' said Pat. 'Do you want to get your change from behind the bar?'

'Oh yes. Could you get it for me, my eyes must be red.'

Pat went to the bar and asked the barman for the change. The man obliged, and she returned to the table and passed it over.

'I'm going to drive back to my mum's now,' the young man announced when she sat down again.

'You OK to drive?'

'Yeah, I'm good. I didn't drink the brandy. Thanks for the Coke and crisps.'

'You're welcome. What's your name?'

He put out his hand. 'I'm Ben.'

'Really nice to meet you, Ben,' said Pat, and she meant it. 'Promise me you'll go to your GP tomorrow and tell them what happened today.'

'Maybe. Oh, I don't know. But thanks.' He stood up and walked out of the pub.

The clouds had dissipated a bit. Pat went to the window and watched Ben get in his car and drive off.

'Thank you.' The chaplain had followed her to the window and was now standing behind her.

'Oh! No worries. Did the barman call you?' asked Pat.

'Yes. When a punter hands over a large note and says "keep the change", the staff always call us. I was watching you. Looks like you did a good job.'

'I'm a psychotherapist.'

'Oh, you are? You're in the right place, then, or the wrong place.' He sighed and stroked his neat moustache.

'How long have you been here? Are you a volunteer?'

'I'm a priest at a parish further down the coast, at East Dean, but I've been volunteering here for about fifteen years.'

'And it's busy?'

'In the chaplaincy? Very.' He shook his head. 'There are so many suicides here. Each as tragic as the last. We find them on the beach. Twenty or more a year. I don't know why they always come here. But, you know, we don't just sit inside waiting for a call or for people to wander in. We patrol the area. Up and down the coastal path all day, keeping an eye out.'

'I've seen you and your colleagues many times. In cars as well.'

'You can spot them, slumped on the edge, fighting with their demons and the body's natural will to survive.'

Pat suddenly looked at him. Of course! Of course! Henry would have been sitting for a while on the cliff edge, his shoulders slumped in despair. Someone would have seen him. Someone would have called the chaplaincy. It was only logical. Humane, even. When you saw someone so distressed, crumpled in a heap, doing battle with themselves, it was human nature to want to help.

'Have you ever seen anyone walk straight out of somewhere like here, or at the Fin du Monde, say, and just run and leap off?' asked Pat.

'No,' he replied flatly. 'There was one teenage girl who I tried to speak to through a closed car window. She refused to look at me, not once. Her engine was revving and eventually I said, I'm very worried about you, I'm going to call the police. It was a terrible mistake. She put her foot down and drove over the edge, screaming her head off.' He raised his eyebrows and bit the side of his mouth. He was clearly still scarred by it. 'But what you did today was amazing.' He nodded. 'It was effortless. How did you do it?'

'It's called steering into the skid.'

'Right,' he said. 'Interesting.'

'It's a technique I learnt on my very first counselling course.' She glanced out of the window. 'I should go. It looks like it's going to rain again, and I haven't got my car.'

'Can I offer you a lift home? I'd like to hear about it.'

'If you're sure?' she said gratefully. 'I'm Pat, by the way.'

'John. And it's no problem, really.'

Pat sat in Father John's navy blue and yellow striped car with the word *Chaplain* in large letters across the back window and yellow and red hazard stripes over the boot. It was warm inside, in the black leather passenger seat; next to the gearstick was a half-eaten packet of jelly babies.

'Pretty village, Westlinke,' said Father John as they drove through the rain, windscreen wipers whipping back and forth. 'So, with that young lad, you steered into the skid?'

'It's a bit of a convoluted metaphor, but when you're in a car and it's skidding on ice towards a wall, your instinct is to try and steer out of the skid. But if you do that, the momentum of the car keeps carrying it forward. So you steer the car in the direction it's already going, aligning the wheels in the direction you *don't* want to go, and then you can steer out, because you're going with the momentum, not against it. It's the same theory when you're working with someone's feelings. They steer out because they sense you're with them, that you're going in the same direction. So instead of yelling, "Stop, don't do it!" you ask how they might want to proceed, what their plan is, and then you slowly change course. Rather than saying, "Don't worry, the sun's going to come out tomorrow", you say, "That sounds bad."'

Father John nodded. 'Then they feel understood, heard. I wish I'd known that when I was talking to the girl in the car, though most of the time I think I do it naturally.'

'The girl in the car wasn't your fault,' replied Pat immediately. 'Honestly. You didn't know how she was going to react to anything you said. Maybe she was scared of the police. Maybe she'd done something wrong and was fleeing from them.'

'Very kind of you to say.'

They remained silent for the rest of the journey, both lost in their own thoughts.

'Here?' Father John asked, pulling up outside Ivy Cottage.

'Thanks, yes,' replied Pat, taking hold of the door handle. 'Can I ask you a question?'

'Of course.'

'The people who jump, the ones you find on the beach, are their faces roughed up, smashed about? Or is that an indication of a prior struggle, do you think? Someone who was forced to jump, or who was in a fight and was pushed?'

'To be honest, I try not look too closely – that's the job of the police – but sometimes they hit the cliff on the way down and they can look very smashed up.'

'Damn,' said Pat.

'Why do you say that?' Father John turned in the driver's seat.

'Well, the young man who died here a week or so ago was one of my clients.'

'Right.'

'And I'm trying to find out who killed him. I can't believe he was suicidal.'

'How can you tell?'

'I asked him.'

'Maybe your patients don't always want to share everything with you. Sometimes other people's private thoughts are just that. Private.'

'You're right, and as my supervisor keeps telling me, just because we feel something doesn't make it true. But I'm like a dog with a bone. I'm not letting go.'

'We can't always be right, we can't save everyone, no matter how hard we try,' said Father John.

'You're right again,' said Pat; then, to herself, *And yet . . .*

CHAPTER 18

Pat sat in the dark kitchen, rain pounding the window, and wept, tears rolling down her face and landing on the pine table. She didn't really know why she was crying. Maybe it was pent-up feeling after absorbing Ben's pain; maybe they were tears for Henry. Maybe it was because Maria and Father John were right and she could not know that Henry had not wanted to kill himself. She did know that Ben had been on the verge of doing just that. The only thing that had stood between him and the rocks below the cliffs had been her intervention, and him answering the call from his mum.

But other things Father John had said also resonated. No one strode across the Downs and straight over the edge; they sat, they waited, they steeled themselves. So why did no one see Henry? Why did no one call the chaplaincy? Why did no one call the police? Because Henry had not behaved like that. If he had attempted to kill himself on Sunday evening, the day before his three o'clock appointment with Pat, someone would have seen him. And they had not.

Dave climbed up next to Pat and rubbed his head against hers. 'Thanks, Dave,' she said.

She opened her laptop where it sat on the kitchen table, the only source of light in the early dusk. The screen lit up her face with its familiar pale blue glow. She clicked through the files until she found it, the first session with Henry. The moment they met. His young face appeared on the screen, his mop of dark hair slightly too long; he seemed both eager and tentative at the same time.

She felt nervous, worried. Had she asked him? Had she properly asked about suicidal thoughts? The question had haunted her recently. She hesitated, heart thudding, then clicked play.

Her own voice filled the speakers. 'Hello, Henry, can you hear me? Oh gosh, I've muted myself. There, *now* can you hear me?'

Henry laughed softly. 'Yes, hello, Pat.'

'Well, here we are. Are you holding your breath?'

He exhaled loudly, blowing through his lips. 'No.'

She asked if it was his first time in therapy. It was. He didn't know how it worked. She explained that there were boundaries – turning up, paying – but otherwise, he could use the space however he liked. He could ask questions or just . . . begin.

He did. Haltingly at first, then with fluency. He told her about his job at a financial firm, working with analysts and clients, calming nervous investors, taking calls late into the night. And then he talked about Derek, his boyfriend, whose jealousy was gnawing at their relationship.

'Sometimes I can tell he's been snooping,' he said. 'It upsets me. My work is confidential. And it feels like he doesn't trust me.' He paused, then added quietly, 'Maybe he thinks I'm cheating. But I'd never do that. I'm besotted with him.'

Pat watched herself lean forward in the video, listened as she asked gently, 'How bad do you feel when that happens?'

'Bloody hell, it's awful.'

'Has it ever been so bad that you've wanted to harm or kill yourself?'

There it was. She *had* asked. She paused the recording, letting out a slow breath. Relief loosened her shoulders. She'd remembered right. And Henry had answered with clarity. She pressed play again.

'Oh God, no,' he said. 'I love my mum too much. We're really close. I could never do that to her, or to me, come to think of it.' He went on, speaking with insight about his feelings, about yearning and discomfort and the way he could sometimes step back and watch his own misery like a separate weather system passing through. 'I don't like it,' he said, 'but it's not me. It's just something I carry.'

Her voice, thoughtful: 'That's interesting. That part of you that can observe yourself being miserable, that's a strength. That's a sane bit watching you.'

He smiled faintly on screen. 'Thanks. Yeah, it feels like that.'

Pat pressed pause again. This was another pointer towards it not being suicide. People who had the capacity to observe their feelings and not be taken over by them, not become them, didn't tend to kill themselves. She pressed play and continued. Henry talked about his mother, who he seemed to have a good relationship with. Then, gently, Pat asked about his father.

'Which one?' he replied.

There was his biological father, distant and disinterested. Never involved. Never there. And his stepdad, kind, warm, a friend. The contrast was sharp.

'I don't really think about my real dad,' he said.

Pat stayed quiet, just waited.

After a long pause, he looked down, almost ashamed. 'I've suddenly gone really sad,' he said. 'It's warm in here, but I've got goosebumps. Fuck. I feel tears behind my eyes.'

And then it all came out: the yearning for recognition, the letters sent with news of promotions, degrees, buying a house. All met with silence. 'Why the hell it should matter, I don't know,' he said. 'But it does. My mum says he is proud of me but was never good with words.'

Pat told him what his mother was probably trying to do, loving him hard enough for two parents, carrying pride for both. Henry nodded. 'I'm lucky,' he said. 'In her. And in my stepdad. But not so lucky with my dad.'

She asked about his partners. About patterns. Was there a connection between the unreachable father and the emotionally withholding men he chose? His eyes widened. 'They don't start out that way,' he said. 'How could I tell?'

But he knew. Deep down, he knew.

They spoke about his friends, those who kept love and sex separate, who didn't get hurt. 'That's not me,' Henry said simply. 'I fall, I get the feels.'

And when Pat asked what 'the feels' were, he laughed and said, 'Derek. His hair, his laugh, how he smells. When he's nice to me, I feel so good. Complete.'

'And when he's not nice?' she asked.

'I'm miserable. But it's so great when we make up.'

Pat called it what it was: an addiction. He agreed. 'I've tried to break it off. But he always reels me back.'

Near the end, she shifted focus.

'I want to talk about the therapy. How do you think it's going today, between you and me?'

His face lit up. 'Really well. Who knew you could learn so much just by saying things out loud?'

She smiled. 'Shall we make this a regular thing?'

'If you wouldn't mind?'

'I wouldn't mind at all.'

The screen froze on his face for a moment before she clicked stop.

She sat in silence, the laptop's glow still lighting her reflection, her square fringe, the faint glint of her glasses. She stared at herself, then down at her hands.

The session had gone well. She had done her job. But there was something about it that stayed with her: Henry's openness, his grief for a parent who never showed up, his longing to be chosen by someone emotionally present.

She was still thinking about it when her phone rang and Prichard's photo glowed on the screen, a small square of light spilling across the kitchen counter in the half-dark.

'Prichard Knowles! It's a swingers' bar!' he declared at the other end. His voice was bursting with delight.

'Hello, Prichard, what is?' Pat was confused.

'Hotel du Cocktail, on Boat Lane in Brighton.'

'Is it?'

'Hell, it is! Well, it's not actual hell,' he corrected. Pat could hear that he was driving. 'But let me tell you, between you, me and that lamp post, it's very, very racy. I was terrified to sit down just in case I was propositioned by some burly chap with a handlebar moustache, or a large lady in a tiny skirt. It was busy and it was only the afternoon. Imagine what happens in the evening! I had a mocktail and some very nice green olives and then I made my excuses and left. Do you think that's the sort of place Malcolm and Fiona like to go?'

'I presume so,' said Pat. 'Otherwise how else would they know Derek and their other hot-tub-loving friends? What road did you say it was on?'

'Boat Lane. Quite a nice part of the city. Smart and expensive. But goodness! Anyway, I'm coming over, is that OK?'

'That would be lovely,' replied Pat. 'I've had a hell of a day.'

'You and me both.'

A little over half an hour later, Prichard burst through Pat's kitchen door and plonked a bottle of red wine on the kitchen table, explaining that he hadn't had time to go home so a Blossom Hill from the garage would have to do. As he marched around picking up wine glasses and a corkscrew, which he didn't need because it was a screw top, he went on to relay in great detail the scene at the Hotel du Cocktail. It was a pretty building at the end of a cobbled street, and apparently the most unlikely of swingers' establishments. Not that, as he was the first to admit, he had any experience of such places. And the names of the cocktails on the long menu were hilarious. He chortled as he listed them: Between the Sheets, Slow Comfortable Screw and Sex on the Beach.

'Imagine ordering that!' His dark eyes were so spherical,

Pat didn't have the heart to tell him that those cocktails had been around since the 1970s.

'Imagine,' she agreed.

'As far as I could tell, everyone there seemed up for it. There was quite a lot of leather and fishnets on display, and one young chap was wearing a black dog collar with a chain attached to it. I was lucky to make it out of there alive.' He wiped his brow theatrically.

'Perhaps we should go there together,' suggested Pat, if only to hear his blustering excuses.

'Hahaha. I mean, do you think I have what it takes to be a swinger?' He took a gulp of wine. 'What sort of person becomes one?'

'Someone who wants to be desired,' replied Pat.

'Well, that's certainly Fiona, isn't it? She wants the whole village to fancy her and gets quite put out when you don't give her enough attention.'

'True, also anyone who wants an ego boost, and adventurous people who really love sex.'

'Do you think that's Malcolm? I mean, Fi is always slightly putting him down and flirting with other people in front of him.'

'He may enjoy being controlled and humiliated. Or maybe he's a watcher. It takes all sorts.'

'What? Someone who just sits and watches other people?' Prichard's eyes went spherical again.

'Oh Prichard, there's a whole pantheon of deviancy out there,' Pat smiled.

'That I thankfully know very little about!' He laughed

again. 'Do you think Henry was a swinger? That he was part of Mal and Fi's hot-tub gang.'

'No,' Pat said gently but firmly. 'I've just been rewatching my first session with him.' She nodded toward the open laptop on the table. 'And what's striking, even then, is how much he wanted to be loved. To be seen, cared for, cherished. He described his mother in warm terms; I'd guess they had a very good relationship. It was with men that things became complicated. Patterns of disappointment, inconsistency. I just don't see him as the Hotel du Cocktail type. That wasn't what he was looking for.'

'Why does Derek go there?'

'Perhaps to find victims for his shenanigans, or maybe he's a sex addict. I don't know.'

'Let's get back to murder-solving,' said Prichard. 'How are you feeling about Dorna now? The evidence is piling up: the bats, the thirty-seven-million-pound development, the damaged hand.'

'True,' said Pat. 'She did also say that she would happily have killed all the protesters from Save the Seashore, of which Henry was a member. But there's a psychological reason why she couldn't have done it.'

'She's not a swinger?'

'I don't know anything about Ms Braddon's sex life, although I suspect she's married.'

'How do you know that?'

'She wears a wedding ring. She's got so many rings on her fingers, on every finger, that actually you don't notice. But women generally don't wear a ring on their wedding ring finger unless they're attached. DS Stevens notwithstanding. The other reason is that I don't think she's the sort of person who would want to get their hands dirty. She strikes me as a delegator of anything difficult.'

'Like murder?'

'Like murder. I get the feeling she's the type who wants the glory but with none of the hard work, and guessing wildly, of course, I can't see her taking responsibility if anything bad should happen. I bet she didn't even kill her own bats. So I could be wrong, but she's not my number one suspect.'

'But you said not to jump to conclusions, and I sense a jump here.'

'You do?'

'Dorna's a delegator and she doesn't like to get her hands dirty, so maybe she delegated and someone else got dirty?'

'Who?'

'Well, Fi, of course!' Prichard picked up Fi's Post-it and slapped it right on top of Henry's, then triumphantly drained his glass.

CHAPTER 19

It was the following Wednesday, and Pat was sitting on the steps of the village hall, letting the morning sun dry her hair. It had been a lovely swim. She had gone earlier than normal, so the beach was nice and quiet. There were no tourists, and no sign of the running club. On her walk back, she had passed the Green Lion and waved to Marcus, who was sitting on a bench outside, seemingly waiting for it to open.

Her eyes shut, she pointed her face towards the sky, quietly soaking up the warm, gentle rays. She had been awake half the night thinking about Derek. He'd had opportunity and motive, and now that all Henry's money had disappeared, there were some concrete facts for her to show to the police. But what she really needed was something that would jolt them into action, something to pull them out of their inertia. Something that would irrefutably put Derek at the scene, with Henry dangling over the edge of the cliff.

'Have you been cold-water swimming already?' It was Dorna, blocking out the sun, peering over a pair of gold-rimmed sunglasses, her painted canvas popped neatly under her armpit.

'No, just swimming,' replied Pat, squinting up at her.

'We should go together,' declared Dorna. 'I need someone

to motivate me, to get me going in the morning, down to the beach, otherwise what's the point of living so close to the coast?'

'And the beautiful Downs,' Pat said flatly, trying to be nice after the pep talk she'd given herself yesterday.

'I've always fancied doing a bit of Wim Hof,' continued Dorna.

'I just like the swimming really,' said Pat. 'The temperature of the water has little to do with it. Isn't Wim Hof more an ice-bath sort of a person?'

'And cold-water swimming,' said Dorna. 'He's king of cold-water swimming.'

'I'm not sure I trust someone who was almost eviscerated giving himself an enema in a municipal fountain in Amsterdam.'

Dorna frowned. 'Sorry? What are you talking about?'

'You're keen.' Prichard had suddenly appeared in the parking lot. He walked towards the two women trailing a multicoloured hand-knitted scarf in his wake. 'I thought I was early. Well, you're always early.' He nodded at Pat. 'Dorna.' He nodded again. 'How are you both?'

'We were just talking about cold-water swimming,' said Dorna.

'Or just swimming,' said Prichard. 'Is that your canvas? Did you take it home?'

Dorna took the canvas out from under her arm. The dark grey Scud missile of a war memorial that she had painted the week before had since, somewhat miraculously, turned into a rather good and accurate depiction of the monument in the middle of the green. Pat was a little surprised. Dorna had even managed to paint in the blades of grass, the yellow and scarlet tulips and the blowsy fronds of wisteria that covered the watchful Bev's house. The level of detail and execution was good, very good. So good that Pat had to squash down a rising suspicion that Dorna might have got someone else to finish it off. Be nice, she told herself.

'Impressive,' she declared. 'What a professional job.'

'Well,' said Dorna, wiggling her right hand in front of Pat's face. 'Now the RSI has cleared up, I can use my hand so much better than before. It's such a relief.'

'Morning!' Jacqui waved out of the open window of her pale blue Fiat 500 as she swung past. 'Are we all excited?' she cried.

'Bursting with enthusiasm!' Prichard said.

'The big day is here!' Jacqui parked her car and rattled the keys to the village hall in front of her as she strode towards them, exuding a joyful efficiency. 'So, we have a couple of hours to finish off our works, and then the photographer for the Westlinke parish magazine is coming to take your photograph. After that we'll hang the paintings, and then at some point our member of Parliament will make time in his busy schedule to judge them, just before we open the show to the public.'

'Our member?' said Fiona, jogging up the steps in a flesh-coloured athleisure onesie that at first glance made her appear stark naked. 'He came to my local launch.'

'Is that one of yours?' asked Pat, taking in the entire bodycon effect.

'It is!' Fiona nodded excitedly and did a little pirouette in the porch. 'Isn't it great!'

'I'm sure it's going to fly off the shelves,' said Jacqui, opening the doors to the hall and gesturing for people to go in.

'Although quite which shelves those are, I have no idea,' said Margot lugubriously as she sauntered up. Her usual twisted Quality Street turban had been replaced by a pale pink towelling variety, as if she'd just left a spa.

All Pat could think of as she walked to the back of the hall and picked up her nearly completed canvas was how interesting the art club photograph was going to be, with a nearly naked Fi standing next to a disapproving Margot dressed for a facial. The only person they were missing was Colonel Thomas. Fortunately, as she turned around, a slow parade of tweed and Viyella walked in through the door.

They all collected up their works, together with easels and chairs, and gathered out in front of the village hall for the finishing touches to their paintings, while Jacqui walked around, pausing at each canvas, giving helpful little hints.

'Detail, detail, detail. It's all about the detail, remember, Colonel,' she said, giving his tweed arm a squeeze. 'That's my motto. Don't forget the flowers, everyone. Make sure you've got all those pretty blossoms and blooms in. We want our village to look nice and pretty. Oh, Pat,' she said, standing behind Pat and looking over her shoulder. She was unable to hide her disappointment. 'My car does rather pull focus in the painting, along with the double yellow lines and the large black wheelie bin.'

'It's what I'm looking at,' Pat shrugged. 'I'm painting *vérité*.'

'Was Michelangelo painting the truth when he did the Sistine Chapel?' Jacqui replied, wrinkling her nose as she walked on. 'I suspect not. Now, Dorna, that's come on in leaps and bounds since our last session. And I'm thrilled that you took my advice on board and have added lots more colour. No one wants to look at a great grey painting, now do they!' She laughed loudly, mainly to herself.

They carried on touching up their creations in silence. They had all naturally taken the same spots as they had done the week before. Dorna was flanked by Pat and Prichard, who kept glancing across at each other.

'Good week?' asked Prichard with a little smile.

'Who? Me?' asked Dorna.

'Yes, you.'

Pat was trying to keep a straight face. As cross-examiners went, Prichard was not the most incisive of interlocutors.

'I've been to the Cairngorms,' said Dorna, holding the thinnest of paintbrushes poised over her work.

'Ah yes, I think I heard your helicopter land this morning. A Robinson R44 Raven II, I believe,' said Prichard.

'I have no idea, it's just a taxi to me,' said Dorna.

'I love the Cairngorms,' continued Prichard, not to be put off by Dorna's dismissive tone. 'Stunning. The birdwatching up there is marvellous.'

'Sadly, I didn't do much of that.'

'Walking?' Prichard asked.

'Working,' Dorna replied. 'I have a Boho Golf & Spa House Club up there too. It was the first one I did, and I went up to see if all was well.'

'You have another one?' asked Pat.

'The Cairngorms and now Westlinke,' Dorna replied. 'And we have plans for three more. Like a franchise. I have my eye on Ireland, potentially Dublin, possibly Marbella and of course Dubai.'

'There's no end to Boho Golf,' said Pat.

'It's just the beginning, actually, Pat. It seems the appetite for Boho Golf is voracious.'

'And now that the bats have gone, there's nothing in your way,' added Prichard.

Dorna smiled, putting down her paintbrush. 'That's the modern times we live in. We've got to invest, update our infrastructure. Well, you know all about that, Prichard, being the Eddie Stobart of the south; nothing moves if you don't have good infrastructure, nothing works. We remain static. It's essential stuff.'

'I wasn't aware that golf was essential.'

'Oh, Pat!' Dorna smiled slowly and shook her head with genteel condescension. 'You'd be surprised. Golf is hugely popular. It's the fastest-growing sport in the world. For some people it literally is a matter of life or death.'

Prichard froze in his seat, unable to move. Pat simply stared straight ahead. She was about to announce loudly that she fancied chilli con carne for lunch. But she could see from Prichard's reaction that he had heard exactly what she had, and she worried that the mere mention of their safe word would cause him to spontaneously combust.

'OK, final touches, please, everyone. The photographer is arriving any minute and we don't want to keep him waiting.

He's got some prize-winning radishes to photograph at the allotments up the road, and he has to do both shoots by lunchtime.'

It took about half an hour of huffing and puffing and shoving for the elderly photographer with an aura of halitosis, flatulence and mothballs to organise the art club into a neat row with their paintings on show, trying not to smudge them, smiling ready for their close-ups. Jacqui insisted on being in the middle, with the near-naked Fi at her side. The rest of them were made to snuggle in together, with Pat very much squashed and squeezed in the centre too.

Prichard's canvas was smart, ordered, traditional but with an air of whimsy. The colonel's was in the Impressionist style, but this was probably due to his smeared specs rather than a desire to ape art history. Fiona's was full of lengthy fronds groaning with fecundity. Margot's was imposing and a little cold. And Dorna's? It seemed apparent that she was more interested in construction than nature, her great grey obelisk dominating the canvas, rising skyward like a poured concrete insult to the landscape. Pat couldn't help but see the painting as an expression of Dorna's love of empire-building, and secretly admired it. The art, that was. Not the proposed empire.

'I think that's it,' said the elderly photographer, with a last click of his camera. 'I believe I've more or less captured the moment.'

'Thank you! Thank you! Thanking you!' Jacqui walked around the hall with a generous swing of her voluminous skirt, clapping the tips of her fingers together in appreciation. 'I do honestly think I love you guys so much. This is the best group I have ever had the privilege of working with. You're all such good artists!'

'Is there a prize for the best canvas?' asked Dorna, zipping up her Patagonia jacket.

'What's better than winning?' asked Pat.

'Winning with a reward,' suggested Dorna.

'Isn't the winning supposed to *be* the reward?' countered Pat.

'Think of the Olympics!' chimed in Prichard unhelpfully.

'They win gold medals that they can flog for a fortune.' Dorna smiled.

'The prize,' said Jacqui, 'is to be featured on the cover of the parish magazine.'

The village hall door slammed shut. Pat swiftly looked around the room. Fi had left the building. Dammit, she thought as she picked her own jacket – Gore-Tex – off a peg by the door. She could kick herself. She had wanted to ask Fi how long her new friend was staying and how useful he had been with her brand. And if the new flesh-coloured all-in-one outfit was his idea.

She left the hall and started to walk home up the lane, turning left at the church, with Prichard trotting beside her firing off questions and jabbing at his phone like a man on a mission. She wasn't really listening, her mind still caught on Fi's outfit. Fi was never one to shy away from a bit of stretch fabric, but what she'd worn today had taken things into full Kardashian territory. Pat half smiled to herself. It was as if Fi had discovered perimenopausal sexual liberation and decided to express it through the medium of Lycra.

'She's got form!' announced Prichard as they reached the top of the hill. His phone had just pinged; he was back online. He'd been frantically googling something and was now flashing the results like a teenager in Pat's face. He pushed the screen right up against her nose.

'Prichard!' she snapped. 'I can barely read that at the best of times, and if you shove it in my face I can most certainly not see a thing. Anyway, slow down, who's got form?'

'Dorna,' he replied. 'Someone else died on her watch.'

'What do you mean?'

'Here.' He flashed the phone again. 'It's in a Scottish local newspaper. I did a search for her and Boho Golf and the Cairngorms.'

'What does it say?'

'That someone connected with that development was found dead too.'

Pat stopped walking. 'At the first Boho Golf & Spa House Club?'

'Yes.' Prichard nodded slowly and raised both his thick eyebrows at once. 'A planner, apparently. He was found at the bottom of a quarry.'

'Was she prosecuted? Does she have a criminal record? Did she do time?' Pat's heart was pounding. Could it have been Dorna all along?

'Well according to this newspaper story, she was never suspected of anything. It was apparently suicide. And it says at the end of the article,' he squinted at the screen, his top lip raised, paintbrush of nasal hair poking out of each nostril, 'that the police aren't looking for anyone else to help them with their enquiries.' He glanced up. 'What do you think?'

'Sounds familiar. Has she got the police in her pocket, d'you think?'

'Police, planners . . . but think about it, both victims died in the same way, falling from a height.' Prichard swallowed slowly. 'Do you think Dorna Braddon is a serial killer?'

'Well! It sure is a possibility.' Pat puffed out her cheeks and exhaled loudly.

'And to think,' said Prichard, shaking his head, 'I've just been sitting next to her in art class. I mean, she's got presence, hasn't she? She's confident. Clever. A bit theatrical, maybe. And I'll admit it, I've warmed to her. There's something . . . magnetic about her.' He paused. 'But then the bats, the pub antics, the damaged hand, and that thirty-seven-million-pound deal to carve up our Downs. It's a lot. And she talks about death like it's a hobby. I keep thinking that as a suspect, she's flashing like a beacon. She did it, didn't she?'

Pat scratched the back of her neck, her mind a washing-machine swirl of theories. 'I have to say, it's all very compelling evidence. We're convinced that Henry didn't kill himself, but I'm not sure it was Dorna who killed him either. On the other hand, she seems so hell-bent on ruining the countryside, she might murder anything that gets in her way.'

Prichard nodded. 'Yes, think about it. Lots of coincidences. Too many! And that hair. Gingers can be devious. We should take this to the police.'

'But none of it would stand up in court,' said Pat.
'Her hair might.'

An hour or so later, after a frantic visit to Pat's office, where they googled and printed everything they could, Pat and Prichard pulled up outside the police station in the moss-mobile with a file full of articles from the *Cairngorms Gazette*, all of which featured the tragic death of the planner found at the bottom of the quarry, a quantity of photographs of the plans for the Boho Golf & Spa House Club, and various close-ups of a younger Dorna Braddon looking 'sad', with a mousy power-bob and red lipstick.

'I'm intrigued that she used to look like that,' said Pat, glancing at the pile of papers on Prichard's lap.

'Before she went ginger? Interesting that she changed her hair colour. One might even say . . . suspicious,' said Prichard.

'It's definitely a noteworthy makeover.'

'Probably means she's good at disguises.'

'Shall we?' suggested Pat, her face turned to the police station.

Inside, she was pleased to see that it was Barry Footer on the front desk. He was head-down, filling out some paperwork and absent-mindedly working his way through a tube of Jaffa Cakes, his hand going back and forth from packet to mouth with barely a pause between supply and demand.

'Dr Phillips!' he blurted when he saw her, spraying the security window with a fine mist of spittle and crumb. 'How can I help you?' He swallowed and then coughed, projecting a gob of chocolate straight onto his admin.

'We have another suspect for the Henry Clayton case,' declared Prichard, stepping out from behind Pat, clutching his file to his chest.

PC Footer blinked frantically as his brain worked through the Rolodex of faces it had stored over his two years of police work. The salt-and-pepper thatch, the crowded smile, the thick eyebrows and the heavy-framed glasses; he'd certainly seen this chap around. But where, he wasn't entirely sure.

'Prichard Knowles!' Prichard stuck his hand out. 'Friend of the venerable Dr Phillips.'

Pat glanced across at him. Venerable? 'Mr Knowles has been helping me crack this case,' she said.

'Except there is no case, Dr Phillips,' PC Footer replied.

'Pat, please.'

'Pat, then. There is no case.'

'That's a matter of opinion,' said Pat.

'It's a matter of fact,' came the clipped tones of DS Stevens, appearing through the door leading to the back office.

'DS Stevens.' Pat's smile was brief. 'How was Lewes?'

'Lewes?' Her pretty nose creased and her left hand, the one with the tight zircon ring, patted the back of her brown bun. 'I'm not sure what you're asking, Dr Phillips. I've not been to Lewes for a while. Bonfire Night a few years back was probably the last time.'

'That is strange. I could have sworn I saw you on the platform the other day with a friend in a camel coat.'

The mention of the coat made Stevens' cheeks pink a little under the heavy contouring. 'How can we help you, Dr Phillips? We're rather busy here today.'

Both Pat and Prichard paused, ears strained for the sound of activity, the clacking of keyboards, the trilling of telephones. But there was nothing but silence. That busy.

'Detective Sergeant Stevens, Prichard Knowles.' Prichard held out his hand.

'Mr Knowles.' She nodded. 'I know who you are.'

'You do?' He sounded delighted.

'I came to your talk on bats in the village hall a couple of years ago.'

'You did! I didn't know bats were your thing, Sergeant.' This time it was Prichard's cheeks that coloured.

'They're not,' she replied, 'but my fiancé likes them.'

'Oh. Right. Well, anyway,' he inhaled through his back teeth, 'we're here to talk to you about another suspect in Henry Clayton's murder. We're aware that the police aren't looking for anyone to help them with their enquiries, but we have some facts that we're hoping might change your mind.'

'Is that so? And what facts would those be?' said Stevens.

Pat was expecting to be led through into the back of the police station to make a statement. But instead DS Stevens stood her ground and moved her weight onto one hip, as if she were bored waiting at the bus stop. She raised her shaped, laminated brows.

'She's got form,' said Prichard.

'Who?' DS Stevens replied.

'Dorna Braddon.'

'The developer?'

'She murdered someone else at her last development, in

the Cairngorms. Look,' said Prichard. Out came the file and the printouts and the articles. 'They even died in the same way. Here. He was the planner, and he fell off the edge of a quarry. There's his photo.' He licked his thumb and extracted another printout. 'And here's the inquest into the accident, and here's Ms Braddon saying how sad she was at his death.'

'Except why would she want to murder her planner?'

'How do you mean?' Prichard looked confused.

'Why would it be in her interest to murder her own planner?'

'Um, maybe she didn't like the plans?' he replied quietly.

'Except that's not the point,' Pat chipped in. 'One suicide on her watch is bad enough, but two might be more than a coincidence.'

'Except . . .' DS Stevens paused and sighed with exaggerated exasperation, 'the first one was an accident.'

'What about her injured hand and her thirty-seven-million-pound-deal and the bats!' said Prichard. 'Don't forget the bats!'

'Well, the bats are no longer there, so the thirty-seven-million-pound-deal is a permitted development and will bring jobs to the area,' DS Stevens replied.

'And her hand?' Prichard insisted.

'If I arrested everyone with a hand injury for double murder, we would be very busy indeed.' DS Stevens gestured around the empty reception area.

'But it's illegal to smoke out bats and move them on; they're a protected species.' Prichard's voice was getting weaker and weaker.

'As are the Downs, surely?' added Pat.

'Not with the new government,' replied Stevens. 'It's all up for grabs now, isn't it?'

'But surely it's worth interviewing Dorna Braddon?' said Prichard.

'On the grounds of what?' Stevens was increasingly impatient. 'Bats?'

'Where she was on the night of the murder?'

'Well,' DS Stevens smiled broadly, her cheeks flushed with triumph, 'if that's your only question, I can answer it for you. Dorna Braddon was in Scotland the night Henry Clayton chose to end his own life.'

'Did you question her?' asked Prichard.

'I didn't need to,' replied DS Stevens. 'Because when we were on the beach the following morning, having been alerted to the body of Mr Clayton being washed up on the shore, I personally watched Dorna Braddon's helicopter land on the cliffs as she arrived back from the Cairngorms. I personally saw her land and I personally spoke to her when she asked me what was going on.'

'Right,' said Prichard.

'Right,' agreed DS Stevens. 'Now, with respect, could you both please leave. PC Footer and I are very busy, and the case of Mr Henry Clayton is closed.'

'Can I just ask?' added Prichard. 'Was her hand bandaged when the helicopter landed? Did you notice if she had a strapped-up hand?'

'Closed!' DS Stevens pointed towards the doors. 'The case is closed!'

CHAPTER 20

Pat had been busy with clients in her shepherd's hut, doing her accounts and sending out invoices, something she avoided until the last minute due to the immense tediousness of it all. She'd also been clearing out her spare room to make Ivy Cottage as comfortable as possible for Sofia's arrival. She was determined not to have a repeat of last time. She was even going to put the heating on in the hope of making the house more barefoot-friendly.

It had amused her, thinking it over. Her mother, Margaret, would have been horrified. Dear, stern Margaret. She wasn't one for comfort, or central heating, or indulgence of any kind. Pat had long made peace with her mother's austere ways. She liked to think she hadn't inherited them (although Sue and Sofia might have said otherwise). Margaret had been shaped by war and rationing and a life edged with loss. Food had been scarce, joy scarcer, and tragedy seemed to touch every household.

Pat could still hear her mother talking about the VE Day celebrations in their Yorkshire village: the tea, the cake, the bread with real butter. How she'd half expected her father to walk through the church hall doors that day. But he hadn't. It had taken months. She'd described how she and her little brother had waited each day, faces pressed to the window, willing him to appear. And then finally he did, walking along the lane. Her brother had spotted him first, but Margaret, aged eight, had run harder and got to him before anyone else. That was the part she remembered most clearly. Not the words, not the reunion. Just the running. The effort of getting there first.

Pat wanted, needed the weekend with Sofia to work. She was looking forward to it. BBC Radio 3 was playing in the kitchen; she'd finished the *Times* crossword and was checking her shares in the *FT*. The weight-loss shares were still climbing. There was some news or other that the drug might become more widely available on the NHS, so they'd gone up again. Maybe she should cash out her profit and invest in something else? Nothing lasted for ever.

She was reading some top tips for investment when Prichard opened the door. Pat hadn't spoken to him since they had visited the police station.

'Knock knock,' he said. His voice sounded despondent. She looked up immediately. It was most unlike him.

'Prichard? Are you all right? Cup of coffee?'

He dragged out a chair from under the round pine table and sat down with the sort of loud 'ouf' you only ever heard in old people's homes.

'Hello, Dave,' he said and scratched the top of the cat's head. Dave's eyes closed as he leant into Prichard's hand.

'Prichard? What's the matter?'

'Oh Pat, I feel such a fool, marching into the police station like that, declaring I knew who the killer was. It was like a very bad episode of *Midsomer Murders*. The way she looked at me, that Stevens woman, and the way she pointed her long fingernail towards the door, it was very humiliating.'

'That's not what happened at all. I've just been on a Zoom with someone who tells herself negative fantasies about what other people think about her. It's a great way of torturing yourself.' Pat snapped down the lever on her espresso machine and pressed the button. 'Personally, I thought you were great. They just refused to listen. They seem to have different priorities. Who knows, perhaps DS Stevens is lazy, or perhaps she's another suspect we should be looking at?' Prichard laughed. 'OK, maybe *I'm* getting carried away with fantasy now,' Pat continued, 'but she's more interested in her friend in the camel-coloured coat on Lewes station than she is in anything else, and although Barry Footer does what he's told, my fantasy is that he was very impressed with you.'

'I'm still feeling like a fool,' said Prichard.

'You're not convinced by my Barry-is-impressed-with-you fantasy, are you?'

'Not yet,' said Prichard

'Come on,' said Pat, putting a cup of coffee down in front of him. 'Do you want me to break this down for you? Maybe we were a little impetuous with our accusation of Dorna Braddon. Maybe we let our dislike of how she gets around planning permission cloud our judgement. I certainly did.' She laughed. 'I can't bear to think of her polluting our Downs. Nothing would make me happier than if her horrific development wasn't happening.'

'The bats are back, by the way,' said Prichard, taking a sip of his coffee. 'I went this morning, early. I saw you swimming, your black bobble hat bobbing around in the sea. But I just wanted to be alone, and then suddenly I found myself there, checking the guano. It was fresh, you know, and I looked up in the eaves and could have sworn I saw a bat. Or two. I couldn't be sure, but the guano was definitely fresh, and there's no arguing with guano, that's for sure.'

They both sighed at the same time and turned to look up at the crime board above their heads. Henry's name was still in the middle, surrounded by other labels – *Fin du Monde, fake suicide note, Birling Gap, Derek, Dorna, Fi, Bats, Boho Golf*. Pat had also written *Missing key* and *No one saw him sitting at the cliff edge*.

'Just think of it like a Sudoku,' said Prichard, squinting at the board. 'We've got most of the numbers, we're just missing a few. All you need to do is tot them up and it will equal murder.'

'Sure, except Sudoku isn't about adding up,' said Pat, 'and currently Derek plus Dorna plus Fi currently equals nada.'

'Well, not really,' declared Prichard, looking at her. 'At the moment, that equals book club.'

'What do you mean?'

'You're not on the WhatsApp, obviously, since you've been banned for being a Trump supporter.' He laughed. Pat was glad that at least something amused him. 'It's this evening.'

'What is?'

'Book club. Everyone is very keen, we're trying to do it every fortnight.'

'What are you supposed to have read?'

'*Fifty Shades of Grey*.'

'Of course!'

'I'm sure you can come along. It was posh Diccon from the *Grand Designs* house who kicked you off the group, and he's not invited.'

'I'm not so sure,' replied Pat. 'I mean, I haven't read the book.'

'I've told you before,' Prichard smiled, 'look at Goodreads and some Amazon reviews, and if you're stuck you can always try the *Guardian*.'

'I'm not sure they reviewed *Fifty Shades of Grey*.'

'You'd be surprised.'

Later, Pat found herself standing in Fi's sitting room, a glass of white wine in hand, her feet slowly disappearing into the white shag-pile rug, watching their hostess, dressed in tight leather trousers, squeak around on her own white leather sofa. Most of the book club had gathered to discuss E. L. James's bestseller, although Dorna Braddon had sent her excuses. She was in London, apparently, having a meeting with her architect about the Boho Golf development. Prichard was on good form, having overcome his earlier mortification, and seemed to be well versed in the goings-on of Anastasia and Christian and the red room of pain, his speed reading of the *Guardian* book review standing him in good stead. But Pat wasn't really listening, because Derek was wandering around between the white hydrangeas and the scented spa candles, serving drinks and handing out canapés. He appeared relaxed, familiar with his surroundings, resting his hand on the back of the sofa, laughing at something Fi said, plucking a crisp from a bowl in front of him and popping it into his grinning mouth.

'So how long are you staying here?' asked Pat, as he approached offering up a plate of pink curls of smoked salmon.

'Me?' He smiled, showing a row of neat blue-white veneered teeth, and ruffled his blonde hair with his free hand.

Pat remained impassive. He was flirting with her, which she presumed he did with absolutely everyone and everything, including the soft furnishings. He smelt of expensive aftershave. Pat remembered Henry remarking on how nice Derek smelt, and he wasn't wrong. Vanilla with a base note of smoke. It was very attractive. Derek himself was attractive; he had charisma and charm and the easy assurance of someone used to being admired.

'Well.' His body swayed a little, his crisp white shirt was unbuttoned just enough for the observer to see the square outline of his waxed pectoral muscles. His chest gleamed, smooth, bronzed. His jeans were well cut and he was wearing an expensive-looking designer belt. 'That all depends on Fifi.' He smirked a little, as if he were remembering an intimate liaison.

'How's that?' Pat plucked a sliver of salmon off his plate.

'I mean, I don't want to outstay my welcome.' He glanced over at Fi, who clocked the heat of his gaze and wrinkled her nose in response.

'You look most welcome to me,' Pat said, understanding the quite basic dynamic. 'Is Malcolm away at the moment?'

'He is,' confirmed Derek. 'And I'm a little bit homeless just now, what with one thing and another, so I'm stopping here for a bit. Just so long as Mal doesn't mind. But Mal's a top geezer, and so far, so good.'

'You're a little bit homeless? That doesn't sound good.'

'Oh, I know.' He rolled his bright blue eyes and smiled his pale blue smile. 'It's all a bit, you know, tricky.' He whistled through his teeth.

'How so?'

'Well, my flatmate and I had a falling-out.'

'Go on.'

'You're not really interested in this.' He laughed and made as if to move away.

'No, no, I am.' Pat nodded keenly and leant in to whisper. 'To be honest, I haven't read the book, so I'm hiding over here to avoid sitting down and discussing however many shades of grey it is.'

'Gotcha.' He grinned. She'd known he'd understand; from one charlatan chancer to another. 'So, my mate Henry, well, he decided I should move out, and so here I am.' He shrugged and took a sip of his champagne, then snatched another glance at Fi, who was laughing loudly, snuggled up next to Prichard.

'Henry Clayton?' Derek was distracted, so Pat went for it.

His head spun back immediately and he frowned, as much as his recent visit to the beautician in Brighton would allow. 'Um . . .' he hesitated, staring at her. 'Yes. How do you know him?'

His use of the present tense was odd. But Pat persevered. 'I was a friend of his.'

'You were?'

'I'm sorry for your loss,' she said, and watched his face for his reaction.

'Very sad,' said Derek. 'Very, very sad.'

His expression appeared to dim for a second as if overwhelmed. Pat was confused. He was clearly a much better actor than she'd thought.

'How long have you known him?' Derek asked.

'A while. You?'

'A while too.' He nodded.

'I can't believe he did that, can you?' Pat didn't take her eyes off his face.

'Well, I can, actually. He was seeing someone for his mental health, I knew that. Some old woman. He'd been seeing her for a while. I'm not sure she helped at all, otherwise he wouldn't have killed himself, would he?'

'Well, no,' Pat agreed with the tightest of smiles. Was that what everyone else was thinking?

'He really enjoyed talking to her, I think. But maybe, well, once you're going to do that, once you've decided to kill yourself, you're going to do it and no one can stop you.'

'I don't think that's true,' Pat said. 'Otherwise what's the point of psychotherapy?'

'Well, exactly,' said Derek with a click of his teeth as he shot her with his index finger and drained his glass of champagne. 'Pointless waste of time if you ask me. Top-up?' he asked, waving his empty flute at her.

Dinner was an excruciating affair. Fi had gone all out with as much themed aphrodisiac food as possible; they had oysters and salmon and asparagus and chocolate mousse, and strawberries dipped in chocolate with their coffees and their birdbaths of Baileys. There was laughing and joking about bondage and S&M, and Fi shared some leather gimp mask story where she forgot the safe word. Pat sat at the other end of the table, observing Derek cavorting around, tapping Fi on the arm or the leg whenever he wanted her attention – a little too often, a little too playfully. At first glance, it looked like neediness, a craving for affection. But as Pat watched, something shifted in her understanding. This wasn't about affirmation, it was about control. He was manufacturing intimacy, laying down charm like honey, knowing that once Fi leant into it, he could start to withdraw. And then she'd chase him and mistake her longing for love. He wandered into the kitchen to fetch more wine, and Pat followed with some plates, as if she were helping to clear.

'Oh, hiya,' he said, looking her up and down. 'Isn't this fun! I had no idea book club could be such a laugh. I just thought it was a whole load of bitchy old Karens sitting around being earnest about books, but no, it's babes on Baileys!' He laughed. He was drunk; his blue eyes were not quite so bright, his cheeks had dropped and he was slack around the jawline.

'Weren't you with Henry the night he died?' Pat asked as she bent down to load the dishwasher.

'Why d'you say that?' He took a step back.

'Weren't you supposed to be with him at Fin du Monde?'

'What did you say your name was?'

'Pat.' She put her hand out. 'Pat Phillips. I knew Henry well.'

'Sounds like you knew him very well, Pat Phillips.' He slowly shook her hand, his grip soft. 'But there was a change of plan.'

'You let him check into the Airbnb on his own?' Pat locked her jaw. Had she gone too far? She had to be careful, not scare him off.

Derek opened the fridge. 'Did Fi say that the white wine was in here?'

'Did Henry check in on his own and you came to collect him a little later? Were you the last person to see him alive? Did you know all his money is missing from his bank accounts?' She couldn't help herself; perhaps she had drunk more wine than she'd realised.

'No.' He slammed the fridge door and stared at her. His slack cheeks were flushed. 'I did not know that. I did not know all his money had gone. That is a surprise! I wasn't there at Fin du Monde, or whatever it's called. I'm not sure if he checked in on his own. I was busy. Something else came up. So I didn't see him that night, and the next thing I know is that my flatmate is dead, found on the beach, having topped himself. Now if you'll excuse me, I have some wine to pour.' His eyes glistened; was he about to cry? Before Pat could press him any further, he'd walked out of Fi's expansive, expensive kitchen and back into the dining room. 'Ladies!' he announced to the room. 'I have wine!' There was a small cheer of delight.

Pat poured herself a glass of iced water from a fridge the size of a wardrobe and sat down in the kitchen. Her hands were shaking as she cupped the glass and listened to the general hilarity next door. Was Derek telling the truth? Did he not know about the money? Did he really not see Henry on the night he died? He certainly looked upset, emotional, or maybe that was just the amount of alcohol he'd consumed. Who could say what his relationship with Henry had really been like? Pat knew one side of the story. There were irrefutable facts, but everyone's angle was different. She hoped she hadn't gone too far with her questioning.

'Pat?' She looked up as Fi weaved her way into her own kitchen and clasped the central unit with her slim, manicured hands. 'Can I have a word?'

'Sure,' said Pat, taking another sip of her iced water.

'Like a proper word.' Fi gestured towards the utility room. 'In there.' She walked ahead of Pat very precisely. She was clearly the worse for Baileys but was making an effort to keep it together. 'Right,' she said, putting her hands on her hips and leaning heavily on the tumble dryer. 'Derek tells me you've been asking questions about us.'

'About you? No. I've been asking him some questions about his friend Henry.'

'The one that died?'

'That's right.'

'Well, the reason why Derek didn't meet his friend in that B&B place on the cliff . . .'

'Fin du Monde.'

'Whatever it's called . . . is because he was sleeping with me.' Pat didn't respond. 'Having sex with me.' Fi's words were slurred and there was plenty of spittle in her mouth. 'Sex,' she repeated. 'We were having a bonk.'

Pat hadn't heard that word in a while. 'Good,' she smiled.

'It was, actually.'

'That wasn't a question.'

'Since you asked, I thought I'd reply.'

'Right, OK.' Pat nodded, keen to leave the Persil-scented confines of the room.

'Malcolm knows, so there's no point in spreading the gossip around. And he's happy for me!' Fi waved a boozy finger in the air.

'Your private life is your private life,' said Pat as she worked her way out of the room.

'And another thing.' Derek was standing in the doorway, holding a bottle of wine, which he swung gently by his side in a manner that felt oddly threatening.

'Yes?' said Pat. Her mouth was suddenly dry and her heart was racing a little. Surely he wasn't about to knock her out among the sheets and dirty towels and Malcolm's Calvin Klein underwear?

'I'd watch it if I were you, Dr Phillips. Oh yes,' he nodded with a flash of his pale blue teeth, 'I know who you are. If I were you, I'd let sleeping dogs lie. I really would. You need to stop digging. Quit while you're ahead, love. Otherwise you've no idea how big the hole will be. And little old ladies are fragile things, aren't they? Accidents happen all the time! Don't have a fall. There's nothing worse than a fall. Especially at your age.'

CHAPTER 21

Pat woke early, annoyed by the events of the previous night. She'd left as soon as she could after the encounter with Derek and Fi in the utility room, brushing past the usual party detritus and Prichard draped like a parody of himself on that ghastly white leather sofa. 'Imagine,' he was saying to the room as she left, 'the Marquis de Sade with a safe word and a signed contract. *Fifty Shades*-type depravity sounds like corporate team-building, hahaha.' Which Goodreads review had he got that from?

The image of Derek waving a bottle of Chardonnay like it was a weapon, delivering half-formed threats with a swagger he clearly thought was intimidating, kept circling back. It was just pathetic. And exhausting. He was, she suspected, one of those men who only ever felt solid when someone else was shrinking. The kind who mistook volume for authority and discomfort for power. Probably a straightforward bully.

The psychology was familiar: brittle pride, hair-trigger temper, a compulsive need to assert control the moment it felt even slightly in question. Underneath all that noise, there was probably something soft and shivering: fear of irrelevance, of humiliation, of not being as important as he told himself he was. And possibly of being found out.

As a murderer, or just as a pathetic little man. Time would probably tell. She exhaled through her nose and muttered, 'Grow up,' to no one in particular.

Sometimes she didn't really fancy a morning swim, but today she needed it. She was buzzing with an angry energy that she wanted to wash off in the waves. She zipped up her dryrobe, grabbed her picker plus a bin bag and marched out of the house, over the cattle grid and straight to the lay-by to deal with the tosser. It wasn't quite slaying a dragon, but it was at least a small achievement, a little win, a victory at the start of the day. She walked briskly up to the bin and stared at the ground. But there was nothing there. Where was the Mars bar wrapper? She turned and looked at the verge. Maybe it had been caught by the wind. Behind the bin? Inside the bin, even? Had the tosser finally made the toss? She looked inside the bin. The wrapper wasn't there. Pat was confused. Was the tosser dead? He was supposed to survive Armageddon along with the cockroaches. She was surprised to find it disconcerting. Perhaps she was having an imaginary relationship with the tosser of the Mars bar wrappers.

She carried on up the hill past Dorna's orange sign and reached the top of the steps just as the sun broke through and the light danced like diamonds on the crest of the waves. She stopped to take in the view. It really was beautiful. She walked slowly down the steps, inhaling the cold sea air, clearing her lungs, listening to the crunch of the pebbles, the hiss and sigh of the sea. She felt better already. Her shoulders were less tense, lowered away from her ear lobes.

She sat down in her dryrobe and pulled down her

leggings, snaking her hips a little as she pulled on her black swimming costume. Old woman? What a prize shit Derek was. Old woman? What age was he? Late twenties? Early thirties? Younger than Henry. He was borderline Gen Z, and while she tried not to generalise, there was a certain self-referential intensity about his age group, as if the world had only just started paying attention when they arrived. Pat sighed. She wanted to avoid confrontation with him from now on, at least until he was brought to justice.

She exhaled loudly and then walked towards the waves, looking up and down the shoreline. The beach was empty. The light was incredible. It was that pure white light that you only got in the morning, clean and clear, before the world had woken up.

As she swam, she ran the conversations she'd had with Derek through her head again. He had seemed – or at least acted – sad that his friend had died, that was true. But in reality it was the money that had got his attention. Fi had obviously told him who Pat was. He'd had no idea at the beginning of the evening, when he was flirting and flashing his eyes and his smile. It was only later that the penny dropped.

Walking out of the sea, Pat wrapped herself in her thick, warm coat and looked up at the old lighthouse basking in the early-morning sun. So if it wasn't Derek who had met Henry at the Airbnb, then who the hell was the man who had arrived to collect him at 5 p.m.? Grace, the landlady, hadn't noticed the colour of his hair, and Derek's hair was really striking. Maybe he'd been backlit so she couldn't tell.

The car park was beginning to fill up by the time Pat

walked up the steps to the top of the cliff. There were already a few tourists standing too near the edge for her liking, smiling and taking their selfies. She was on the verge of telling them to step away from the precipice, to watch out for erosion, but somehow she didn't have the energy. She walked back across the Downs, her hands in her pockets, deep in thought. If Dorna had an alibi and Derek really was otherwise engaged, then what were her options? Who else was still in the frame?

As she crossed the lane and walked down the track towards her cottage, Malcolm's golden Aston Martin crawled up alongside her. He lowered the window.

'Nice day for it,' he said. Pat must have looked confused. 'For a swim.'

'It was,' she smiled. 'Back so soon?'

'I thought I'd surprise Fi,' he said. 'I took an earlier flight.'

'Oh good. I'm sure she'll be delighted.'

He waved as his car purred off, and Pat paused by the cattle grid, imagining the scene back at the house: the bedroom door creaking open, Malcolm walking in with a fresh cafetière and mugs, only to be confronted by the unmistakable tangle of Fi and Derek mid-thrust, the beast with two backs in full motion. She suspected Malcolm had meant it in principle when he said he didn't mind the fling. But principles had a way of buckling under the weight of sweaty reality. She could just see him now, standing awkwardly on the threshold, blinking, the tray still in his hands, unsure whether to retreat, clear his throat or ask if anyone took sugar.

As she wandered through her garden gate, still imagining

the scenes unfolding next door, she stopped in her tracks. Why was the door to the shepherd's hut swinging in the breeze? Surely she had locked it last night after her final Zoom session? She would most certainly have shut it at least. She felt oddly trepidatious about approaching the wooden steps as the door swung backwards and forwards, slamming against the frame in the wind. It was unnerving. A few sheets of paper flew out in front of her and spiralled in the air. The wind gusted again, and more and more pages were sent soaring.

She ran inside and quickly shut the door. Someone had been in there. Her papers were in a mess. Her metal cabinet was wide open, and the intruder had worked their way through the files, chucking the ones they were not interested in on the floor, while others were open on the desk. Was there one missing? Who knew? She leafed through the cabinet. It was hard to be sure with the mess and the sheets of paper everywhere, but it looked as though Henry's file was gone. It could be a coincidence. But it was unlikely.

Something crunched underfoot. She looked down. Her parched spider-plant pot had been smashed on the floor. They were in a hurry, she thought, bending down to pick up the pieces. It was difficult to break a pot on a wooden floor unless it had been pushed off the desk with some force. She was suddenly struck by a terrible thought. Maybe she had disturbed them. Maybe they'd been watching her, waiting for her to go for her swim before they broke into the place. She felt sick and scared, and Pat did not usually scare easily.

Her first thought was to call the police. But the idea of D S Stevens' neat bun and her banal questions and her achingly slow brain wandering around the place filled her with dread, and she was not sure she had enough stale biscuits to entertain PC Footer for more than twenty minutes.

She called Sue. Sue was busy, but she stopped her work calls as soon as she heard about the break-in.

'It's very odd,' she said. 'Why would someone want to steal someone else's file. What's in there?'

'It's different for each client. Normally it's just the basics, but sometimes I might add a small progress report. It depends.'

'What was in Henry's report?'

'Quite a bit, actually, but only because he liked to talk a lot.'

'That's worrying. Are you all right?'

'I'm a bit shaken up. It's an odd feeling being broken into, it's a violation. Oh God, WHY didn't I abide by the governing body's code of ethics and keep everything in code?'

'They would've stolen all the files then,' said Sue. 'You'd be even more violated.'

'I might have done something unwise last night. I told Henry's so-called boyfriend, who is now the lover of the next-door neighbour, that the money had gone.'

'It's probably him who broke in, then, looking for a file about the money. Look, don't you think you should book into a hotel for a bit?'

'Don't tell me, there's a lovely B&B down the road.' Pat's laugh was hollow. She scratched the back of her neck. She was on edge, that was for sure.

'I could come down at the weekend if you want? Let me

rephrase that. I'd love to come down for the weekend and look after you for a bit. Spoil you. We could go out to the pub for supper – the Green Lion, isn't that what it's called? I seem to remember they do some nice fishcakes.' Pat didn't reply. What to say? She didn't want to offend Sue, especially after she'd offered. 'Or not?' added Sue, as she sensed the reticence down the line.

'The thing is, Sofia is coming for the weekend...'

'Your Sofia?'

'Yes.'

'Well, that's great,' said Sue. 'I know how much you miss her, and you haven't seen her for ages.'

'Why don't you come too?' suggested Pat, with mild enthusiasm. 'It would be nice for you to catch up.'

'Well,' Sue sighed. 'Maybe not.'

'I know, how about you come for Sunday lunch? You can take the train. It's easy, and that way I can have Saturday night with my daughter and then both of you on Sunday. Two of my favourite people.'

'It sounds like a good plan,' agreed Sue. 'Then at least I get to check that you're OK.'

Pat hung up and felt a little better. But her office was still a mess and Henry's file was missing, and she had an uneasy feeling that she was being watched or observed in some way. How else could the criminal have managed to get in and out of the hut so quickly? She had only been gone an hour or so. She sat on the floor and started picking up the pieces of loose paper. Some of the clients' notes that she was looking at were quite a few years old. Some of them she remembered clearly, some of them she had almost forgotten.

Her mobile rang.

'Prichard Knowles!' he announced. His voice sounded a little jaded.

'Hi, Prichard, how are you?'

'Not well, Pat, not well at all. I ended up playing party games, spin the bottle and all that, until past midnight. I'm exhausted. I also drank Baileys, which should only ever be drunk at Christmas; it's not something one should indulge in outside the festive season. Anyway, you left early?'

'Well, I was somewhat threatened by Derek in the utility room with a bottle of wine.'

'That sounds like a very grown-up form of Cluedo,' laughed Prichard. 'I'm not sure I comprehend.'

'Derek threatened me while I was in the utility room with Fiona, and he was holding a bottle of wine and swinging it around.' The more Pat explained the situation, the more bizarre it sounded.

'I'm sorry. You're going to have to rewind. What were you doing in the utility room with Fiona in the first place, and more importantly, where was I?'

Pat talked Prichard through her evening, including Derek and Fiona's liaison, the admission of their dalliance, and Derek's menacing words by the tumble dryer.

'Well, I am shocked!' declared Prichard. 'I had no idea.'

'And the shepherd's hut was broken into this morning.'

He immediately offered to come over and help her tidy up, and to stay as security. But Pat could tell that he was not in the finest of fettles, and she would clearly have ended up looking after him as he moaned around the kitchen asking for paracetamol and craving salt, fat and carbohydrates.

'Don't worry, Prichard,' she said in the end. 'I'm a big girl, and I can look after myself.'

She tidied the hut, put everything back where it belonged, had a cereal bar in the kitchen, then returned to the hut for the day's Zooms.

It was still light when Pat decided to have a bath. She stood in the avocado suite, waiting for the plastic bath to fill up, and found herself locking the door. It was an odd feeling being scared in her own house. Somewhere she'd lived very happily for ten years. She added some bubbles. She was not normally that type of person. She'd been given them for Christmas and they had sat unopened by the bath ever since. She was tempted to climb up onto the edge and have a look next door. But as she turned off the taps, it was all quiet the other side of the leylandii. What scene had greeted Malcolm on his return, she thought as she slipped into the bath, was anyone's guess.

She didn't stay in there long. She'd planned to lounge around for a good half-hour, having a luxurious soak, but in the end, she was in and out. She told herself it was the oversweet smell of the bubble bath. Truth was, she felt vulnerable, exposed; each time she ducked under, her mind told itself either that Derek would be there when she surfaced, or that she would be held under by some violent criminal and would flail around in the water until she drowned.

They were just thoughts, she told herself. Ignore the thoughts.

Dressed in her fluffy dressing gown, with a mug of herbal tea, she sat down with Dave to watch TV, which as far as she could work out consisted of back-to-back panel shows. She called Sue. The phone went straight to answer machine. She wasn't sure she could manage Prichard's laugh tonight. She was fine. This was her sitting room after all. She dozed on the sofa and listened to her purring cat as he kneaded the fluffy edge of her dressing gown with his sharp nails.

The tapping on the window was light, like raindrops on glass. Pat went rigid on the sofa and held her breath. What was that? Was it a branch, a twig on the window? Or was it someone clawing at the glass trying to get in? She lay motionless, her ears straining, her whole body stiff, on high alert. Fight? Flight? All she could hear was the pounding of her own heart as it hammered away against her eardrums. There it was again. The noise. Even Dave stopped purring and looked across at the window.

Pat inhaled and then sat bolt upright on the sofa, spun her head to stare at the window and screamed loudly. The apparition at the window also screamed. Pale skin. Bright pink lips. Black hair. Hands either side of the face. For a nanosecond, she believed she was looking at Edvard Munch's *Scream*.

It was a Korean tourist. Tapping the glass with acrylic nails, asking for help: how did she get back to London from here? Eventually Pat sent her on her way to the village bus stop, then drew all the curtains, turned off the lights, bolted the doors and windows, picked up Dave and went to bed, pulling the duvet right up under her chin.

CHAPTER 22

Sofia parked her large red 4x4 right up on the grass verge outside Ivy Cottage, blocking out the light from the kitchen window. Prichard, who was sitting at the pine table, turned to look at Pat, eyebrows raised, waiting for her reaction. But Pat did nothing. She simply smiled, rubbed her hands together with excitement and rushed out of the house to meet her daughter.

'Darling!' she said as Sofia came down the path wearing a pink and white checked seersucker dress and dragging a heavy wheeled suitcase in her wake. 'Let me help you with that.' She picked up the bag and resisted the temptation to ask how long Sofia was staying or what she had in there. 'It is so very lovely to see you,' she continued. 'You look well.' She kissed her on both cheeks. 'Really well.'

'Sorry about the suitcase.' Sofia smiled. 'I didn't know what to wear, what the vibe was, so I packed the lot.'

'No problem,' Pat puffed as she hoicked the bag over the threshold.

'Hi, hi, hi,' said Sofia with a little wave as she walked into the kitchen and dumped her pale cashmere wrap and a large paper bag in the middle of the table. 'I'm Sofe,' she said, going straight to give Prichard a hug. 'So very nice to meet you.' She squeezed him tightly, while Prichard stood stiffly with his arms by his sides, his ear lobes turning scarlet. 'Oh Mum,' she exclaimed, turning back to watch Pat battling to squeeze her suitcase into the kitchen, 'I had forgotten quite how homey this little cottage is. It is so sweet, so cute, so totally homey. Here,' she said, opening the paper bag on the table and bringing out a glass-based Tupperware with a blue plastic lid. 'I made you a little lemon drizzle cake with hand-candied curls.' She unclipped the lid and the room instantly filled with the sweet, sticky, sharp scent of sugar and lemons. 'It's all organic,' she added as she flopped down at the kitchen table. 'Gosh it's nice to be here.'

'How was your journey?' asked Pat, turning on the coffee machine.

'Boring, long, tedious. Gosh, it's miles from London, isn't it? Miles. All the way down here. I had to listen to a whole podcast to pass the time so I didn't fall asleep. How are you? What have you been up to?'

'Oh, you know, this and that,' said Pat, collecting three mugs together. 'The usual, really, it's quite busy at work actually.'

'And you, Prichard?' asked Sofia. 'You live down here, don't you?'

'I do,' he nodded. 'Not very far away.'

'Mum said. I haven't been here for ages. It's nice to properly meet you.'

They all sat down around the table with their cups of coffee, and Sofia sliced up some of her cake and offered Prichard a slice, which he devoured within a minute.

'Oh my goodness,' he said, a few escaped crumbs still clinging to his lips. 'That is a sensational drizzle. Where's that recipe from?'

'It's Nigella's lemon syrup loaf cake, but I made it round. I always think cakes should be round.'

'Oh, I adore Nigella for cakes, but also Nigel, he does a lemon cake with pistachios, have you done that one?'

'No, but it sounds marvellous. Didn't he do one with lemon confit on the top as well?'

Pat sat at the table, blowing on her hot coffee as she listened to Sofia and Prichard discuss the merits of which lemon cake recipe was better. Nigella or Nigel? The jury was out. Sofia was animated as she spoke, her hands carving the air with familiar movements; the echo of Martin was unmistakable. Pat took a sip of her coffee and watched, struck not just by the likeness but by how patterns seemed to outlive context. The gestures, the timing, even the cadence: inherited or absorbed, it was hard to tell. Sometimes people weren't so much blank slates as layered manuscripts, stories written over stories, filled with echoes of those who came before. Sofia in that moment was more Martin than Martin ever managed to be.

She looked well. She had dyed her hair a bit blonder, Pat noticed, with some stripy highlights, and plucked her eyebrows, and her skin was looking good, all glowy. But that was the fashion these days, wasn't it? It was all flat and matt and black when Pat was young. But now you had to look like you were straight out of a sauna. She was smaller than Pat, at least four inches shorter, slimmer, more of a pear shape than her sturdy mother. Pat smiled as she observed every minuscule detail of her daughter's face. It was good to see her.

With great tact, Prichard said he'd got a hundred things to do – he really did need to run a feather duster over his diecast car collection – and then it would be time for the art competition judging in the village hall. Pat had already declared her lack of interest in the outcome of that, and her painting was definitely not going to win. Prichard left them to it.

After he'd gone, Sofia pointed to the noticeboard. 'What's that?' she asked. 'Didn't it used to have my baby photos on it?'

'Yes, yes,' said Pat. 'That's all over there on the side. Don't worry, I would never throw those out.'

'Good. That would be awful.'

'I'm not completely heartless,' she said, laughing as lightly as she could. This was an age-old accusation. Along with the *Pat was never home* story.

'So is it some kind of game?'

'Kind of. I'm investigating a murder.'

Sofia's eyes widened. 'What?!' She sat up and stared up at the wall, her mouth slightly open. 'Who?'

'Well, actually it isn't a game. His name was Henry, and he was a client of mine.'

'Oh my gosh.'

'I know. It hasn't been exactly fun.' Pat smiled briefly. 'Maybe you could help?' She stood up.

'Me? Help you?' Sofia's voice was raised in surprise. Pat could see her furiously trying to decipher the Post-it notes.

'You might see something I missed.' Pat nodded. 'Your fresh eyes, you'll have a different take on events, see things from a different angle, which would be very helpful, as we're stuck.'

'Right,' said Sofia, putting her elbows on the table. 'Go on then.'

Pat started from the beginning. She went on to fill in as many blanks as she could, finishing up with the altercation by Fi's tumble dryer and the breaking and entering of the shepherd's hut. Sofia was intrigued and asked all sorts of questions about why Henry was in Westlinke in the first place and what would Derek have to gain by killing him.

'Surely he was in a good situation? Free flat? Boyfriend? Why rock that boat?'

'True, but Henry was getting a cease and desist order out on him, and they were splitting up and Derek was being kicked out of the flat in London.'

'Were they really, though? Splitting up?' Sofia shrugged. 'We've all heard that before. They'd broken up and got back together many times over; why was this time different? Henry had already consented to the date night in the lighthouse. Derek didn't turn up, but Henry would have forgiven him anyway, he'd always done so before.' She paused. 'I don't think Derek is your guy. It doesn't make sense.'

'Well, he did threaten me and then my office was broken into. It doesn't sound like a coincidence, does it?'

'True,' agreed Sofia. 'But I still don't think he's got enough of a motive. It seems too . . . obvious.' She pointed to a curled yellow Post-it. 'Tell me more about this Dorna Braddon.'

'I've met my match with her,' replied Pat. 'She wants to pave over the Downs. She's got this awful development called Boho Golf & Spa.'

'Oh, I know that company,' replied Sofia. 'It's quite cool. Hip. Adam has stayed at the one in the Cairngorms, it's absolutely gorgeous apparently.'

'I didn't know Adam played golf,' said Pat with a fixed smile.

'Avidly,' replied Sofia, still looking at the board. 'It's the fastest-growing sport in the world.'

'Talking of sport, did you bring your cozzie? The sea is definitely warming up and it's a lovely day.'

'I certainly did. And my dryrobe is in the back of the car.'

Pat and Sofia gathered up their swimming things and headed for Birling Gap, marching up over the Downs towards the cliffs. Pat set a quick pace, but she soon realised that Sofia was not quite so fast.

'I thought I was fit,' puffed Sofia as she climbed the hill behind Pat. 'I do spin classes twice a week, and yoga and Pilates.'

'That's London fit, though, isn't it?' replied Pat, standing with her hands on her hips waiting for Sofia to catch up. 'The ground is nice and smooth and even, and there's no wind or rain to ruin the cycling and no lumps or bumps in the road.'

'Yep,' Sofia huffed. 'What's that orange sign near the barn about?'

'That's Dorna Braddon's thirty-seven-million-pound Boho hell development.'

'What, right here? On these Downs? Next to your house?'

She looked across at the miles of long silvery grasses and the numerous wildflowers bending in the breeze, shimmering a thousand different shades towards the horizon. 'Surely that's illegal?'

'It used to be,' said Pat. 'These days, who knows? Henry was fighting the development just before he died.'

'Well, there's a motive. How much did you say it was worth?'

'Thirty-seven million.'

'An expensive motive!'

'Except according to the police, Dorna wasn't here in Westlinke the night he died.'

'She could have hired a hitman, though.'

As they walked down the hill, the car park and the National Trust café looked remarkably full. It was a glorious Saturday afternoon in May and the sky was a cobalt blue with the occasional fluffy white cloud; of course it was going to be busy. Over half a million tourists visited a year, and today they all seemed to have come at once.

'I had no idea this place was so popular,' said Sofia, watching the hordes lining up to have their photographs taken at the cliff edge. 'And why are there so many tourists? Is that a Korean flag?' She pointed at a tour guide who was holding the flag on a long stick, trying to regulate the photo queue.

'South Korean,' Pat corrected. 'It's something to do with a pop band who filmed a video here with the Seven Sisters in the background. They've been coming ever since.'

'They must be a very popular band,' remarked Sofia,

looking up and down the cliff. 'Kind of like One Direction,' she added.

'I suppose so. Can't say I've ever been a fan.'

'It's definitely got busier since I was last here.' Sofia's mouth twisted into a disapproving expression.

'They're always getting lost, knocking on my door all hours of the day.'

'Don't they know these cliffs are dangerous?' Sofia watched as the seemingly oblivious groups posed, one leg in the air, pretending to fall.

'There are signs everywhere. I'm not sure what else you're supposed to do.' Pat paused. 'Henry was discovered on this beach at eight a.m. After the high tide.'

'He was pushed from here?' asked Sofia.

'Sometime after five the previous evening, we think.'

They walked down the steps to the sea. Their progress was hampered by the amount of traffic to and from the beach. There were a few people in the water, one serious lady swimmer in a full-length wetsuit and rubber cap ploughing up and down the shoreline attached to a large red float.

'That doesn't look much fun,' said Sofia as she hopped from one leg to the other on the pebbles, wrapped in a towel, putting on her swimming costume.

'Just so long as she's enjoying herself,' said Pat, striding into the sea. 'Come on!'

They stayed in for precisely fifteen minutes, one minute for every degree Celsius, laughing and joking and bouncing around in the waves, treading water, watching the tourists take their snaps. Pat tried to remember the last time they'd swum together. Maybe eight years ago? Perhaps longer. They emerged pink with cold and giggling with exhaustion, and flopped down on the beach, rubbing themselves with towels: shins, shoulders, back of the head. Sofia lay back on the pebbles and stared up at the sky.

'Mum?' she said, sitting up suddenly. 'If all these tourists are here all the time, taking photos of Birling Gap, surely someone will have taken a picture of Henry?'

'What do you mean?' asked Pat, rubbing her face with her towel.

'Well, you know, accidentally snapped him, like in the background. He'll be there in their selfies or landscape photos. If you think someone pushed him, they may well be in the shot too.'

'Do you think?' Pat slowly put down the towel.

'Well, it's worth a look. If you type Birling Gap or Seven Sisters into Instagram, all the photographs tagged with that will come up, and you can see if he was there on the day he died.'

'Really?'

'Let's give it a go.'

Back at the house, Sofia set up Pat's laptop to trawl through the hundreds of photographs that responded to the search tag. Sofia offered to do the scrolling, as Pat kept getting distracted by the images people were posting. Ice creams, dancing, cartwheels, walking through clouds; it was some sort of special effect, apparently. Pat was old enough to remember when being invited over to see someone's holiday snaps was the punchline to a joke, the ultimate social endurance test. There was even a time you had to sit through grainy home cine films, nodding politely. Now people queued up willingly to scroll through strangers' sunsets and breakfasts. But she understood it really. It wasn't about the photos; it was about being seen how you wanted to be seen. About curating a version of yourself that felt shinier, more coherent. A life with edges tidied and light carefully filtered.

While Sofia kept working her way through endless images, Pat chopped cucumbers and avocados for the chicken salad she was making for supper.

'It's certainly popular,' said Sofia as she scrolled. 'What was he wearing?'

'A suit, a smart suit, Armani, like what you'd wear to go to dinner.'

'Black? Blue? Striped?'

'Black. White shirt.'

'Like this?'

Pat stopped chopping and bent down to look at the screen, squinting slightly, her knife still in her hand. 'What's that?'

'A sleeve and a shoulder in the background of this photo. Dark hair?'

'You're amazing,' said Pat, slowly sitting down, heart thumping. 'It certainly looks like him. The light is greyish, it's turning, so it could be around five p.m.?'

'Yes, it could be, but a glimpse of someone's shoulder doesn't prove much.'

'It proves that he wasn't sitting on the edge waiting to jump. It has him standing, moving, walking around. Not sitting round-shouldered, hunched to the world, contemplating his own death. Is anyone else there?'

'In this photo? Not that I can see. But I can tell you the exact location, if I click through here. It's near the car park. See?'

Pat peered at the map that was now on her screen. 'That's just above where his body was found.'

'I'll keep digging.'

Pat chopped and laid the table while Sofia carried on scrolling and back-referencing all the images she could find. But when they sat down to supper, it was still just the sleeve and the shoulder. Proof of life sometime during the late-afternoon light of 21 April.

Pat sighed. 'Well, thank you, darling, for all your help.' She poured herself a glass of red wine from the open bottle on the table. 'Would you like a glass?'

'Maybe later,' replied Sofia.

'So what else have you been up to?' asked Pat.

'I could show you if you want?' suggested Sofia, turning the computer around.

'Sure, that would be great,' said Pat, hoping her tone sounded upbeat. 'I'd like to see what you're doing.'

'You don't have to.'

'No, no, I'd love to.'

'Only if you're sure?'

'Sofia, I would like to see your work.' Pat took a swig of wine. 'Is that affirmative enough?'

Sofia tapped into her account. *Sofe, 28-year-old wife to the wonder that is Adam, homey hosting, London lifestyle and food. All organic and guilt-free!* Pat didn't say anything. Sofia had done some updating since she'd last looked. There were now more than seven hundred thousand people following the account.

'So, it's about recipes and having fun and going about my business in London,' explained Sofia. 'It's not my everyday, obviously, but that's how I sell it, so I'll do like "Trad Tuesday", where I'll show all the stuff I do during the day. But I usually spend quite a lot of time setting all these things up.' She clicked on a recent video at the top of her profile.

'Hi!' said the social-media-perfect version of her. 'My name is Sofe and I've been very happily married to my gorgeous hubby Adam for the last four years. We love our home in Battersea, it's our safe place. I'm a stay-at-home wife and influencer. I absolutely love to cook, especially for Adam, who works *so* hard.'

Pat sat at her kitchen table watching her daughter explain her life to her hundreds of thousands of followers, going through recipes and her handy hints to uplift and elevate seemingly dull domestic chores, such as putting lavender in the laundry and spritzing pillows with a little scent for a good night's sleep. She made a bath oil with fresh rosemary, preserved some lemons, made wild garlic pesto with activated pine nuts and went flower shopping at Columbia Road market on a Pashley bicycle complete with wicker basket. She played another reel where she learnt how to embroider stars into the holes in a cashmere jumper and tried her hand at knitting a pair of bed socks, which proved to be much harder than it looked. She churned butter, made cheese, and batch-cooked some salmon dish for the freezer. There was a kombucha and sauerkraut session, and lots of pickling. By the third or fourth clip, Pat was bowled over by the amount of hard work involved in the filming, the editing, the music and the endless ideas to keep her audience entertained.

'Sofia,' she said, 'I can't believe how hard you work at this. It's incredible.' She was quite pleased with herself for swallowing back the words 'Not quite my bag, but . . .'

'Thanks, Mum.' Her daughter smiled brightly.

'Seriously. I don't how you manage to do it all. Cheers, darling.' Pat smiled, leaping out of her chair and heading towards the cupboard. 'Let me get you a drink.'

'Mum.'

'What?' She turned around.

'I'm pregnant.'

'Oh my goodness!' She beamed from the other side of the kitchen. 'That is good news . . . It's great news!'

'You think?'

'Oh.' Pat was a little stunned. 'It normally is.'

'Is it, though?' Sofia bit her lip. 'Given the track record of this family.'

Pat sat slowly down in her seat. 'Really? Is it that bad?'

'Come on, Mum! I mean, no one could have fucked up quite as much as you.'

'Oh.' That hit Pat hard, straight in the solar plexus. She had to remember to breathe. It was a stark contrast to the camera-ready Sofia she had just watched on Instagram.

'I'm not really sure I want this baby,' Sofia mumbled out of the side of her mouth.

'Oh,' Pat said again. As a statement, it didn't come tougher than that.

'It seems unfair on the poor little thing. Another basket case waiting to happen. I really *don't* want to do a bad job.' It seemed to Pat that what Sofia actually wanted to say was 'as bad a job as you did'. 'The idea of history repeating itself, it's too much,' she concluded.

Pat sat there for a second. *Don't react, reflect*, she told herself. She knew that. 'Well,' she replied in as measured a way as possible, 'you don't have to make the same mistakes I did.' She smiled. 'Although I did try.'

'Did you? Did you really? Well that's even more worrying!' Sofia laughed. 'You tried your best and you still fucked it up! And here I was thinking you were just phoning it in, from your work, or the divorce, or night school or your PhD or your dissertation or your clients, all the other things you did except be at home and be a parent.'

'I was absent, I'm sorry. I was always at work, and then I was training.'

'And selfish.'

'Oh? Probably. And selfish.'

'And self-absorbed.'

'Isn't that the same thing?'

'I'm just making my point!'

'OK, I was all of those things. But just because I was doesn't mean you need to be.'

'But I've learnt from the master, haven't I? What if my childcare abilities are inherited? What if I do the same as you, give it all up for my career?'

'The whole point is that we can change. Human beings are intelligent, we can learn from our mistakes. I recommend a brilliant book by a colleague of mine, *The Book You Wish Your Parents Had Read (and Your Children Will Be Glad That You Did)*. It's great, I wish I had read it before I had you. I wish I'd been a therapist back then, and then I would've known that I should have been more present for you. I think I was assuming you would be a child for ever and there would be another time I could see a nativity play, or pick you up from school. I'm sorry, darling. You will get it right for your kid. I've got a copy of that book somewhere. Read it before you decide anything. It will show you how not to repeat the mistakes Granny made with me and I made with you. The pattern of seeing your child as a chore to delegate rather than a person to relate to. I know I did that, and I'm sorry. I did fuck up and I wish I could do it again.'

'OK,' Sofia replied flatly.

'You are aware of what you needed and didn't get; I was not aware of what I needed as a child and didn't get. That will make all the difference.'

'Oh Mum,' said Sofia, and she went up to Pat and they hugged.

When they separated, they looked at each other's red eyes, smiled and hugged again, then Pat said, 'Does Adam know?'

'Not yet.'

'He'll be over the moon when you tell him. *I'm* over the moon!' She leant over and kissed her daughter on the forehead. 'I am so, so happy for you! I really am. You'll be fine. You'll be a natural.'

'Will I? Why?'

'Because you're not me. You're different.' She smiled. 'You are better.'

CHAPTER 23

'Who the hell has parked on your verge! Oh my God, you must be furious! They're practically in your kitchen!' Sue breezed through the front door in well-cut jeans and a crisp white shirt, with a Liberty silk scarf tied loosely around her neck, clutching a large bunch of blowsy pale peach peonies that she dumped on the kitchen table.

'Sue!' Pat leapt out of her chair. 'I was supposed to pick you up!' She glanced over at the round brass wall clock above the kitchen sink.

'I took the earlier train. It's a nice day, no point in hanging around, and there were taxis at the station.' Sue kissed her on one cheek and then the other. 'Terrifying taxi ride. The driver kept looking at me in the mirror while he moaned about his life and didn't appear to concentrate on the road at all.' She ruffled her blonde hair and looked over to the doorway to the sitting room, where Sofia had wandered in with wet hair, barefoot, wearing Pat's old pale pink terry dressing gown and blowing on the large mug of tea she held cupped in both hands in front of her. 'Sofia, very nice to see you, it's been a while.'

'Hello, Sue, I'm the driver who's parked in the kitchen!'

replied Sofia. 'I can't believe you didn't say anything, Mum. I'll move it if you want.'

'Don't be crazy,' said Sue, going to give her a hug. 'You can't do anything wrong in her eyes. She'd let you reverse into the sitting room if she thought it would make you happy!'

Sofia returned Sue's hug. 'Lovely to see you after so long.'

'It seemed an opportunity too good to miss,' smiled Sue. 'You're down here for the weekend, the sun is out, and it's so easy to get on a train. Now,' she picked up her flowers off the table, 'where shall I put these hand-picked cottage-garden peonies that I bought at vast expense this morning in Islington and were probably from your next-door's garden anyway? Talk about coals to Newcastle. Do you have a vase?' She began foraging along Pat's dusty shelves, rootling among bowls and pots that had not been moved in years. 'Christ!' she coughed. 'This place needs a bit of a sort-out. When was the last time you threw anything away? I mean, that orange Le Creuset can go for a start.' She nodded over at the fridge. 'It's practically a museum piece. Are you a hoarder now, Pat?'

'We both know I have very little emotional attachment to possessions and my levels of anxiety are hardly abated at all by holding on to trinkets and biscuit tins. Anyway, that orange Le Creuset is Prichard's favourite; he uses it to make his boeuf bourguignon.'

'Does he now?' said Sue, lifting the hefty lid. 'Well, he needs to give it a damn good clean.'

'I shall let him know.'

It took Sue less than five minutes to notice the murder

board above the kitchen table, and it wasn't long before the three of them were sitting down working their way through all the possibilities. Sue obviously knew all about Derek and his devious ways, although there was still no update from the bank as to how the money had managed to go missing without anyone knowing who had taken it.

'They're worse than useless,' she complained. 'We've been on to them on a daily basis, and still the fraud department haven't managed to come up with any explanation other than that it's gone to Guernsey. And it's that much harder because, you know, Henry's dead and the accounts are in his name. It's madness really. They used a shell company to move the funds through that and then on to the Channel Islands.'

'So it's complex *and* sophisticated?' asked Sofia.

'It appears that way.'

'Is Derek clever enough to pull that off on his own? He doesn't sound like the sort.'

'But it's not Dorna Braddon, is it?' said Pat. 'She's got a thirty-seven-million-pound deal going through, so she won't need another one hundred and twenty thousand, and anyway, as I said, she wasn't here the night of the murder.'

'Unless she's short of actual cash,' said Sue. 'You'd be amazed how people who present as wealthy can have so little money in the bank. It's all in assets. I see it all the time, especially when I'm doing divorce cases that require full financial disclosure, when I have to find out exactly how much money has been loaned to people or given away. People so often live hugely beyond their means. The most surprising people have savings, and the even more surprising have not.'

She sighed deeply. 'I'm not sure if our murderer is even on the board. Why is next-door's Fi up there? Has she been having her parties again?'

'Derek is staying there,' said Pat.

'Well, there's a turn-up,' replied Sue.

'He's been kicked out of Henry's place. I suppose it's only natural that he's found some other place to lay his hat.'

'Ah, he's prolific.'

After Sofia had got dressed in a red pinafore and white shirt with puffed sleeves and her pale pink cashmere wrap, they decided to walk to the pub for lunch. They set out along the lane and over the cattle grid. At the layby, Pat stopped. She wanted to make sure that the tosser had moved on permanently, but suddenly out of the corner of her eye she spotted a Mars bar wrapper around the back of the bin.

'You're not still picking rubbish up, are you, Mum?' asked Sofia. 'I remember once when I was a child and we were walking along the street, I threw my juice box into a garden that was full of litter already and you made me knock on the door and ask if I could get it back. The woman who answered the door thought I was completely mad. It was traumatising.'

'Well,' shrugged Pat as she dropped the wrapper in the bin, 'you never did it again, did you?'

'I never dared.'

They carried on along the lane, past the church and down the hill towards the green. As they walked towards the village hall, Pat suddenly wondered if it might be open.

'Do either of you want to come and look at the results of the painting competition?'

'I don't mind if I do,' declared Sue. 'Do we have skin in the game?'

'We most certainly do.'

'In which case . . .'

The door to the village hall was unlocked. Pat entered, followed by Sue and Sofia. The place was eerily quiet, and felt oddly cold after the warm sunshine outside. The art club easels were stacked up at the back of the hall and the beanbags were still out from Sunday school earlier that morning. There was a whiteboard on wheels shoved up against the wall, with a question written on it in red pen: *What's the best news you've ever heard?*

'I see they're still spreading the word of the Lord,' nodded Sue. 'This place looks like it's well used,' she added, glancing around.

They'd hung the art club canvases all down one wall of the hall. Pat could see Prichard's immediately, with its tiny, delicate strokes and fine lines. It appeared to have a blue rosette stuck on one corner.

'Looks like Prichard's come second,' she said, sounding both delighted and amused. 'The honourable member came to judge them yesterday. Second place! I can't believe he didn't call me to gloat.'

'I have to say I don't think much of first, if we're being frank,' said Sue. 'It's a bit grey and phallic for my liking.'

'That's Dorna Braddon's masterpiece,' said Pat, walking over to stand next to her.

'Well, she certainly knows how to make an impression, doesn't she? She moves in, concretes over the Downs and wins the art club painting competition. It's one way to make friends and influence people.'

'I have to say, I quite like this one – the colours and the flowers and the wisteria. It's very pretty. I wouldn't mind that on my wall,' said Sofia.

'That's Margot's,' said Pat.

'Well, it's very decorative. Which one is yours, Mum?'

'Good question,' replied Pat as she looked around the hall. 'It doesn't appear to be here.' She started to count the paintings, ticking them off on her fingers as she worked out who each belonged to. 'Mine's the only one not here.'

'Is this it?' asked Sue, pushing the whiteboard out of the way. 'I'd recognise that rebellious belligerence anywhere.'

'I don't know what you mean.' Pat smiled.

'While everyone else has painted a nice pretty picture, you've done the parking lot.' Sue laughed. 'No wonder they've hidden it in the corner!'

'Don't be so rude,' replied Pat. 'I painted what I saw, that's all – wheelie bins, cars. If you don't take note of what's right under your nose, you're inviting trouble.'

'I see your painting didn't make the team photo either,' said Sofia, standing at the entrance to the hall.

'What?' said Pat, walking towards her daughter. 'I was holding it up with the rest of them.'

'Not here you weren't,' Sofia replied.

'I was!'

'You weren't!'

Pat and Sofia stood side by side and stared at the framed photograph of Westlinke Art Club. There was Prichard and Jacqui, Margot and the colonel and Dorna Braddon, the nearly naked Fiona and the rest all standing together, holding up their paintings for the village to see and appreciate. They were all there except Pat's. Her piece of art had clearly been Photoshopped out and in its place was the repeat pattern of her checked shirt.

'Most bizarre,' she whispered under her breath. 'I was definitely holding it.' She pointed. 'Right there.'

'And now you're not,' replied Sofia.

'I'm really sorry,' said Pat. 'Do you two mind going to the pub and getting a table? I've just got to make a quick phone call.'

As Sue and Sofia walked slowly off across the grass towards the Green Lion, Pat sat down on the steps in front of the village hall. She felt a little strange. What hit her was how invisible you became after a certain age, with people looking right through you. Having her painting rubbed out made her feel a bit like she herself had been rubbed out. She got out her phone.

'Prichard Knowles!' he answered.

'It's Pat.'

'How are you?' he began. 'I'm on the B2066 on my way to Brighton.'

'I'm in the village hall. Congratulations on your blue rosette.'

'Oh, I know! Can you believe it? Stone the starlings! You could have knocked me down with a cricket bat, I was so thrilled. A rosette, an actual rosette. I know it's blue and not red, but I don't think I've ever won one of those. Dorna was first, but then her work was truly well done and fine, and Margot was third. Fi was a little annoyed not to be placed, but, you know, we can't all be winners.'

'Well, yes, we can't all win, this is true,' replied Pat. 'I wanted to ask a question.'

'Fire away.'

'The photograph of all of us on the wall by the door.'

'Yes?'

'Well, my painting's not in it.' As she said it, Pat realised quite how childish she sounded, but there was no getting away from how strange the situation was.

'Oh, I know,' said Prichard. 'I meant to call you to warn you about that, but then I got distracted. Don't be too cross. Jacqui thought it pulled focus too much and it wasn't in keeping with the idea of Westlinke in bloom, which was the brief, I think.'

'I wasn't aware we were given a brief.'

'Well, anyway, sorry about that.'

'It's not your fault.'

'No, it's Dorna's.'

'How could it be Dorna's?'

'She was the one who cut your painting out of the photo.'

'She did what?'

'She offered to help make it disappear and Jacqui accepted. It's on the WhatsApp.'

'I never seem to get the WhatsApps.'

'I can add you if you want?'

'Thanks, but don't worry,' sighed Pat. 'It's bizarre. How did she do it? It was right in the middle of the photo.'

'She's incredible with a computer, apparently. She cut your picture out and then stuck the photo back together again; it's like an extreme form of Photoshop. You can literally do anything these days. No one puts anything on their social media, according to Dorna, without it being filtered or doctored or tweaked. I mean, look at Fi. She looks much better on the phone than she does in the flesh.'

'True,' replied Pat.

Once she'd hung up, she sat on the steps of the village hall, deep in thought. She was surprised by how upset she was at her painting being edited out of the art club photograph. How dare they! Especially as the quality of their own work was so underwhelming. She'd been cancelled by mediocrity, and it was galling. She laughed at herself and looked up across the green. She shouldn't leave Sue and Sofia in the pub on their own for too long; they had both come to see her after all.

As she stood up, she saw two figures walking across the grass towards the pub. The first she recognised instantly. The dirty-blonde hair, the worked-out physique, the smart tight blue shirt opened just lower than necessary, the wide smile and those pale-blue veneers. He was striding with confidence, his arms swinging, his hips swaying as he pointed towards the pub door. He was flirting for sure. Pat stood still. If she didn't move, he wouldn't see her. He was too absorbed in his conversation. But who he was with?

The second man was a bit taller, but not much. His suit

appeared oddly dark in the bright, shiny light of a spring day. A chocolate-brown shirt and matching tie that looked as if they'd been bought together in a package. Pat caught a glimpse of a golden sleeper earring as they got closer. Marcus? What was he doing with Derek? They seemed friendly, if a little awkward. Pat thought it interesting that Marcus was wearing a tie and not his usual casual attire. It looked like a first or maybe second date. His body language was tense, while Derek's . . . well, he was shameless, that was for sure! First Fi, now Marcus. Maybe Malcolm had kicked him out and he needed a new place to stay. It wouldn't be long until he'd weaselled his way into every house in the village.

She watched them walk through the door of the pub, and gave herself a couple of minutes before following them in.

Sue and Sofia were sitting in the far corner, at the table with the banquette seat and the row of stools, as favoured by Dorna Braddon. Sue was sipping a glass of red wine and Sofia had a half-pint of lemonade with plenty of ice. The table was laid for lunch, with burgundy-coloured mats and matching paper napkins. In the centre was a pale wicker basket holding slices of white baguette and a plate of individually wrapped servings of Kerrygold butter.

'I hear congratulations are in order,' said Sue as Pat sat down. Pat looked from Sue to Sofia; what had they been talking about? 'We're a grandmother,' grinned Sue. 'To coin a phrase.'

'Margaret Thatcher?' queried Pat.

'Well, why not!' Sue raised her glass of wine. 'You must be thrilled!'

'I am,' agreed Pat.

'Does it make you feel old, Mum?' said Sofia, with a shrug of her shoulders.

'It makes me feel very happy, actually. Although I do think you should tell your husband before you start telling my friends,' said Pat, pouring herself a glass of fizzy water.

'A, Sue is not just any friend, and B, I want to tell Adam to his face, at the right moment, in the right place, so he'll always remember it. It will be amazing to video for my Insta too.'

'I am extremely happy for you,' said Sue, tapping Sofia's lemonade with her own glass. 'And I for one think you will make a wonderful mother.'

Sofia and Pat looked at each other and smiled, both of them reliving last night's reconciliation.

Pat's expression changed suddenly, and she took a quick intake of breath. 'Don't both look at once, but over there,' she said nodding her head in their direction, 'Derek is having lunch with our local barfly. I wonder if Malcolm had enough of the swinging shenanigans and told him to leave him and Fi alone. I wouldn't be surprised if Derek is already on to his next victim.'

'Derek!' Sue spun around and stared straight at him.

'For Christ's sake, Sue! Be discreet,' Pat hissed under her breath.

'So that's the little shit in the flesh. I fancy going over and giving him a piece of my mind. He ruined Henry's life, rinsed him for cash, and now he's laughing and flirting away as if he hasn't got a care in the world. In fact . . .' Sue stood up, but Pat was quicker, grabbing her jeans and pulling her back down into her seat.

'Please! Watch and see what they're doing,' she said. 'I can't really look, as he knows me, and last time he saw me, he threatened me with a bottle of Chardonnay in a utility room. Oh, and probably broke into my office.'

All three of them leant over the table, backs rounded, with Sue occasionally glancing sideways to give a running commentary.

'They're drinking large glasses of Aperol spritz,' she said. 'And studying the menu.'

'Do they look like close friends?'

'It's a bit touchy-feely. They're definitely . . . into each other, I'd say. But Derek is *really* trying it on.'

Sophia chimed in. 'Does the other guy seem into—'

'Ladies!'

'Oh my God!' Pat leapt in her seat and pulled back from the table. 'Where did you come from?'

'The bar? I've brought you some menus.' Johnno was standing behind Pat, clutching three laminated sheets of paper to his chest. 'I'm afraid we're out of the roast pork,' he said as he handed them round. 'But the chicken and the beef are still available. Do you want to order now, or do you need more time?' He squatted down next to Pat, so close she could smell a waft of Lynx Africa. 'That's him,' he said out of the side of his mouth, mumbling through his facial hair.

'Who?' Pat asked.

'The bloke who whacked your bloke the other day. Remember? You were asking about it the last time you were in here.'

'Right, thanks,' nodded Pat. 'His name is Derek, I know that now. And do you know Marcus?'

'What, the bloke with the earring?'

'Yes.'

Johnno turned slowly and looked across the room. 'I never asked him his name, actually. He lives next door and comes in every day. His drinking is single-handedly covering the pub's energy bill,' he added, half grinning. 'I'm digging the chocolate-brown shirt.'

'You are?' asked Sofia, slightly astonished, from the other side of the table.

'Very retro,' said Johnno

'Do you know what he does?' asked Pat.

'Seemingly very little,' he said with a shrug.

They ordered their food and tried valiantly not to be distracted by what was going on in the opposite corner. Poor Sue was forced to brief Pat on every nuance and every rattle of laughter. There was one moment when both men disappeared, only to return a few minutes later, wafting in a gust of cigarette smoke, fresh from their fag break.

'Phew,' said Pat. 'I was worried they'd gone!'

Shortly after, there was the sound of raised voices and laughter. It took all her willpower not to turn around.

'What's happening?' she hissed.

'I think they're leaving,' said Sofia. 'Derek's thrown down his napkin and is heading for the door, and the other guy is finishing off his third Aperol spritz and marching after him. Oh, he's just paused at the bar . . . Now he's pulled out a wad of cash and seems to be paying the bill.'

'That's a big wad,' said Sue.

'It doesn't surprise me that Derek doesn't pay for dates,' said Pat.

The two men were talking animatedly as they left, but with all the noise in the pub it was hard to make out what they were saying. Pat, Sofia and Sue watched, their faces close to the window, as the pair stood and finished their conversation outside. They parted ways with a brief hug, then Derek headed for Mal and Fi's house, no doubt to the frantic twitching of Bev's curtains.

CHAPTER 24

The three of them elected to walk back from the pub along the coast. As they strolled down the lane towards the car park and Birling Gap, Pat's brain was churning. Why was Derek still here? Why was he going on dates but still living in Fiona's mansion? And how could he be so careless, so brazen about it? Picking the village alcoholic as his next victim was a new low.

When they reached the car park, the queue for the Mr Whippy van curled around the café and all the wooden picnic tables were full of families working their way through piles of sandwiches and sharing large bags of crisps and litre bottles of Coke. The place was rammed, and there was a line of people waiting to go down the steps to the sea.

'How could nobody have seen Henry?' asked Sue, frowning, as she stood next to Pat, watching the swirling sea below. It was high tide, and the waves were crashing on the beach and then frothing and foaming swiftly back.

'Well, it was off-season in April, so that makes a difference,' Pat replied. 'But I agree with you. The volunteers from the chaplaincy patrol the coast all the time, and there are the walkers, who are the first to stop and help people. They notice if someone is sitting with their legs over the edge, looking down rather than out and not moving.'

'So it was here, then?' asked Sue, looking up and down the cliff, her blonde bob blowing in a light gust of wind. 'I'm not a religious person, as you know, but I feel like I should say a prayer or something. He was a such a sweet boy.' Her face crumpled for a second, and she sighed loudly into the wind. 'It's all so very upsetting.'

'His mother called me the other day – I think I told you about it,' said Pat. 'She was inconsolable.'

'I've spoken to her too. It's heartbreaking, and now that she's found out all the money is missing, she's convinced it wasn't an accident. I think they had a good relationship,' added Sue.

'Yeah, he mentioned several times during our sessions how close they were,' agreed Pat.

They walked a bit further along the coastal path and sat down on one of the many benches that looked out to sea. The wind had dropped, and it was surprisingly still and calm, although the crashing waves could still be heard below.

'This is where I found his phone,' announced Pat, her eyes closed as she turned her face towards the sun.

'Right here?' Sue stood up, walked tentatively towards the edge and peered over. It was a long way down.

'Sue, get back here, those cliffs are made of crumble!' shouted Pat.

'Do you think he could have been pushed from here and then washed up on the beach a few hundred yards along, what with the current and the undertow?' asked Sue.

'I don't see why not,' said Pat. 'It would explain why no

one has any photographs of him actually at Birling Gap, except his jacket sleeve and his arm. Not many people can be bothered to leave the car park and walk up this way, unless you're local, I suppose.'

'Do you fancy an ice cream?' asked Sofia, leaping off the bench.

'What? After all that lunch?' replied Pat.

'When you're eating for two, Patricia Phillips,' said Sue, pulling Pat up, 'there is no rhyme or reason to what you want, or when you might fancy eating it, or so I have read. Cravings, darling, cravings!'

Sofia didn't even ask if the ice cream was organic. Which was lucky. They wandered back over the Downs eating their cones with the Flakes she had insisted they all have as an added extra, and headed up the hill towards the barn with the red roof and the wooden fence.

'I've seen the plans,' said Pat, dipping her Flake in her ice cream and licking it. 'All this is going, Sue. All of it.' She pointed about with her stick of chocolate. 'She's going to put cabins here facing the sea, and a swimming pool and a nine-hole golf course, if I remember correctly, and there's a spa, obviously, with pump rooms and a sewage bit right over there, next door to Ivy Cottage. There was probably one of those planning notices in a plastic sheet, but that's long since blown away, but the sign is here.' She gestured, then looked. But Dorna's orange sign had disappeared. 'That's weird,' she said. 'It was here yesterday.'

'It was,' confirmed Sofia. 'I saw it.'

'Maybe it's fallen off,' said Sue, looking the other side of the fence. 'No. Nothing.'

'Do you want to go and see if the bats are back?' asked Pat.

Sofia glanced at her watch. 'I think I need to get home. It's a long drive, and the traffic on a Sunday night away from the coast is awful.'

'True,' agreed Sue.

'You're not wrong, although I'm sad you're leaving so soon,' added Pat. 'But the M25 can be gridlocked.'

'Adam will be worried,' continued Sofia. 'He doesn't like me driving on my own.'

'What, in between the twelfth and thirteenth holes?' Pat laughed drily. Sue shot her a look. 'Of course he will,' she corrected herself quickly. 'And you can tell him your news, though only if you want to. Of course.'

'I want to.' Sofia nodded.

'Well, it's the best thing I've heard all week, all month, all year.' Pat gave her daughter a tight hug.

When they got home, it took Sofia fifteen minutes to pack. Pat wheeled her heavy suitcase of mostly unused outfits back up the path to her red 4x4, which was still parked on the verge of pain, still blacking out the kitchen window.

'Thank you, Mum,' Sofia said as she climbed up into the driver's seat. 'Thank you for your help, and support, and for helping me make up my mind.'

'It was a pleasure,' replied Pat, feeling a wave of emotion as she grabbed hold of her daughter's soft arm and gave it a gentle squeeze. 'And here's that book I told you about. Let me know what you think of it.'

'Good luck with your murder,' said Sofia with a smile, placing the book on the passenger seat. 'You'll find out who did it, I know you will.'

'Thanks.' Pat smiled. 'I really have enjoyed seeing you, and I'm so happy at your news. You should tell Martin too, after you've spoken to Adam, of course. I'm sure he'll be thrilled.'

'Dad?' Sofia started the ignition. 'He already knows. He was the one who told me to come and talk to you about it all.'

'Oh,' said Pat, taking a step away from the car.

'And he was right. He said you'd have the answers, and you did.' Pat simply nodded, a light smile on her face. 'I love you, Mum, see you soon.'

Sofia waved as she drove down the lane and turned around in Mal and Fi's drive, then, honking her horn, she waved again as she headed back past the cottage, over the cattle grid and towards town.

Pat returned slowly to the kitchen.

'Cup of tea?' suggested Sue.

'Probably,' Pat replied, putting her hands on the table. 'Apparently it makes everything better.'

As Sue pottered about making the tea, Pat sat at the table and stared in silence at the board in front of her.

'Well, it was nice to see her,' said Sue, sitting down and handing Pat her cup of black tea. 'And it's great news about the baby. Exciting. Babies are always exciting.'

'They are. She told Martin before me.'

'Did she? She's always been a daddy's girl,' said Sue with a shrug as she blew on her own tea.

'We had a talk last night about how absent I was when she was growing up, working full-time and doing my psychotherapy training on top of that, and what's more, being preoccupied. It was good she could tell me and I could validate how she felt; that's gone a long way to healing our relationship. And, you know, I parented better than I had been parented, and she will do better than me. It's going in the right direction.'

'Oh, I'm sure you were a great parent,' said Sue. 'I think she's got that thing about her childhood – you'll know what it's called, false memory something.'

'False memory syndrome.' Pat took a sip of her tea. 'No, she hasn't got that. Truth is, I probably wasn't a great parent. I found the whole thing quite boring. For some people pushing a swing in the park on a drizzly Sunday afternoon is what they dream about. I didn't really. I didn't mind changing nappies, that was just something you had to do, and I was happy reading her books and telling her stories. But there are hours and hours of trying to soothe crying, and tedious playgrounds. I think I'd be better at it now; I've learnt that parenting is a long game and those hours are a valuable investment. My attitude was wrong then; I saw them as a waste, I didn't realise how important they were. I delegated being with her.'

'What about Martin? He was busy too.'

'He was better at being present when he was with her. I was too easily distracted.'

They drank their tea in silence for a while, Pat still staring at the murder board.

'What are you thinking about?' asked Sue.

'Do *you* think Derek's clever enough to have emptied Henry's accounts all on his own?' Pat asked. 'I mean, you know him.'

'I know *of* him. On paper. But no, I don't know whether he's clever enough.'

'He's more fisty than cerebral, isn't he?'

'He's highly manipulative, and that usually requires a certain amount of intelligence.'

'Why would he go for Marcus while he's still staying at Fi's, though? Does he think he can scam both of them at the same time?'

'Marcus doesn't look like he's part of Henry and Derek's crowd, does he? The handsome, successful young metropolitan men who drink cocktails and go on holiday to Mykonos.'

'Except Derek wasn't one of those types either; he was just pretending to be one. He was a fraud, who found Henry online and set out to exploit him. Pretended to want what Henry wanted then tried to rinse him for his money and contacts. Henry was waking up to that, and it seems it was enough to get him killed.' Pat put down her tea and glanced up at the wall clock. 'You're going to miss your train if we don't hurry.'

'I was putting off getting into your car,' said Sue with a smirk.

'Oh come on,' said Pat. 'You love my driving really.' A statement they both knew was not entirely true. Sue was not a fan of the moss-mobile at the best of times, but the way Pat scraped past – or sometimes, it felt to Sue, through – thorny hedges to let a car get by the other way amused and annoyed her in equal measure. 'You'll scratch the paint,' she often laughed.

'I know,' Pat would reply, 'and it makes it completely not worth nicking. People are far too precious about their cars.'

By the time Pat came home from dropping Sue off at the station, she felt quite low. Sunday nights were always her least favourite night of the week; they were dull and boring, punctuated with bursts from *Songs of Praise* that still seemed to reverberate down the decades. She wished she'd spent more time with Sofia and Sue and been less distracted by Henry's murder and trying to solve it. She found herself thinking, *I did it again. I was distracting myself instead of being present with people.*

She went into the sitting room and turned on *Antiques Roadshow*, hoping to be diverted by some diamonds rescued from a box of tat at a car boot sale, or Granny's old Fabergé egg. Maybe Dave sensed her low mood, because he sat upright on her lap looking at her, giving her head bumps.

'Knock knock!' came a voice from the kitchen. 'Pat? Are you in?'

'In the sitting room, Prichard.'

'Marvellous! I thought you might want to try this bottle of joy I have just found at the back of the cupboard.' He poked his head around the door. 'Damson 2021,' he grinned. 'How vintage!'

CHAPTER 25

Pat wasn't entirely sure there was such a thing as a vintage gin. An artisan gin, a nice gin, but gin was gin, surely? Wine was subject to the vagaries of the weather, the soil, so could be improved by a good year, a delicious harvest, but a spirit was distilled in a sealed system. It was exactly the same every single time. But as she walked into the kitchen to meet a rather ebullient Prichard, she didn't have the heart to disabuse him of his enthusiasm.

'Vintage, you say? Well, then I suppose it would be rude not to have a small glass.' She smiled as she sat down at the table, edging her laptop to one side.

'Rude?' declared Prichard, popping the cork and inhaling the heady aroma. 'It would be obscene not to!' He sighed loudly with evident satisfaction. 'I can't believe I found it right at the back of the cupboard, winking at me like a goddess.' He paused, plucking two small glasses from the shelf behind him. 'I thought you might need cheering up, what with the art competition and your painting's exorcism from the team photograph. And I know how you don't like Sunday nights.'

'Exorcism?' Pat sniffed as he gave her a glass. It smelt oddly like elderly alcoholic jam. 'Well, that's what it felt like. It was like some sort of voodoo. A kind of excommunication.'

She took a sip and felt the strong, fiery liquid slip down her throat. Her whole body shivered briefly. It was indeed vintage stuff.

'What did Jacqui say?' she asked.

'It was very long and complicated, but she didn't want her car and the car park and the giant wheelie bins destroying the bucolic nature of all the other paintings, so she went over to Dorna's, and Dorna did some weird computer thing, and then poof! Your painting was gone!'

'Right,' replied Pat, taking another swig. 'Well, she certainly sent me packing.'

'To Coventry, hahaha,' Prichard laughed. It wasn't funny. 'Congratulations again on coming second.'

'Oh, thank you, it was nothing.' He smiled broadly. It clearly was something. 'How was your weekend?'

'Sofia's having a baby,' Pat announced. It sounded surprisingly emotional, momentous even, when said out loud.

'Stone the starlings! Congratulations, Granny!' grinned Prichard. 'Granny!' he giggled, mainly to himself.

'I'm looking forward to maybe being a better granny than I was a mother.'

'You'll be one those proud grannies who tells everyone about their grandchild's first steps, first words, how talented they are and how they are really, actually, very special indeed.' He smiled. 'You're going to be a terrible bore!'

'I saw Derek in the pub with another man,' said Pat. 'That Marcus fellow.'

'Now that *is* news,' pronounced Prichard.

She went on to describe the scene, with Marcus in

his chocolate-brown shirt and matching tie, and the flirting-turned-tiff-turned-hugging.

'They looked as if they knew each other, but to be honest, I couldn't focus as much as I wanted to; I didn't want Derek to see me. Luckily he was too busy giving Marcus his come-to-bed eyes. Oh, and we also found evidence that Henry was on the cliff on the afternoon of the nineteenth of April.'

'You did!' Prichard leant forward. 'How?'

'It was Sofia's idea. We looked through all the images that were taken in Westlinke and posted that day on social media using various hashtags and things, and we managed to spot his hair and his shoulder and a sleeve.'

'Really! Let's have a look.'

Prichard and Pat began scrolling through the various Instagram photos taken around Birling Gap. They were all smiling faces and ice-cream cones and beaming groups with their hands pointing in the air, which was apparently the universal pose for tourists to show that they were having fun.

'I'm much slower at this than my daughter,' said Pat, hunched over the keyboard, peering at the screen. 'But you have to find the hashtag Birling Gap or Seven Sisters and then scroll through. Ah! There.' She pointed. 'You see. There's Henry's dark hair and the shoulder of his suit. A glimpse of his white shirt cuff. If you look again, there he is in the background.'

'So he is,' agreed Prichard, his nose edging closer and closer to Pat's screen. 'You can see his nice shoes too.'

'Oh, I missed those. You're right. He was wearing them when they found him on the beach. The question is, what time was this? I'm not sure how any of this works really.'

'I know, me neither,' agreed Prichard. 'I'm a total tech-tard. And what's that?'

'What d'you mean?'

'There? On the ground?' He pointed. Their heads moved in closer together. 'Is that a shadow? Someone else standing next to him?'

'Oh God!' said Pat, flopping back in her chair and draining her glass of damson gin in one. 'If only we knew someone who could help with all this stuff.'

'Well . . .' Prichard paused and raised an eyebrow. 'There is someone we could call.' He hesitated for another moment. 'Dorna!'

Pat groaned. She admired that about Prichard: the way he stayed civil and didn't write people off just because they'd done things he disagreed with. He could still see the whole person, not just the offence. It was a valuable reminder, she thought, that people weren't all good or all bad. However difficult she found Dorna, perhaps she needed to be a little more like Prichard sometimes.

But she wasn't quite there yet.

'No,' she said flatly. 'I don't want that woman in my house.'

'Even if she can help? She's amazing with computers.'

'Surely there's someone else?'

'At eight fifteen on a Sunday night?'

'But she might have murdered Henry!'

'In which case she can sit here and quietly incriminate herself. Come on, you'll enjoy that. And then we can perform a citizen's arrest in the kitchen.'

'Dorna Braddon doesn't do anything quietly.'

'Well, she can noisily incriminate herself and then we can arrest her.'

'Except obviously, on the night of Henry's disappearance she was in the Cairngorms, at least according to the police.'

'The choice is yours.'

It took Dorna half an hour to arrive, during which time Pat had almost worn a groove of irritation from the back door to the sink, as she paced up and down her kitchen muttering, 'I can't believe you made me do this.'

Inevitably, Dorna parked her enormous Audi Q9, more suited to an LA rapper than a village lane, right on the verge of pain, blocking the last sliver of evening light eking through Pat's kitchen window. Pat sat rigid at her pine table, breathing deeply, summoning images of calming landscapes. The garden gate clattered open, then shut, and moments later came a hammering on the kitchen door.

'Yoo-hoo!' called Dorna through the letter box. 'I bring bubbles!'

Pat opened the door slowly. 'Dorna.' Her voice was clipped and tense. 'Good evening.'

'Two bottles!' With a shake of her bangles, Dorna shoved the bottles of Bollinger champagne straight at Pat and proceeded into the kitchen. 'Oh,' she sighed as she stood by the table in the blaze of a bright spot from the overhead lighting. 'It looks bigger on the outside.' She ran a hand through her cropped red hair as she glanced around the kitchen, then smiled at Pat. 'Have you just moved in?' Her hand was poised quizzically in the air. 'Although I could have sworn you've been here for years.'

'Years,' said Pat, and in the ensuing silence, she opened the champagne with a loud pop.

'Fizz!' announced Prichard. 'Who doesn't love that?'

He leapt into action, blowing the dust off some flutes that were lurking at the back of one of the shelves and handing Pat and Dorna one each.

'Cheers,' he said, clinking Dorna's glass with his own. 'Thank you for coming.'

'Well, I felt a little guilty about cutting your painting out of the art club photo, to be honest,' replied Dorna, looking at Pat. 'So it's good to know that you don't bear a grudge.' She turned back towards the kitchen table and took a sip of champagne. Both Pat and Prichard watched as she took in the contents of the noticeboard. Pat's heart sank and Prichard's face tightened into a rictus grin. In their haste and damson haze, neither of them had thought to take the thing down.

Dorna's eyes moved from her own name to the mention of Boho Golf & Spa, to the death of Henry and her possible involvement with Fi and Derek and the word *Swinging* appearing haphazardly next to her Post-it. *Bats* was written in bold marker pen, *Injured hand* was also on the board, as was the Fin du Monde guest house. She drained her glass and slowly placed it back on the table. Her cheeks were suddenly very flushed, eyes glimmering with what Pat guessed was shock and perhaps a little – or a lot of – rage.

'Well, well, well, haven't we got a couple of Poirots in the room! So where have you got me? In the lighthouse with the lead piping, while swinging with Fi and eating bats? This is madness! What *are* you doing? The poor man's death was deemed a suicide. Is this some sort of elaborate trap? A stitch-up?' She laughed so loudly that Dave got up from his cushion and left the room. 'Seriously?' Her lip curled in confused astonishment. 'What's going on here? What are you doing?'

'We're trying to find out who murdered Henry Clayton,' said Pat, sitting down at the table. 'And we were hoping you might help.'

'Why would I help you?' said Dorna. 'You've been nothing but unpleasant since the day I first met you. Bossing people around on the Downs. Shouting at them to put their dogs on leads. It's as if you own the place!'

'We didn't get off to the best start, I admit,' replied Pat, pouring herself some more champagne and giving Prichard a beseeching glance.

'We thought you might want to help out of the goodness of your heart.' Prichard beamed from one woman to the other, a terrible frisson of panic growing inside him. It felt as if they might come to blows at any point. He loathed confrontation.

'Are you sure I *have* a heart?' asked Dorna, topping up her own glass and pulling up a chair.

Prichard laughed lightly. 'Of course you do, Dorna. A huge one pumping away in there.'

'If not for kindness,' said Pat mildly, 'then maybe because it's good sense. Murder isn't great PR, and refusing to cooperate when something's unresolved tends to create a vacuum. And vacuums attract suspicion. Eventually the police will have to reopen the case. Money is missing. The narrative isn't closed. And other stories might resurface, like the man who died on your Cairngorms site. It only takes one journalist with a long memory. And with your new Downs project already as unpopular as it is, well, it wouldn't take much to tip it further off course.'

'Except,' Dorna said with a flat smile, 'there is no development.'

'Oh?' said Pat, and sat back in her seat.

'No development?' queried Prichard. Had he heard her correctly?

'No.' Dorna sighed. 'It's too bloody windy.'

'It is?' Pat asked. 'It is,' she agreed with herself quickly. 'Not a great place to play golf.'

'You're not wrong,' agreed Dorna, taking a gulp of fizz. 'In fact, it's a terrible place to play golf. We've had some professionals come and have a look, and while, you know, they like a hazard, a bunker and some open water – all very entertaining – if you can't control your shots eighty-five per cent of the time, then apparently it's too frustrating.'

'So there's no development?' Pat asked again, just to make sure. 'No sewage works and pump room right by my house?'

'No,' said Dorna with a shrug. 'Sorry about that. It must have been a bit of a shock.'

'A shock? It's kept me awake ever since I saw your model.'

'I was never a great fan of that model. It wasn't very sympathetic to the environment. And weirdly, having lived down here for a bit, I think I've fallen in love with the place. I like the wind, I like the fact that the weather can change in a heartbeat, I like that pub where the barman takes twenty-five minutes to warm up a sausage roll. Turns out I even quite like being shouted at by madwomen, banshees who patrol the Downs looking for hapless fools who don't have their dogs on a lead.' She smiled.

'To be fair, I suspect there is only one proper banshee,' Pat acknowledged.

'And she'll scare the living daylights out of anyone. Even hard-nosed property developers from London.' Dorna drained her glass again. 'Now, what do you need me to do?'

Pat sat next to Dorna as they worked their way efficiently through the second bottle of champagne, even more efficiently served by Prichard, who stuck to his usual poison and was quietly nursing what he claimed was his finest damson vintage yet. Pat found that Dorna made her laugh. She was sharp, funny, self-deprecating, with a keen eye for the ridiculous. As Dorna scrolled through her phone and laptop, hunting down every possible glimpse of Henry on the cliff, Pat found herself softening, and gently checked her own earlier reaction.

The narcissism of small differences, that was the term. Freud, of course. How easy it was to resent in others the very qualities we didn't like to acknowledge in ourselves. That prickle of dislike, often reserved for people most like us. She smiled. It was entirely possible that the person she'd initially written off might turn out to be a real friend.

Pride and prejudice getting in the way again, she thought.

After a while, Prichard excused himself and retired to the sitting room to snore, quite loudly. Dorna and Pat stayed hunched together at the table, drinking their champagne and trying to find any more photographs of Henry on that fated afternoon. But there was nothing.

'I'm not sure we're thinking out of the box enough,' announced Dorna eventually. 'The tourists might have edited their photos before uploading them on Instagram. Facetuned people out and all that. And the South Koreans are more tech-savvy than most. So Henry may very well have been removed from most of these.'

'Like my painting?'

'Exactly like your painting.' Dorna sat back in her chair and looked up at the noticeboard. 'I see you have my injured hand down as a clue.'

'Well . . .' Pat raised an eyebrow and looked down at the now healed hand. 'How's the RSI?'

'I can tell you it wasn't attempted murder!' Dorna's voice had increased in decibels with every glass she'd drunk.

'And there was I thinking you'd beaten Henry up and hurled him over the cliff, hurting your hand as you did so.' Pat smiled briefly.

'You're not far off,' replied Dorna. 'There *was* a fight at the cliff edge, except it was between me, Trigger and a poor terrified sheep.'

'The dog was off the lead again, wasn't he?'

''Fraid so,' she sighed. 'It happened about twenty minutes after you told me off. I was keeping him off the lead because I didn't want to do as you said.' She looked up at Pat and smirked. 'I had to hurl myself between him and the sheep, and my hand got in the way. He didn't mean to bite it. I didn't want to admit it, because, you know, you'd already reprimanded me. In this case, RSI stands for rabid, stupid, imbecilic.'

'Glad to have cleared up that mystery,' said Pat.

'Trigger has gone to live with my sister in London,' said Dorna. 'Fewer sheep there.'

'I would pay good money to see a video of the fight, though,' said Pat.

Dorna laughed, then turned to the murder board and stared at it for a few seconds, to the accompaniment of Prichard's snores.

'Wait . . .' she said slowly.

'What?'

'Oh my gosh. Maybe someone filmed it!' There was victory in her eyes when they met Pat's.

'What, Henry falling?'

'No, that would've gone viral. I mean vlogging. That's where we need to look. The vlogs!'

'Vlogging?'

'Reels, vlogs, whatever you call them. People film videos of themselves while on holiday and put them up on the internet.' While Pat was trying to decipher these tech terms, Dorna was already bent back over the computer, furiously tapping at the keys. 'YouTube. All that sort of stuff. You can't tamper with videos as easily as you can with photos. If someone was filming the day Henry died and posted a vlog of it, they probably couldn't edit him out of the footage.'

She typed and clicked, and typed and clicked, as various fresh-faced tourists appeared on the screen, chatting away and pointing animatedly to the white cliffs behind them.

Neither woman could understand a word, but the enthusiasm was contagious. Pat stood up to get her old, scratched Brita jug from the fridge. She needed to sober up. Her eyelids felt heavy, but her body was buzzing with anticipation.

'There!' Dorna shouted, ignoring the glass of water in front of her, and pointing at the screen. 'Right there!'

Pat sat down and they both stared. There he was. Henry. The whole of Henry. Walking in the background of some influencer's vlog.

'Oh my God,' whispered Pat. 'How did you find that?'

'Methodology and luck,' said Dorna. 'So that's the suit. That's him.'

'Absolutely, that's correct. Play on.'

They watched the screen, brows furrowing in concentration. As Henry walked past the vlogger, he was smiling. The wind caught his hair. He was beautiful and young and alive.

Someone else entered the frame. A man with dark hair and the hint of a gold earring.

Pat's heart dropped.

'Well,' said Dorna, folding her arms. 'Do you have any idea who that might be?'

'No . . . it can't be,' Pat whispered.

'Do you know him?!' Dorna sounded astonished.

'It's Marcus. Oh my God, it's Marcus.'

'Wait. Let's not get ahead of ourselves. Shall we look for more?' said Dorna, barely able to hide the excitement in her voice.

Henry and Marcus appeared again in the background. Henry wasn't smiling any more. He was walking backwards, his arms crossed in front of him as Marcus got closer. And that was it. Another tourist moved into the frame, fully covering the scene behind her. Dorna replayed the clip again and again.

'It seems like Marcus is trying to get something. His arms are extended. It's like he wants to touch him or grab something off him,' Pat said.

'His phone? Wallet?' There was a deep line between Dorna's eyebrows as she peered at the screen.

'Could be.' Pat paused. 'Wait, stop the video. Do you see that?' she asked, pointing at the two figures as they left the frame.

'Can you tell what direction he's gone in?' Dorna sounded rather thrilled now.

'Well, judging by the background, the picnic tables and the car park . . . towards the lighthouse. Where the tide is strong and there's a rip,' said Pat.

'Strong enough for the body to travel a few hundred yards back towards Birling Gap?'

'Certainly. Do you think that's enough evidence to take to the police?'

'Yes, but maybe we need more. Should I look into Marcus properly?' Dorna suggested.

'How can you do that?'

'Easily.'

For the next few minutes, Dorna silently clicked away on the computer, while Pat tiptoed next door to see exactly where Prichard was. The lights were off and the room was dark, and both the sofas appeared to be empty, yet the snoring continued, deeply in and gravelly out. Pat stood in the doorway with her hands on her hips, confused. Finally she realised where the noise was coming from, and walking softly around one of the sofas, she found Prichard curled up fast asleep in Dave's bed, with Dave cosily curled up on top of him.

Pat returned to the kitchen. 'You won't believe—' she began with a broad smile.

'Found him,' interrupted Dorna. 'Here he is. His full name is Marcus Ellis. He's thirty-three years old and he says he lives in London.'

'Well that's a lie. He lives in Westlinke, next door to the Green Lion.'

'This is his Instagram page. He definitely lived in London up until very recently.'

'How did you manage that?' Pat sat back down at the table.

'I'm surprised you don't know how to do any of this. It's basic internet sleuthing. I should teach you one day.' Dorna drained her glass. 'I simply followed Henry Clayton on Instagram, and then Derek, then I found a photo where he had tagged Marcus, and boom! Got his profile. It wasn't hard. But look at him. He looks like a murderer to me, with his smug face and his smug smile and his smug little earring. Look at him in Ibiza with a smug cocktail. You'd be amazed what sort of information people let slip on these platforms. All it takes is a few clicks and you can find almost anything. Where did you say the money had gone?'

'The Channel Islands.' Pat couldn't control the thoughts

rushing through her head. So when she had seen Marcus and Derek at the Green Lion, that hadn't been a first date. They knew each other from somewhere else, and somehow Marcus knew Henry too. Henry had never mentioned him to her, though. Pat was certain Marcus had something to do with his death, but the full picture wasn't clear yet.

'Look at this one. The background and the geotag at the top.' It was a photo of Marcus, pint in hand, at a beachfront restaurant. 'Our dear friend Marcus has certainly been to Guernsey!'

The realisation hit Pat like a ton of bricks. 'It's got to be him,' she said. 'God.' She paused. She felt oddly upset and relieved at the same time. It was a strange feeling looking at this Marcus, the likely-to-be-a-killer version of Marcus. Her mouth was dry. She'd thought she might feel more euphoric than this. Elated. In tears. The idea of closure would smell sweeter, and it would certainly sound better than the incessant snoring from next door.

'Shall we send him a message!' Dorna raised her eyebrows conspiratorially. 'Put the wind up him a bit!' She grinned. 'Tell him we're on to him!'

'I'm not sure that's a good idea,' Pat heard herself saying.

'We need to flush him out.'

'Why do we need to do that?'

'What's your account?' asked Dorna, ignoring her.

Pat logged into her Instagram account, surprised that she even remembered her password. With Sofia's encouragement, she had posted a photo of Dave a few years ago, when he was a bit slimmer. It was only slightly out of focus. She only followed four accounts, which she never remembered to look at: two that posted cat content, one about open-water swimming and, of course, Sofia's.

Dorna took over. 'OK, so I'm sending him a direct message. He probably won't get it, but I've written: "We know what you did." Is that OK to send?'

'We shouldn't send him anything. He's potentially dangerous,' suggested Pat, who had drunk rather less than Dorna and seemed to be the only person in the room who realised that texting a killer wasn't a great idea.

'Too late!' Dorna said with a wide grin. 'That'll teach him to mess around with middle-aged ladies!'

'Except he hasn't messed around with middle-aged ladies; he's probably murdered a young man!' The stressful knot in Pat's gut was growing by the minute now. 'Can we delete it? Get rid of it? How do we do that?'

'Sure. You just scroll through here and then press . . . Oh shit, that was quick,' declared Dorna, and looked at Pat, her mouth slightly open and her hand covering her chin. 'Oh shit, shit, SHIT!'

'What shit?'

'Look,' she said, turning the laptop to face Pat. 'He's seen it.'

'Shit,' said Pat.

'Shit,' agreed Dorna.

And they both just stared at each other.

CHAPTER 26

Did they finish all the damson gin? Probably. Did they drink the two bottles of champagne? Most certainly. Did they solve the problems of the world? They solved a murder, and they toasted that fact quite a few times. So much so that they both fell asleep on the sofas. Pat was sitting upright, her head lolling backwards, her nose towards the ceiling and her mouth wide open, catching flies. Dorna was curled up on the cushions like a baby, knees under her chin, her short red hair nestled into the chintz as she shivered quietly without a blanket.

It was dawn when Dorna woke and tiptoed, very quietly, out of the house. She started up her Audi Q9 and headed home slowly for a large glass of cold water and a fistful of paracetamol. Had she looked in the bushes before she got into her car, she might have been able to warn Pat. Had she closed the front door properly, heard it click shut, rather than leaving it slightly ajar, she might have made it a little less easy for him. But she didn't see him. She didn't notice the glint of a gold earring hovering in the undergrowth. She was focused on getting home as soon as possible and crawling under her duvet on her expensively sprung bed from Selfridges.

*

Pat woke with a terrified start and a sharp intake of breath, grabbing her chest in fear as she became aware of his presence. He was in the room, sitting opposite her on the soft cushions of the chintz sofa.

'Jesus Christ!' she gasped, leaping up. 'What the hell are you doing here!'

'Well, well, well. If it isn't the shrink detective,' he said, his voice dripping with sarcasm. 'Bit of a heavy night?'

This Marcus was something far more unsettling than the village alcoholic with sweaty palms. Controlled. Still. And it was that stillness that got to her. His eyes gave away nothing; not anger, not fear, not even curiosity. They were just blank. Pat felt her stomach tighten. When someone's expression didn't line up with what was happening around them, it sent a signal. But Marcus wasn't just unreadable. He felt absent, dead behind the eyes.

'You couldn't leave it alone, could you? Poor old Henry Clayton, jumping to his death. Right place. Right time. Famous suicide spot. The police believed it, why not you?'

Smack, smack, smack. He was hitting the palm of his hand with something. Pat shot him a terrified glance. It was a hammer. He was slapping it into his open palm. Her hammer? From the tool shed next to the cold frame? What the hell did it matter! He had a hammer, and he looked like he was prepared to use it. He had form. He'd murdered once before. Why not again?

'You couldn't leave it alone, could you, Dr Patricia Phillips? Oh yes, I know your name, and . . . oh!' He feigned surprise, looking around the room. 'Apparently where you live. Although to be fair, I was hoping for something a bit swankier, bearing in mind all the studying you must have done. All that swotting. Anyway, what's Henry to you?'

'A patient,' replied Pat defiantly, and then immediately regretted it. Why had she given him anything? Dammit!

'Oh,' he said, slowly standing up. 'So that's it. He was your patient. Were you worried about the suicide thing being on your watch?' He moved towards her, slapping the hammer into his hand again. 'Was it guilt? Were you annoyed that his death would be on your record? Ha!' He made as if to hit her on the side of her head. Pat flinched and sent up a prayer even though she really didn't believe in God. He laughed again, then slowly placed the smooth, flat surface of the hammer against her temple. It was deathly cold. 'Tap, tap, tap,' he whispered.

Pat didn't move, but she maintained eye contact. She could smell his breath on her face, and it wasn't pleasant. She had read somewhere that if you were being mugged, it was best to distract your attacker. 'Do you speak French?' she asked. '*Parlez-vous français?* A friend of mine has got this app for teaching himself French.'

Marcus's face twisted in a puzzled look.

'Going anywhere nice for your holidays?' she continued. 'You like Ibiza, don't you?'

'Will you shut up, woman!' he shouted.

Wrong strategy. *Think, think!*

'What was Henry to *you*?' she asked.

'What do you mean?' Marcus lowered the hammer, just a fraction.

'Why him?'

'Why not?' He glowered. 'If you're that much of an easy target, you're fair game.'

'But it doesn't make sense. I thought Derek . . .' She didn't even know what to think any more, let alone say.

'Do you think Derek is clever enough to do all those things on his own? The money? The love-bombing? The grooming? He doesn't even know it was me who did it! He thinks Henry offed himself. Derek's a pretty twink. He's not smart, he's only good in bed.' Marcus smiled creepily. 'He'll swing any way I tell him. He's a weak little thing who likes easy money, easy drugs, a nightclub podium and nice cocktails when he can get them. He hasn't got two GCSEs to rub together.'

'So Derek works for you?' Pat suggested, attempting to smile. 'You're his boss?' She needed to keep him talking. When he was talking, he wasn't pummelling her temples with a hammer.

'Boss!' He laughed loudly, baring yellowing teeth. 'Derek is the picador to my matador.'

'Wow.' She tried to sound impressed. 'You've murdered other people before? Or was Henry a mistake?' She so hoped he had been.

'You really don't get it, do you? So much for our little village detective!' he laughed. 'Derek was supposed to meet him at the lighthouse under my instructions. He'd managed to get the passwords and ID for the bank accounts, but we needed the username for the trading account. He couldn't do it, wasn't good enough at it. He was busy with that needy woman, Fiona. She's got pots of money, way more than

Henry. I knew as soon as I moved to Westlinke that she'd be an easy one to get. We'd picked up her and her desperate husband at the Hotel du Cocktail.'

'So that's why you moved here. Did you run out of people to scam in London?'

'I like the beach. And yes, village life seems to make people stupider. You're all the opposite of street smart.'

'But why stay after killing Henry?'

'Why not? It was ruled as a suicide, remember? And I have unfinished business.'

'Right. So Mal and Fi are your Plan B.'

'Once I've tidied up Plan A.'

'Tidied?' Pat raised her voice just as Marcus raised the hammer. 'Did you always intend to kill Henry, then?'

'I'd met Henry a couple of times with Derek, after they started dating. I pretended to be Derek's best friend. Derek was getting attached, you see, he's a softie! He didn't want to take all Henry's money, not really. Poor Derek, falling in love with his victim. He kept making mistakes, getting too emotional, trying to steal investors' information off Henry's phone, changing his mind and breaking up with him. He got sloppy. I had to step in. It was such a perfect set-up, you see. I just had to go to the bar in Soho where the two of them always went together, and there he was! Poor little Henry. Heartbroken and lonely, desperate for attention. It was almost easy. I convinced him to give it another go with Derek.'

'How?' Pat's lower lip trembled. She clenched her jaw. *Don't show any weakness*, she told herself.

'He thought we were friends! That I was giving him good

advice. The poor lad. Does it even matter? He still came to Westlinke for a romantic weekend, didn't he? And Derek, so silly, he thought he could still make it work. But he felt guilty about it all. I thought he might come clean to Henry, and I couldn't let that happen.'

'So Derek . . .?'

'What is your obsession with Derek! Did he have his way with you too? I didn't think you'd be his type!' Marcus laughed again. 'Derek had nothing to do with it. I made it so it looked like I ran into Henry when he arrived in Westlinke. I told him we'd go for a detour before Derek arrived. I took him for a walk near Birling Gap, told him I'd take a photo of him. I just needed to take the phone and run. But Henry got suspicious and wouldn't give it to me. He was seeing a lawyer and was paranoid. So we went back to the lighthouse.'

'And that was where you did it.' It wasn't a question.

'Yes, just behind it. It's too steep even for tourists, I knew it would be quiet.'

'How . . .?'

'How did I kill him? I hit him on the head with a rock. Just like I'm going to hit you with this hammer.'

Pat's blood ran even colder than she'd thought possible.

'But he hadn't got his bloody phone on him, only his room key, so I took that and kicked him over the edge.' Marcus shrugged. 'I thought I'd write a suicide note for him for good measure. I might do one for you too, Dr Pat.' Madness flashed in his eyes. 'What would you like me to say in it?'

'PRICHARD!' Pat yelled.

And suddenly, as if out of nowhere, Prichard leapt out of the cat's bed and over the chintz sofa, roaring like a tiger and pouncing on top of Marcus, wrestling him to the ground.

'What the hell!' shouted Marcus as they rolled around on the Axminster carpet.

'Careful!' shouted Pat. 'He's got a hammer!'

'Ouch!' screamed Prichard as Marcus hit him in the ribs.

'Watch out, old man!' shouted Marcus.

'I'm not bloody old!' Prichard grabbed his neck and attempted to throttle him.

Marcus yelped at the top of his voice as Dave launched himself across the sitting room and sank his teeth into his leg. In a flurry of fur and claws, the cat went in for another deep wound. Pat took the opportunity to step on Marcus's wrist and grab the hammer. Such was the pain, and the anger, and the shot of adrenaline, that Marcus arched his spine in roaring agony and managed to throw Prichard off with renewed determination and vigour. 'GET OUT OF MY WAY!' he screamed, running for the kitchen to escape through the back door, the cat still attached to his leg.

But Pat was there, blocking his path.

'Move!' he barked.

'No!' She stood her ground.

He shoved her hard against the fridge. 'Piss off, you old bag!' he snarled.

Pat reached for the top of the fridge and grabbed the first thing that came to hand: the lid of the orange Le Creuset pot. She whacked him hard over the head with it. 'I'm of a certain age, not old!' she shouted.

'Oh. My. GOD!' exclaimed Marcus, feeling the side of his head. Stunned, he looked at Pat, and the lid, and back at Pat again. 'Ouch,' he said, 'that really hurt!'

Pat didn't know what to say. She had never done anything quite so violent in her life. 'Sorry,' she replied.

'Well, yes, I should think so!' he said, and opening the front door, he staggered out, one hand on his head, the other dragging his leg. Swearing in disbelief, he limped up the garden path and out of the gate, leaving a trail of blood as he went.

'Pat, Pat!' exclaimed Prichard, rushing into the kitchen, arms wrapped around his ribcage. 'Are you all right! Who was that? I have never been more terrified in all my life!'

'Prichard,' said Pat, struggling for breath. 'I had no idea you were so brave.'

'Brave?'

'You threw yourself across the sofa like a panther with its claws out. You were incredibly heroic. I didn't know you had it in you!' She smiled.

'Frankly, my dear, neither did I!'

'I think you saved my life.'

'I think I might have done!'

'And Dave,' they both said, turning to look at the cat, who was sitting in the middle of the kitchen table trying to look nonchalant, though his hackles were still up and he was twice his normal size.

Pat locked the door and opened a packet of cat treats, counting out six.

'Is that all he gets?' said Prichard.

'He's on a diet.' She scratched Dave's head. 'By the way, Prichard, what took you so long to come to my rescue?'

'I woke up to the sound of Marcus's voice and thought I was dreaming, then I realised he was confessing, so I turned my phone on and pressed record.'

'Oh my God, genius!' said Pat.

'What if he comes back?' Prichard asked, eyes darting to the door.

'He'd better not, or I'll use the whole Le Creuset pot next time!'

It was just gone 8.30 a.m. when Pat and Prichard walked into Southbourne police station. PC Footer was already at the front desk, slowly tearing bits of croissant out of a paper bag while checking the messages on his phone. The reception was quiet, the floor still damp from its recent mopping. The smell of bleach hung in the air.

'Dr Phillips!' Footer said, sitting up straight and scrunching the paper bag shut. 'What are you and Mr Knowles doing here?'

'We'd like to talk to Detective Sergeant Stevens,' said Pat, leaning on the front desk a little for support. She'd had no idea quite how exhausted she was. What with the late night and her early-morning caller, plus the amount of champagne and damson gin she'd imbibed, she was completely thrown off her schedule and had rather a poor head and dry mouth to boot.

Prichard, on the other hand, had had a delightful snooze in Dave's bed and was pumped up after his fight with Marcus and his astonishing, reckless bravery. Saving one's dearest friend from certain death did things to a man.

'We demand to see DS Stevens!' he declared, thumping the front desk with his clenched fist. 'And I guarantee she wants to see us!'

'Not again, surely,' said PC Footer, shaking his head.

'I know my rights.' Prichard nodded. 'And we also know who murdered Henry Clayton.'

'That case is closed,' PC Footer replied.

'Then reopen it!' Prichard swung his arm dramatically out in front of himself, as if he were sweeping aside great hordes.

'I think it would be better for all of us if you just let us in to see her,' whispered Pat. 'Otherwise there is no telling what Mr Knowles might do.'

'Sure,' said PC Footer, pressing the entry buzzer under the desk. 'Although she does have someone with her at the moment.'

'We won't take long,' said Pat, opening the door to the open-plan office.

'It's our local MP!' he called after them as the door swung shut.

The back room, despite the paucity of coppers, smelt strongly of milky coffee and bacon sandwiches. But Pat and Prichard were on a mission as they marched between the empty desks towards the glass office at the back, where DS Stevens was sitting, ankles crossed, one heel on the ground, while she swung from side to side, laughing up at a figure who was standing in front of her, leaning on the desk, still wearing his camel-coloured coat.

'Honourable Member,' announced Prichard with a broad grin, his hand extended forward. 'Prichard. Prichard Knowles. We met the other day, when you judged the art competition in the village hall in Westlinke.' He shook the MP's hand vigorously. 'Very nice to see you again, and thank you very much indeed for the second place.'

The MP stood to attention and looked at Pat and Prichard, seemingly confused by their sudden interruption.

'Right, sorry, who did you say you were again?'

'This is Dr Patricia Phillips, and I'm Prichard Knowles MBE. And we have solved the case of the murder of Henry Clayton.'

The MP had thick grey hair and a sports-car tan. He was wearing a smart navy suit, a Savile Row shirt and a pair of gold cufflinks, with portcullis lapel pins on his coat and his jacket. Pat watched as DS Stevens stood up and straightened her skirt, then smoothed down the stray hairs in her neat brown bun. She looked from one to the other, noticing the tension in the air, the flushed pink of Stevens' cheeks. Yes, she thought, the honourable member was definitely the man who'd dug his fingers into the detective's buttocks at Lewes station.

'You've solved a murder?' asked the MP. 'How extraordinary, Mr Knowles! How could you possibly have done that! DS Stevens is all ears, aren't you, Amanda?'

'Except that the case is closed.' Stevens smiled tightly.

'Ms Stevens has the highest clean-up rate in the south,' added the honourable member.

'Well, here's another one to add to that lengthy list,' said Pat. 'I'm sure she won't mind that.'

'Listen to this,' said Prichard, and he got out his phone and pressed play.

'I can't hear anything except muffled sounds,' said Stevens.

'Wait!' said Pat, and they continued to listen. Suddenly the sounds became clearer.

'That's when I pushed my phone under the sofa, nearer the action,' said Prichard.

They listened to the confession, the threats, the fight, the sounds of Dave's contribution.

After the recording stopped, there was silence.

'What was that all about?' said the MP.

Pat ignored him and looked at DS Stevens. 'As you can probably hear, I hit Marcus with an iron casserole lid. Do you want to arrest me for actual bodily harm?'

'Who is he?' said Stevens.

'Marcus Ellis, he lives next door to the pub. He's probably packing up right now and making his way back to London. This is how we caught him – these are the vlogs we've found on YouTube or Instagram or TokTok or whatever it's called.' Pat put a sheaf of paper on DS Stevens' desk. 'And I think he would probably be an interesting person to run through your police computer.'

'One thing I don't understand,' said the honourable member, 'is why he would confess to you, Dr Phillips?'

'It certainly wasn't guilt,' Pat replied. 'It wasn't a slip, either. It was about control. About recognition. He wanted me to know. Not just what he'd done but how clever he thought it was. He needed someone to bear witness. And not just anyone – me. Because I'd seen through him. I'd challenged him. I think that in his mind it gave the whole thing weight if I understood. That's why he chose that moment – when he thought he was about to kill me. He thought it would be him having the last word on the matter. People like Marcus don't want to get away with it quietly. They want to be admired for getting away with it. That's what this was. A performance. And I was the audience. It wasn't enough for him to win. He needed a witness.'

'How d'you know that?' asked DS Stevens.

'It's just my professional opinion,' said Pat solemnly.

'I'm not sure what to say to you, Dr Phillips.' The detective smiled briefly and patted the back of her tight bun. She exhaled a deep sigh. 'Except thank you, I suppose. Thank you for helping us catch a murderer. The Downs are a safer place with you here.'

Pat couldn't believe what she was hearing. Amanda Stevens finally listening to her? Thanking her? She blinked at the detective. Was she dreaming? Had she heard that right? Amanda Stevens. Thanking her. Maybe she needed more sleep. Or stronger tea.

Prichard had to hand over his phone, as it was now evidence. He was rather miffed about this. 'We'll get you a burner to use until you get it back,' said Pat.

'But I've just downloaded Duolingo and I'm getting really good at Korean now,' he protested.

The MP butted in. 'We should think about giving you both some sort of award.'

'No thank you,' smiled Pat. 'I think we've had quite enough excitement as it is.'

CHAPTER 27

Pat later heard that Marcus Ellis was arrested just an hour after she and Prichard had left the police station, having completed their witness statements following that morning's breaking and entering and threatened violence – which was tantamount to a prison sentence all on its own. He had been found cowering in the waiting room of Polegate train station with a half-packed suitcase, a one-way ticket to London and a terrible black eye. He was dragged kicking, screaming and spitting along the platform in full view of some terrified passengers and a small group of tourists (who naturally filmed the whole episode to put on TikTok), into the police van and straight into custody. When the police went through his case, they found a key with an orange fob labelled *Cabin Room*.

Detective Sergeant Stevens had taken all the credit for catching her man. She'd appeared on the local news wearing pearly lip gloss and speaking with the authority of someone who'd spent the day rehearsing in front of a mirror. She reminded viewers how important it was for the public to stay vigilant, and added, 'If you see something that doesn't look quite right, report it. See it, say it, and we'll sort it.' She nodded solemnly, as if quoting from scripture rather than adapting the words from a train station poster.

Marcus had indeed emptied Henry's bank accounts, and all the money was found in Guernsey. Not that that was much consolation to Henry's devastated family. The police picked up Derek a week later. All they could charge him with was fraud by false representation for gaining Henry's trust under false pretences, and as it was a first offence he got a six-month suspended sentence and a community order. He'd rapidly abandoned his grooming of Mal and Fi in the wake of Marcus's arrest, but old habits, it appeared, died hard and he was back online within a week, looking for the lonely, vulnerable and hopelessly romantic. He was also frequenting Hotel du Cocktail to see if there were any more hungry cougars good for a bob or two. Mal and Fi decided their marriage had been spiced up quite enough and decided not to go there again. They also drained the hot tub and asked Caroline to see if she could plant something in it.

Even with Marcus in custody, on remand with bail refused, Pat found it hard to settle. Sleep came late, and when it did, it was shallow and broken. She'd wake suddenly, heart racing, certain she'd heard something. Her thoughts no longer obeyed her. They arrived without warning: flashes of his face, the precise way his jaw tightened before he smiled, the cold weight of his voice. Sometimes she found herself right back in that moment, as if no time had passed at all. She would blink, breathe, remind herself it was over, but her body stayed coiled, alert, as if waiting for the danger to return. Her own mind had become a room she couldn't quite leave. She realised that she was the one needing help now. She booked six sessions with a psychotherapist specialising in trauma and went to the therapy centre above the pub in Vauxhall once a week to work through the recurring fears that had descended on her since the incident with Marcus. She found a better place for her house key than under the plant pot, and obeyed her governing body's code of ethics to the letter when it came to keeping the records of her clients.

One Tuesday in the middle of June, Pat woke horribly early. It was hot. Sweaty hot. But she felt different than she had these past few weeks, like she could breathe again. She was lighter, energised, alive. She rolled over and tried to go back to sleep. But sunlight had already broken over the horizon and it seemed pointless, a waste, to stay in bed. She went downstairs and made herself a strong cup of coffee, then sat at the kitchen table with Dave, who was trying to convince her with meows and rubbing her legs that he hadn't just been fed, which he had. It was just gone 5 a.m. She grabbed her elderly bathing suit off the radiator and changed in the kitchen, put on her dryrobe and stepped out to greet the morning.

She walked out of the house and over the cattle grid, and was about to turn right and march up over the Downs when she heard something, she wasn't quite sure what. She stopped, her ears straining.

'Viking... North Utsire... South Utsire... Forth... Tyne... Dogger...'

She carried on up the path, and the closer she got to the lay-by, the louder it became. Someone was listening to the Shipping Forecast, at quite a volume.

'Fisher... German Bight... Humber...'

There was a car. The engine was running, a low, throaty growl, a plume of pollution wending its way towards her.

'Lundy... Fastnet... Irish Sea...'

Pat felt her heart beat faster as she approached. Could it be, finally, after all this time? Red-handed? But as she drew closer, she realised that the car was very familiar. Golden. Expensive. An Aston Martin. She came round to the driver's side.

'Malcolm! What are you up to?' she barked through the open window.

'Jesus Christ!' There was a mad fumbling inside the car. 'Pat!' he squealed, pulling at his clothes, his shirt, as he tried to rearrange himself. 'It's not what you think!'

'You have no idea what I'm thinking!' she said.

'I promise you, it's not what it looks like. It really isn't what it looks like.' His face was puce, his skin sweaty, and his eyes were spherical with terror. 'I'm not... I'm not doing what you think I'm doing.'

'You're a man on his own, at dawn, with his engine running in a lay-by; what else am I supposed to think?' she replied, placing her hands on her hips and peering through the open window. The interior of the Aston Martin was immaculate, all cream leather and walnut, which made the presence of a half-eaten Mars bar on the passenger seat all the more bizarre. 'What's that?' She nodded.

'OK, you've got me,' he said. 'But please, please don't tell Fi. Mars bars are banned from our house. I'm not allowed chocolate or anything like that, so every morning I come up here early and listen to the Shipping Forecast and eat a Mars bar. Old habits, I suppose.'

'What do you mean, old habits?'

'My commute to work. I used to leave just after five. A

Mars bar and the Shipping Forecast. God, I miss it now I'm retired. I'd slowly nibble the chocolate one shipping area at a time. The combination of the two is heaven.' He closed his eyes for a second.

'ASMR,' said Pat. 'Autonomous sensory meridian response. Interesting. Tell me, does the Mars bar taste better when you're listening to the Shipping Forecast than when you're not?'

'Oh yes!' He looked at her, slightly amazed. 'How did you know? It's the only time I eat one. Sometimes I'm lucky and the weather is good, but most of the time it's dark and it's just me and the radio.' He looked up at her, his eyes clouded with self-pity. 'Please don't tell Fiona,' he implored. 'She wouldn't understand.'

'Fine. I won't. On one condition.'

'Anything. Absolutely anything.'

'When you've finished your Mars bar and you know what's happening in Rockall, or whatever the last one is . . .'

'Southeast Iceland.'

'. . . when that's finished, you get out of your car and you carefully put your wrapper in the bin.'

'Is that it?'

'That's it.'

'And you won't tell Fi?'

'I won't tell Fi.'

'OK,' he agreed. 'Absolutely.'

'Finish up. And bin it!' and turning on her heel, she pulled her dryrobe tightly around her and marched up over the Downs, heading for her early-morning swim.

EPILOGUE

A few weeks later, at the beginning of July, after they heard that Marcus had got life with no chance of parole for twenty-five years, Pat received a letter from Rebecca Clayton thanking her for her tenacity, for never giving up on Henry when the rest of the world had. Pat had invited her to the ceremony she, Sofia, Prichard and Dorna had planned: a naming ceremony for a bench to commemorate her son's life. But Rebecca had understandably declined. She did not want to visit the place where he had lost his life, at least not just yet, and she was also not inclined to do so with an audience of strangers.

'Darling, you really shouldn't be carrying that,' said Pat, rushing around the side of the moss-mobile to relieve Sofia of the large tin she had in her hands. 'Not in your condition.'

'Well, firstly it's not a condition. It's not an illness, it's a pregnancy. Secondly, I'm as fit as a fiddle, and thirdly it's a strawberry pavlova, and I don't think you'll find anything that's lighter than meringue. And anyway you shouldn't be carrying it with your hip. When are you having the operation?'

'I'm on a list, any time soon.'

'Why don't you pay to have it done?'

'It's a way of putting it off.'

'You two, stop bickering,' said Dorna, who was lugging two straw picnic hampers with a rug tucked under one arm.

'Here,' said Prichard, grabbing the tin from Sofia's hands. 'Happy now, Pat?'

'Don't you bloody fall over carrying that,' said Sofia. 'I know how clumsy you are, Prichard!'

'You sound exactly like your mother,' he said, turning and marching up the coastal path towards Fin du Monde. 'The apple didn't fall far from that tree, did it!' he added over his shoulder.

Pat stood in the car park, taking the rest of the picnic out of the boot. She thought for a second about locking it, but a cursory look around made her realise no one was coming anywhere near it. She smiled. Not locking the car – another sign she was over her trauma.

It was a beautiful afternoon. One of those clear, warm days when summer finally decided it was serious and the grass smelt like baked goods and the heat from the warm earth seeped through Pat's flip-flops and the yellow rays of the sun toasted her shoulders either side of her vest top. She should have worn a shirt.

She walked slowly along the path carrying the heavy freezer box full of ice and soft drinks. It had been her idea to name a bench in Henry's honour. There were many along the coast, quiet memorials from husbands, wives, children, friends, each one marking a life that had mattered. Somehow it felt right that Henry should have one too. She had managed to persuade the council to engrave the bench where she'd found his phone, the place where he'd dropped it, or hidden it from Marcus when, as it turned out, he'd been trying to defend himself. The honourable member of parliament himself had intervened and facilitated all the paperwork.

'So what do you think?' she asked, putting down the cold box and looking around. 'The location? The engraving? Do you think he would have liked it?'

'I like it, Mum,' replied Sofia, helping herself to a cucumber sandwich from Dorna's basket. 'And I'm sure he would too.'

'Well, cheers!' Pat raised her can of San Pellegrino. 'Here's to you, Henry Clayton, you charming, funny, clever, handsome man.' She took a sip and sighed.

'And I for one am thrilled you caught the bastard!' said Dorna.

'I couldn't have done that without your help.'

'I'm sure you would have caught him in the end,' Dorna smiled.

'I'm just lacking the tech skills,' replied Pat, taking another sip of her drink.

'Have you thought about those computer classes in the village hall?' Prichard suggested helpfully.

'The ones for the elderly?' asked Pat.

There was a long pause.

'Anyone for pavlova?' asked Sofia.

'Try stopping me!' said Prichard, helping himself to a plate.

Dorna flapped out the rug and they all sat down in the sun, looking out to sea and spooning in mouthfuls of Sofia's delicious pavlova.

Pat helped herself to a little more. 'I have to say, this is one of the most delicious things I have ever eaten. You really do have a talent, Sofia.'

'Thanks, Mum.' Sofia smiled up at her, her large hat shielding her face. 'I'm glad you like it.' She turned her head to look down the hill towards the car park. 'I think your policeman friend is coming this way.'

'Really?' asked Pat, straining her neck.

She watched as PC Footer made his way towards them, stopping once to catch his breath.

'Good afternoon,' he said when he finally joined them. 'Sorry to disturb.'

'Would you like a sandwich? Or some pavlova?' asked Dorna. 'Join us – come and sit down.'

'Oh, no thank you. No eating between meals for me,' he said proudly.

'Wow,' said Pat. 'What's brought about this change?'

'I'm on the pen,' he announced.

'You mean the weight-loss injections?'

'That's it. I don't even think about food any more. You really got me thinking about my eating.'

He nodded towards the wooden bench with Henry's name carved in the middle.

'You've done a nice job. It's a good spot.'

'Thank you.' Pat looked at him, her eyebrows raised questioningly.

'Anyway, your gardener, Caroline, said you'd be here,' he said. 'I wonder, Dr Phillips, if I might have a word about another case? I think we might need your help.'

Acknowledgements

Thank you to my Mexican psychotherapy colleague Norma Zoia Cabrera Reyna, who knows a lot about psychological autopsies. Thank you to the real police detective Amanda Barry (now a psychotherapist), who told me about police procedure which my fictional police detectives did not follow. I'd also like to thank my friends and relations for their company, encouragement and inspiration, especially Helen Bagnall, Natalie Haynes, Yolanda Phillips, Jonny Phillips, Suzanne Moore, Janet Lee, Richard Coles, Lorna Graddon, Grayson Perry, Flo Perry – I need those cheerleaders. Thank you to my agent Karolina Sutton and publisher Venetia Butterfield and their brilliant teams, whose judgement and support is invaluable.

I'm grateful for the beautiful South Downs, its visitors and their inspiring love for Instagram.